the Stone Circle

ALSO BY GARY GOSHGARIAN

ATLANTIS FIRE

ROUGH BEAST

the
Stone
Circle

A NOVEL BY

GARY GOSHGARIAN

DONALD I. FINE BOOKS

New York

DONALD I. FINE BOOKS
Published by the Penguin Group
Penguin Putnam Inc., 375 Hudson Street, New York, New York 10014, U.S.A.
Penguin Books Ltd, 27 Wrights Lane, London W8 5TZ, England
Penguin Books Australia Ltd, Ringwood, Victoria, Australia
Penguin Books Canada Ltd, 10 Alcorn Avenue, Toronto, Ontario,
Canada M4V 3B2
Penguin Books (N.Z.) Ltd, 182-190 Wairau Road, Auckland 10, New Zealand

Penguin Books Ltd, Registered Offices: Harmondsworth, Middlesex, England

First published by Donald I. Fine Books, an imprint of Penguin Putnam Inc.

First Printing, September, 1997
10 9 8 7 6 5 4 3 2 1

We gratefully acknowledge permission to quote from the following:

''Bad Moon Rising'' © 1969, Jondora Music BMI. Words and music by
John C. Fogerty. Used by permission. All rights reserved.

''Saturday in the Park,'' Written by Robert Lamm. © 1972 Lamminations
Music / Big Elk Music. ALL RIGHTS RESERVED. Used By Permission.

DIF REGISTERED TRADEMARK—MARCA REGISTRADA

LIBRARY OF CONGRESS CATALOGING-IN-PUBLICATION DATA
Goshgarian, Gary.
The stone circle : a novel / by Gary Goshgarian.
p.   cm.
ISBN 1-55611-533-4 (acid-free paper)
I. Title.
PS3557.O77S7   1997
813'.54—dc21   97-23043
                                                         CIP

Printed in the United States of America
Set in New Baskerville

PUBLISHER'S NOTE
This is a work of fiction. Names, characters, places, and incidents either are the
product of the author's imagination or are used fictitiously, and any
resemblance to actual persons, living or dead, events, or locales is entirely
coincidental.

For Kathleen, Nathan and David
— my circle.

Penetrating so many secrets we cease to believe in the unknowable.
But there it sits, nevertheless, calmly licking its chops.

— H. L. MENCKEN

Author's Note

Because this is a work of fiction I have taken liberties with both place and history. There are no islands of Kingdom Head or Shepherd's Island in the Boston Harbor. Nor did the early leaders of the Commonwealth commit the specific acts attributed to them here. But Mystery Hill in North Salem, New Hampshire, is real, and so is its mystery.

For their assistance in the background research of this novel I would like to acknowledge the following people: Brona Simon, State Archaeologist, Massachusetts Historical Commission; Professor Peter Wells, formerly of Harvard University; Professor William M. Fowler, Jr., of Northeastern University; Professor John Pendergast of the University of Massachusetts (Lowell, Mass.); and Samuel Andonian, M.D. Also, a special thanks to Mary Blue Magruder of Earthwatch (Watertown, Mass.) and to Robert Krueger of New England Industrial Truck. To them I offer my gratitude for their kind help and apologies for any inaccuracies.

I am also grateful to the Office of the Provost at Northeastern University for the research and development grant which provided me the time to bring this book to completion.

Finally, a very special thanks to my agent, Susan Crawford, for standing behind this book and its author.

Prologue

"He looks spooked."

Vinnie was on his knees with a flashlight in the bow hole try-ing to coax Carla's puli onto shore. Just minutes ago they had to restrain him from jumping off the boat at the sight of land. Now he was a trembling gray muff trying to hide in his paws.

Carla hung over the edge of the boat. "Maybe he's seasick?"

But, as far as Vinnie knew, dogs didn't get seasick. And if it were some other ailment, it had hit very fast. "How about we just leave him here? He'll be fine."

"He's probably got to go." She clapped her hands. "Come on, Bilbo, come to Mommy."

Ordinarily her call would transport the dog into tongue-lolling flight, but he just whimpered and nuzzled down.

"I think he's just tired," Vinnie said. But Bilbo was shaking as if he'd been dumped into a freezer. "What's the problem, boy?" he whispered. Through the fur a single eye burned like an ember.

Carla looked down the beach. In the obscure light, huge con-struction machines along the dunes brooded like prehistoric beasts. "Maybe it's the island." But they'd been island hopping all day.

As Vinnie clipped the leash to his collar, the dog let out a growl and nipped his hand. There was no break in the skin, but the reaction shocked Vinnie. In two years of dating Carla he had never known Bilbo to snap at anybody. On the contrary, he was a big happy, good-natured animal.

"I don't know what your problem is," he muttered, "but if you mess my boat you're going to wish you had fins."

He wrapped the looped end of the leash onto the cleat. As he backed out, a low menacing growl bubbled out of the dog's throat. In the light, a slit of fiery jelly regarded Vinnie through the curls, sending a cold rash up his arms and across his back. He crawled out of the boat, half wondering if maybe they should get the dog to an animal hospital.

He took Carla's hand as they walked down the beach. The water was a sheet of black glass, and in the distance the Boston skyline glowed like jewelry. All down the beach were silhouettes of the construction machines that were turning Kingdom Head into an island Las Vegas—casino, hotels, condos, golf course, and marinas—its completion slated for July 4, 2000.

They spread a blanket not far from where they'd anchored the outboard. Under a three-quarter moon Vinnie and Carla settled into each other's arms. Soon they were breathing heavily, their bodies moving in deliberate cadence with the night waves. After a few minutes Vinnie began to remove Carla's top, when a high-pitched yowl sent a bolt of lightning through him.

Sounds of splashing, another yowl, and Bilbo dashed by them up the sands.

"Bilbo. *Bilbo!*" Carla jumped to her feet.

Vinnie scrambled on his back trying not to snag himself in his zipper.

"He'll get lost!" Carla screamed.

"Let him for chrissakes." His heart felt like a kettle drum doing rolls.

"Vinnie!"

"He can't get lost, Carla. He's got a nose like radar and can see in the dark." He flicked on the flashlight. The dog was running up the beach, its leash trailing him. "There," he said, and in a side thought he wondered how the hell the dog had pulled free of the cleat. The strap was leather and metal.

In the dim light the dog came to a dead stop, looking like one of those stop-action movie shots. One instant Bilbo was scurrying up the sand like the Tasmanian devil, the next he was stunned in his tracks. Suddenly, as if picking up direction, he snapped his head and shot up a high sandy slope toward the top, his legs driving him like a robot dog following orders beamed from some invisible master. Over and over they called but he wouldn't respond. Halfway up, his legs hit a soft pocket as sheets of sand cascaded over him, but he moled his way out and to the top.

Vinnie had no idea what Bilbo was running down. His reaction seemed so purposeful. Whatever, Vinnie was certain that chasing him was a colossal waste of energy. No doubt he'd come bounding back after working the heebie-jeebies out of his system. But Carla was half hysterical. So they trudged after him in loose sand to the top of the cliff.

"It's probably just a rabbit," panted Carla at the top.

"That, or he's gotta take one serious leak."

Only at the top did Vinnie realize just how high they had climbed—maybe sixty or seventy feet above the beach on a wide mesalike flat that formed the eastern head of the island. As he scanned the layout, his eyes fell on something that made his heart freeze: a dark human figure on the far side of the plateau. He swung the flashlight around across the open flat.

Nothing. Just the stars and the deep indigo eastern sky. But he could have sworn somebody was there a moment ago. He took a deep breath to clear his head, telling himself it was a combination of the scant night light and the blood throbbing in his eyes. A simple illusion.

But the movement just to their right was not an illusion.

He swung the light onto a large dome-shaped mound just in front of them. On it, Bilbo was yipping and running in frantic circles after something. Carla called his name, but again no response. The dog was locked in chase around that wide, flat dome of sand. Maybe a rabbit or field mouse. But as they closed in, they could see it was no night critter, just a little vortex of dust. Bilbo was in madcap pursuit of what looked like a thin spiral of dead leaves and sand that waltzed across the mound as if looking for a place to settle. Suddenly the thing screwed itself into a pinpoint and disappeared.

Then silence. Dead imperturbable silence. No whirring wind, no yipping, not even the chittering of crickets. Even the lapping waves had ceased. It was as if somebody had switched off the audio.

Vinnie moved closer to within ten feet of Bilbo. He was frozen in another stop-action trance in the middle of the mound staring, muzzle down, at where the dust had disappeared.

"Bilbo? Bilbo . . . what is it?" The dog glared at the ground as if he had cornered something he would snag on the next move.

"Bilbo, it's all right, baby. Come to Carla." She moved to within five feet.

Suddenly the animal snapped its head around into the full beam of the flash. And he let out a growl too heavy for him—an awful deep-throated roar that sounded as if it rose from something huge below. Its eyes blazed at them through the fur and its mouth was drawn back so the sharp teeth were fully exposed and champing furiously.

"My God . . . he's rabid."

Vinnie said nothing, but he thought: not rabid, something else. He looked possessed.

Suddenly, the dog snapped his head back toward the ground and began digging madly with his front paws.

"What's he doing?"

"After a mole, or something." But Vinnie didn't believe that either. Even if something in the air had sent Bilbo on a wild chase, it didn't explain the drooling mouth or gnashing teeth. Or that roaring. *What in God's name was that?*

"Vinnie, I'm scared."

He wanted to console her, but the words wouldn't come. His brain strained to process what his eyes were taking in: Bilbo was pawing up sand, shells, and pebbles, resembling a cartoon canine whose body remains fixed while the legs become a blur of high-speed rotors. Except this was no Road Runner chase-down. From all appearances Bilbo was digging himself into the ground. He'd tear a rock out with his mouth and snap it away with a snarl—rocks that barely fit in his teeth, that looked too heavy for a dog his size to be flinging around like walnuts. His legs raced as if what he was after lay just beyond reach, as if he'd lose it were he to let up in the slightest.

"What's wrong with him?" Carla screamed. His head was nearly out of sight. *"Stop him!"*

She lunged for the animal, but Vinnie pulled her back and grabbed the leash. Bilbo was no more than forty pounds, but it was like pulling against a bear. Sand spit up from the hole as Bilbo worked his way into the earth. With all his might, Vinnie yanked on the leash.

Suddenly, the animal froze. Another growl and he pulled himself out of the dirt, his head swinging into the light, bared teeth snapping wildly at him.

"Jesus!" Vinnie scurried backward like a crab.

It looked nothing like Bilbo. Its face was a mask of mud and fur, its snout shaved and bleeding from boring into the dirt. One eye was a gaping socket drooling thick ocular fluid from where a shell had sliced through it. The other blazed red. It growled and snapped blindly in the air, its white teeth dripping a gruel of blood and dirt. The only sign that it was the same animal was the red collar.

Carla let out a cry, but the animal did not regard her. It did not regard anything they were aware of. It swayed its head in the light and made another awful growl. In the next instant it threw itself back into the hole.

"The leash!" Carla yelled. "Get the leash!"

But Vinnie couldn't move. For a stunned moment he just watched the animal burrow itself into that ancient mound, its hind legs kicking out debris, the red leash trailing like an intestine.

Before it disappeared, Vinnie leaped for the leash. But the tug was so violent that it snared his wrist like a noose. The next instant he was on his face being pulled into the ground.

It all happened so fast that he barely registered Carla grabbing him or the sensation of the skin being scraped off his arm. All he could process was the huge force pulling from below—a force that had nothing to do with Bilbo or anything that made sense. What did make sense was that his arm was in up to the shoulder and that his face was pressed into the dirt and that he was fighting with all he had lest his neck snap. The strap was too strong to break, and his only hope was that it would slip free. But the way he was pinned, he could not twist his hand. So with his last scrap of energy, Vinnie made a corkscrew twist.

So exquisite was the pain that it sucked the air out of his lungs. Vaguely, he felt himself come free. He rolled to his knees and pulled. His arm came out of the ground like a dead root.

A muffled growl rocked the mound, and the ground closed up under him like a rapidly healing wound. Someplace behind him Carla let out a long scream that Vinnie failed to note. All that registered was the pain and the spurting blood. His hand had been torn off at the wrist.

chapter
One

THREE MONTHS LATER—
MEMORIAL DAY

Peter was not sure what to make of the call or where it would lead. All Dan Merritt, state archaeologist, had said was that an anomaly had been unearthed out on Kingdom Head—nothing they'd ever seen before. Or, as the joke went, Peter's kind of thing. All of Merritt's people were booked on other digs, and the hotshot Indian colonialist from U.Mass. said he was not interested. So Merritt had turned to him.

Yes, it was a hand-me-down dig, but that was better than no dig. And as Peter Van Zandt pulled the Jeep out of the cemetery and headed for the Boston waterfront, he told himself that this was a new start.

It was Memorial Day, and it had begun at Mount Auburn Cemetery in Cambridge. It was the first time Peter had brought his six-year-old son to visit Linda. Although Andy dimly remembered her, he wanted to see where she had been buried. Peter had put off bringing him because he felt that Andy was too young. What finally changed his mind was the fear that avoidance was making death a taboo—the supreme boogeyman—and he did not want the boy growing up with a mortality phobia. Dying was as natural as living, and six years old was time to learn, even if it meant confronting it over the grave of his mother.

"Was she pretty?" Andy had asked, looking up at Peter with those dark liquid eyes. Linda's eyes.

"Yes, very pretty."

"Like that picture in my room?"

"Yes."

Andy clutched a bouquet of pink geraniums. "Will I see Mom when I die?"

"Sure, but not for a long, long time."

"But, how come she had to die, Dad?"

The question squeezed Peter's heart. *Because I killed her.*

"Why don't you put the flowers down, Andy?"

He sniffed the bouquet, then laid it at the base of the head-stone, looking around, half-expecting to see a grateful sign in the trees or bushes. There was none.

"You can go to hell, Peter."

It had happened two and a half years ago. A fight over child-proofing the kitchen, and she had stormed out of the house and driven off. It had been a night of freezing rain and she took a turn too fast. A large oak tree stopped her, and flames had claimed her life.

Peter could not change what had happened. He could not bring Linda back. She had died in the heat of the moment. And he had nearly died of grief, for his love for Linda had been a funda-mental condition of his existence. For months following her death, Peter was certain he would not survive. He had never guessed that guilt and despair could be so ravenous. He had tried to throw himself into his work, but he was always a membrane away from the black vortex. What saved him was Andy. The boy needed a father. So Peter focused all his efforts on bringing up his son without a mother—efforts not in a small way fueled by a sense of expiation.

"You can go to hell, Peter."

She had worn lavender tights the night she died. And white aerobic shoes. And her mind was full of venom.

Peter would always wonder what she had thought when he raised the knife—if she actually feared he'd use it on her. He would also wonder what her last thoughts were before the flames claimed her.

"Daddy, remember how Mom used to tickle-wrestle me?"

"Yes, she really made you laugh."

"But you can play monster best in the whole world."

He could still feel the knife clutched in his hand—that six-inch molybdenum steel piece with the staghorn handle and initialed gold escutcheon. It had cost nearly three hundred dollars, even back then. It was his last Father's Day gift from Linda. She had signed the card: "Keen and esoteric, like you, Big Daddy."

He had been in the cellar cutting the leaking drainage hose from the washing machine.

"Goddamn it, he could have suffocated."

Linda had died because of the kitchen cabinets. There were eight rooms in their house, yet Andy was drawn to the crawl space under the sink. No matter how many times he'd been reprimanded, he went back. He took to it that night while Linda was upstairs changing and Peter was in the cellar cutting the hose from the washer. By the time Linda came down, Andy was among the cleansers and SOS pads and halfway into a thirty-gallon Hefty bag.

"Andy!" Her scream was so horrible that Peter was certain he'd come up to find him dead. "Goddamn it, Peter, he could have suffocated."

"How the hell can I fix the washer and babysit at the same time?" His reaction rose out of raw horror at what could have been his baby's death. The knife was still in his hand. "And where were you?"

"Where was I?" Linda was so flustered she could barely get the words out. "Jesus! . . . I told you I was going upstairs. Did you have to be told to watch him?"

"He knows he's not supposed to go in there. I told him a hundred times."

"Peter, he's three years old!" she cried. "He wouldn't get in there if you'd put the damn locks on you've been promising for months."

"If you're so anxious about the cabinets, put them on yourself. You're not helpless. All it takes is a fucking screwdriver."

Linda's black eyes blazed. "You can go to hell, Peter." Her voice spit gravel. "It's because of me you can spend all bloody day sifting dirt."

She had smacked a nerve, and Peter saw red. He came at her, knife in hand, and stabbed it into the butcher block between them.

For a long moment she glared at the knife. "How dare you?" she said. "How dare you!"

Her last words.

Then she stomped out of the house, her disbelief trailing her, Andy wailing. The rear door slammed and her car raced down the driveway and onto the street. Andy climbed out of his chair and ran to the door screaming. Peter's stomach was a fist. While she drove around to cool off, he'd be left to calm Andy down, finish cooking the dinner, feed the boy, then bathe and dress him, read him a book, and somehow get him to bed. At about the time he'd wash the last pot, Linda would come rolling back, ready to make up—an old pattern of storm and reconciliation. They'd kiss and make up and later make love.

"It's okay, little guy." He clutched Andy to his chest. The baby was hysterical. "Mommy'll be right back. Just don't go under the sink anymore, okay? Please? And everything will be all right."

A telephone call from Mount Auburn Hospital at 8:10, and life as he knew it was over. Two days later Linda came back in a casket. She had died, her heart full of fire.

While the pain of Linda's death never lost its sting, over time Peter had learned to cope. And excavating Merritt's anomaly would help get him through the summer.

"Dad, are we going on the ferryboat now?" Andy asked as they left Mount Auburn and headed for Storrow Drive.

"You bet, Pooch."

"But, Dad, they're not real fairies."

"The words sound the same, but they mean different things."

"But, you know what? I wish there were real fairies."

"Me, too."

"And ghosts."

"And ghosts."

In less than half an hour Peter pulled the Jeep into the garage near the New England Aquarium. Because of the holiday, the waterfront was mobbed, mostly with tourists and college kids out for the summer. Under the afternoon sun Peter led Andy to the Harbor Cruise kiosk, where they bought two boat tickets. They walked to the waterfront park, past an unassuming statue of Christopher Columbus and down Atlantic Avenue, where a small marching band played music. They strolled through the crowd to the Aquarium plaza and they watched the seals feed in the outside tank. They bought popcorn and ginger ale and, because the sun was strong, a white cap for Andy with green lettering: BOSTON—HOME OF THE CELTICS.

Hand in hand, they walked down the pier toward the long white boat. Out in the harbor, where Peter and Andy would spend much of their summer excavating three strange boulders, the scattered islands made translucent humps in the blue mist.

Peter taught field archaeology and American Indian cultures at Samuel Adams College, a small liberal arts school north of Boston. The pay was low, so on weekends and summers he would do small contract digs for industry. But as the years passed, he lost interest in excavating old root cellars and Victorian toilets. And though he still enjoyed teaching, Amerindian archaeology, his specialty, had lost its hold on him. Compared to high cultures such as the Greco-Roman or Mayan or even Bronze Age Europe, it was little more than dirt digging. A dozen years, and all he had to show were a few spearheads, arrow points, and pottery shards. Nothing glamorous, nothing to bring in the *National Geographic* film crew— no Mohegan Troys or Winnebago palaces of Knossos to excavate. The field allowed few surprises.

Dan Merritt's offer couldn't have come at a better time. School was out for three months, and three weeks ago, the New Hampshire Historical Commission had pulled the plug on the one dig that had excited Peter. They mumbo-jumboed him about funds drying up, but the truth was he had been fired. He had violated professional skepticism by announcing to the press that it was possible ancient Europeans had migrated to America long before Columbus. The interview had centered on his excavation at Mystery Hill—a famous site he had excavated for three years, and one which the Establishment maintained was the creation of some early nineteenth-century farmer, who in his spare time constructed the twenty-acre complex of stone slab chambers, walls, and dolmens. Yes, the statement was dumb: He had let himself be lulled into public speculation to impress a young reporter; and he had broken the ultimate taboo of challenging orthodoxy out loud. There simply was no evidence of pre-Columbian settlement of America—not the Europeans, Vikings, ancient Greeks, or Phoenicians. Furthermore, no legitimate scholarship indicated that local Indians, remote or recent, ever undertook stone constructions. That made Mystery Hill the work of New England farmers, who were famous for building stone chambers for root cellars, smokehouses, animal pens, and whiskey closets. An anomaly. A big stone hoax—Peter's kind of thing—which became known as "Van Zandt's Folly."

In light of that, it was damn decent of Dan Merritt to offer to set him up on the Kingdom's Head dig—a kind of pardon for Peter's indiscretion in the press. And Peter gladly accepted because he needed this dig, no matter what was out there. He needed something to throw himself into again—something to help him get larger around that egg of pain he had been nursing for the last two and a half years.

The boat let out one long blast as Peter walked Andy up the gangplank.

If nothing else, it would be a nice getaway. Andy could swim and look for crabs and pirate caves. And Peter would shovel up an old foundation and maybe place an article in some obscure little newsletter. Nothing special. Despite some silly rumors of odd occurrences, all they had were three granite boulders—maybe a Colonial oddity, maybe an Indian fishing site. Whatever, it would be a nice, safe dig. A new start, and another opportunity to keep Linda's death at a distance.

Or so he thought.

chapter
Two

They took to the rear upper deck for the view. All seats had been filled, but Andy wriggled his way portside, pulling Peter behind him. With a long blast of the horn, the boat pulled out of its berth. And the captain's voice rang out in nasal clarity over the PA system.

"Even before America was a country, European explorers recognized Boston Harbor as a mariner's dream—a port both large and remarkably safe."

The boat pulled into the inner harbor and the waterfront spread out before them like a movie set.

"By the 1630s, the harbor was a key to the establishment of Puritan culture here. It was in these waters the founding families established their fortunes, where in America's infancy great businesses and banks of the nation's future began to raise capital. Three hundred and eighty years later, the harbor is still a crucial element in the evolving culture of Boston and the state of Massachusetts.

"What makes the harbor unique is that its islands surround a major metropolis. Nowhere else in America do you find such a primitive and pristine community so close to the modern world, yet so removed."

Against a delft-blue sky countless sailboats filled the horizon, their colored jibs bellied out in the sultry breeze. The harbor air felt wonderful, and the blue openness was a liberation. Peter was happy they'd be on an island for six weeks, free of the mainland clutter. They would watch the sun rise overland and set on the sea,

and reclaim some elemental harmony so rare in the modern
world.

". . . On the right is Shepherd's Island, site of a state correc-
tional facility. . . ."

Throughout the trip Andy sat beside Peter. In his hand he
clutched Lambkin, a soft stuffed doll, now a little ratty, but which
still went to bed with him each night. A cross between a lamb and
farmboy, it had big sloe eyes and a sweet face, and was dressed in
bib overalls with a red-and-white gingham shirt. It was Andy's first
toy. Peter and Linda had bought it at a shop in Harvard Square the
afternoon they first glimpsed Andy in the fuzzy shades of a
sonagram at her doctor's office. Peter could still see Linda at home
later stepping naked out of the bathroom, her breasts huge pink
melons, her belly button pressing out like a nose. "Ever do it with a
Beluga whale?" she had asked.

"Call me Ishmael," he said. And they made love while Lambkin grinned happily at them from the bureau.

Large sections of Peter's brain still lived in the past, when
Linda was alive. And at moments such as these, adoring his son, he
took refuge in them.

"Coming up on our right is the only other privately owned
island in the harbor—Kingdom Head. We're not certain of the
origin of the island's name. Some say it was the stamp of a zealous
minister three centuries ago, who had dreams of America as the
biblical Promised Land. Apparently the local natives didn't agree,
since it's the one island in the entire harbor the Indians never
inhabited. And, yet, rumor has it the island is haunted by a ghost
known as the Indian Witch Bride. . . ."

Cutting across the view was a large sleek power boat that
seemed to come from nowhere. It was all of sixty feet and had a
long deep bow and open stern deck, a cabin that could sleep eight
or ten, and a flying bridge sporting an impressive radar unit. It cut
through the blue, tossing up high silver fans. Peter watched it race
alongside the Bay State ferry, then cut a hard arc toward Kingdom
Head.

"With its two hundred and seventy acres, Kingdom Head is
the largest island in Boston Harbor. It is also the most wooded,

although many of the massive oaks will be making way for the extensive construction. . . ."

There were three figures in the boat—two in the cabin, and a third dressed in white riding alone on the flying bridge.

"The heavy equipment along the shoreline gives you some idea of the scale of construction Kingdom Head is undergoing. Those of you from the Commonwealth are probably aware that the island is being converted into what developers hope to be the vacation hub of the Northeast—a cross between Hilton Head and Las Vegas. Besides a complex of condominiums and hotels, there will be restaurants, shops, tennis courts, a golf course, marinas and, of course, a casino planned for the eastern head of the island, right up there on that cliff known as Pulpit's Point. That casino, as you might know, gave rise to some controversial legislation. . . ."

The ferry cut south to George's Island, and the cabin cruiser shot toward Kingdom Head, leaving a long milky wake from a wide stern whose stylized gold script read KINGDOM COME.

Kingdom come.

The letters blazed in the sunlight as the water taxi entered the cove. The cruiser, now empty, filled the small dock below Pulpit's Point. Maybe sixty-five feet from stem to stern, it sported several antennas, a large radar unit, and high-tech radio dishes. Whoever owned it, thought Peter, didn't teach archaeology for a living.

"Donald Trump in town?" Peter asked Dan Merritt, who met them at the dock.

"Close enough," Merritt said. "E. Fane Hatcher, *Mister* Kingdom Associates."

"More like Mister Bugsy Siegel Two?"

"Well, we can't look a gift horse in the mouth now, Peter. Besides, all that payola stuff never stuck."

"Maybe not, but isn't it odd how the state's first non-Native American casino license went to Hatcher?"

Until Fane Hatcher, the only way to bring casino gambling to the Commonwealth was on an Indian reservation. While nobody could prove it, or dared to, everybody knew that Hatcher had bought off a pile of politicians to get the necessary zoning, gaming, and alcohol permits for the island, along with a couple dozen other permits to turn it into a casino resort.

Merritt smiled. "No comment."

It was the typically politic Dan Merritt response. E. Fane Hatcher had the reputation of being the godfather of Boston real estate, but there was no way Merritt would bite the hand that fed them. Not even in a slip to Peter. If you wanted archaeology to happen in Boston, you could not dis the local land barons, especially one whose billion-dollar gambling resort would be a revenue bonanza for Boston and the Commonwealth. In fact, you might even consent to kiss their backsides. Otherwise, precious artifacts might go the way of the bulldozer. There were just too many occasions when out of fear of a work-stop order, developers simply destroyed some ancient foundation or, as happened six years ago with the remains of an intact seventeenth-century British man-of-war buried at the site of a Back Bay office building. So Merritt played it cool, and he suggested Peter do the same.

Peter liked Dan Merritt, but always felt a little self-conscious around him. Merritt looked like the hottest archaeologist in the state. He had an aggressively ordered appearance, one that whispered *I've got my act together!* His head was neat and round like an owl's. His hair, which seemed to have been parted by a laser, magically resisted the breeze. Perfectly arching eyebrows added to the owly demeanor, giving him a touch of disdain. His chinos still showed their razor crease, his blue work shirt looked new, and his yellow work boots held an impossible shine. Merritt lived his life by the book. He was never sloppy, never unorthodox, never given to wild speculations or yearnings. He was the soul of correctness. Everything he did had significance and polish.

Peter's life, on the other hand, was a rough draft. His appearance snorted *rebel!* His hair was wild black ringlets that always looked in need of shearing. A front tooth was chipped, and he had a small scar on his upper lip from a street fight as a kid. He stood about six feet, and because of a daily workout routine at the Sam Adams gym, he had maintained the athletic form of his college wrestling days. His usual outfit was faded jeans, sneakers, and a pullover. Today it was black. Linda once said he looked like an exotic thug.

"They're waiting for us." Merritt nodded at the hill.

It was five o'clock, and except for a few seagulls squawking overhead, nothing moved. The last of the construction crew was filing onto a large utility boat from a jetty on the opposite side of the cove.

Merritt led Peter and Andy up the slope, along a packed trough cut by the wheels of backhoes and trucks. Peter carried Andy on his shoulders.

As they climbed, Peter was struck by the extent of the construction. It was vast, reminding him of one of those World War II movies he had seen as a kid, showing Navy Seabees and a fleet of earthmovers turning a south Pacific island into an air base overnight. Construction stretched as far as he could see. Offshore sat two huge barges, one floating a high dredging crane; the other a dump bin to collect the soil of a sandbar to make way for a hundred-boat marina. Opposite them was the shorefront, now a twenty-foot-high bank of dirt and rocks excavated from someplace in the interior. Behind the dirt mounds were bulldozers, front-end loaders, and huge dump trucks basking in the sun.

Peter felt sorry for the island. It looked wounded. If the place had a ghost, she was no doubt spitting fire. "I don't get it," he said. "They're ripping to beat a winter deadline, yet they offer excavation rights. Why didn't they just push the stones into the sea?"

"Hatcher seems to think they've stumbled upon the foundation of a chapel one of his ancestors built in the late seventeenth century. I think he's hoping you'll find enough of the original to make a replica. His plan is to turn the island into a reproduction of a Colonial village, complete with town hall, village green, shops, as well as the marinas, condos, casino, and church."

"A Club Med for high-rolling Pilgrims."

"Something like that."

"What's your reading of it?" Peter asked.

Merritt shook his head. "I don't know. If it's a foundation, the place must have been another Westminster Abbey. Three granite slabs three feet wide, ten feet long, a foot and a half thick. It had to take a small army to haul them up this. The same for an aboriginal drying station for fish. And the question, why all the way up here and not down by the water where they make more sense?'' Merritt shrugged.

Peter rubbed his jaw in cunning speculation. "Mmmm . . . three stone slabs, three-by-ten-by-a-foot thick? Sounds to me like a Martian landing pad."

Merritt laughed quietly. "Still preaching Erich von Daniken?"

"Hell no, he's passé," Peter said. "I've graduated to *The X Files.*"

Merritt laughed as they headed up the slope. At least they could joke about it.

chapter
Three

The top of Pulpit's Point was a wide plateau of exposed soil, where three men were waiting for them. Two stood by a yellow front-end loader on an incline near the edge. The bearish man in work clothes was explaining the controls to the man in a blue blazer.

It was the third man who caught Peter's attention. He was dressed in white—footwear, pants, T-shirt, and a billowy windbreaker—except for a red silk paisley scarf around his neck. He stood on one of the exposed stones, his hands behind his back, legs spread slightly, and he regarded them through black sunglasses. E. Fane Hatcher. He didn't look thirty, yet he owned his own Boston Harbor island. His complexion was fresh and evenly tanned with no hint of a beard. His hair was golden blond and sat in spikes over his brow. A preppie Caligula. It was hard to imagine him cutting deals with the Commonwealth Gaming Commission.

"Suppose I shouldn't be standing on the evidence," Hatcher said, stepping off the stone. A deep, crisp voice belied the boyish demeanor.

He introduced the big-bellied, red-faced man in the blazer as Fred Goringer, his attorney cousin. Goringer had a wide clubby handshake. "Hey, nice to meet you, Professor."

The other man with the bearish body and soggy cigar stub was Mike Flanagan, the superintendent. His face was a cement scowl.

"Dan says you're the local expert on colonial archaeology," Hatcher said.

"Dan's being kind," Peter said. He introduced Andy.

"Hey, Dad," Andy said, his eyes saucering, "look at the front-end loader."

"Like to sit behind the wheel?" Hatcher asked.

"Behind the wheel?" Andy squealed. "Yeah. That's a great idea. Can I, Dad?"

"Okay by me."

"Mr. Flanagan will show you how it works." Hatcher nodded at Mike Flanagan, who did not look happy suddenly playing baby-sitter. Andy raced to the payloader, with Flanagan slogging behind him.

"I'll get right to the point, Professor. My family records indicate that a small chapel sat here in the late seventeenth century. Supposedly it got blown away in a storm." Hatcher moved so Peter could inspect the stones. "I'd like you to see what you can find."

"Okay."

Peter squatted beside one of the slabs—three giant cobblestones. He ran his hand over their flanks, looking for any signs of human craft—paint or mortar, incised glyphs, tool marks or even fire cracks. Nothing. They looked like Easter Island blanks. But they had been dressed, pounded into rough rectangular slabs, which seemed unusual for foundation stones. Also, the overburden—the material they had been buried under—was mostly beach sand speckled with pebbles and shells. That was odd, since the beach was sixty feet below.

"A little outsized for a foundation, but it's possible." Peter did not mention other possibilities—an Indian fish-drying station or even part of a colonial farmer's corral—for he sensed the risk in dealing with Hatcher. The man wanted an heirloom; and if Peter downplayed the ancestral potential, Hatcher might have second thoughts about the excavation.

"My family's always done things in a big way."

"So I've noticed."

Flanagan swaggered back from the payloader, leaving Andy playing the wheel and gear shifts and making growling engine sounds. "If you ask me," Flanagan said wiping his brow on a handkerchief, "you got three big rocks that're gonna fuck up my work schedule." He looked at Peter and spit into the dirt.

"I don't recall anybody asking you, Mike," Hatcher said.

Flanagan's large, flat face flushed. "Well, I'm gonna say it anyway. I don't like a lot of people wandering around that don't belong here. I got enough men and machines I'm responsible for without worrying about some archaeology people." He looked directly at Peter. "You got a kid—he could get where he shouldn't be or fall in a hole or something. Dig someplace else. It's dangerous here."

"We'll keep out of your way," Peter said.

Flanagan snorted and spit a clammy wad of mucous just inches from Peter's foot.

He's trying to unnerve you, Peter told himself. Don't let him in. It's Hatcher who's paying the bills. He glanced at Andy sitting behind the steering wheel of the payloader. He was about to say something conciliatory when he felt his mind suddenly slump.

Andy froze at the wheel.

The smell of smoke.

Bad feeling.

Andy waved, and in a snap Peter was back out, the feeling gone. A momentary fugue, Peter told himself. Probably Flanagan working his menace on him. He turned to Hatcher. "It's nice of you to let us excavate."

"Well, I like contributing to the advancement of science, although it isn't all altruism. The island's been in the family for eleven generations—some three hundred years. Corny as it sounds, I've got a sense of destiny about the place—something that runs in my family. An early ancestor claimed he was personally appointed by the Almighty to rid the land of heathens and demons. A little silly, but his intention was to convert the island into heaven on earth."

"And you're completing the job," Peter said.

"In a manner of speaking. Besides the obvious commercial venture, this represents a moral commitment to my family and to the Commonwealth. It will raise the quality of life in the state."

Peter glanced toward the low skyline of Dorchester and South Boston and wondered how many people in those sweltering three-families were grateful a yachtsman's paradise was being forged out here.

"If you find anything connecting to my ancestry, I want to

preserve it." Then he added, "You know, Professor, I've got a hunch about this place." He scanned the stones and the golden mound of sand. "I've got a feeling there's something very special here."

"We can only hope," Peter said. "According to Dan, you're allowing us six weeks."

"That was before our latest timetable," Hatcher said. "You've got from June twenty-fourth to July fifteenth."

"That's only three weeks."

"Three weeks too much," Flanagan growled. He pulled the cigar stub out of his mouth and crushed it under his boot. "I got two fucking months to stabilize the hill to take a foundation, and another three to do a shell. A three-week cut at this end bumps us to the ass-end of November. The place freezes up, and I get the shit for it because you archaeology people come dicking in the sand."

"We'll double the work load when they're through," Goringer said. "Simple as that."

"Yeah, simple as that," Flanagan said. "What about the twelve men who get laid off?"

"They'll manage," Hatcher said.

Flanagan was about to say something, but Hatcher's gaze changed his mind.

Peter studied the mound of dirt. It made a flattened dome of some fifty feet to the far side of the hill, where it dropped sixty feet straight down to sea rocks. If the three exposed stones sat at ground level, there would still be some fifteen thousand cubic feet of debris to sift through.

"It'll take six months to excavate this properly," he said.

Hatcher nodded. "Then, you'll have to cut corners."

"With brushes and trowels?"

"What do you need?"

"That front-end loader's a good start."

"What?" Flanagan's eyes cue-balled in their sockets.

"That can be arranged," Hatcher said to Peter. He nodded to Goringer to make note.

"Over my dead body," Flanagan said.

Hatcher's black-glass stare snapped at him like twin barrels of a shotgun. "That can be arranged, too."

"Jesus Christ!" mumbled Flanagan.

Hatcher took off his glasses to clean them. He had hard, bright sapphire eyes that made Peter wonder if he were wearing tinted contacts. He wiped the lenses on the edge of his jacket. "Mike, Professor Van Zandt and his assistants will be here for three weeks excavating this hill at my invitation. Consider them under my employment. If there are any reports of interference, I will hold you responsible. Is that clear?" He slipped his glasses back on. "I asked you if that was clear!"

"Those machines are the property of Poro Construction, and they don't job them out to just anyone off the street. That's all I gotta say."

"Make that a promise," Hatcher said. Then he nodded to Fred Goringer. "Call Tony Poro in the morning and make the arrangements—the front-end loader with the backhoe and an operator on call." Then he turned to Peter. "There's an old abandoned caretaker's place about half a mile up the beach. It's going to be redone for our pro shop. But you and your assistants can hole up there. Nothing fancy, but it beats living out of a tent. Dan, I'll see you at the boat."

Hatcher left with Goringer and Flanagan for the cruiser. The water taxi would be back for Peter and Andy in a few minutes.

"Never thought I'd come to this," Peter said to Merritt. "Archaeology by backhoe."

"It's better than no archaeology."

"I guess, but won't three weeks with Flanagan be fun? I'll probably spend most of the time trying not to get spat on."

Merritt chuckled. "Could be worse. You could have Hatcher mad at you."

Peter nodded. "He does seem to carry all the guns."

When Merritt left, Andy was still behind the wheel of the payloader, his Celtics hat on backward the way the big kids wore them and his little belly filling the red stegosaurus T-shirt. He was working the wheel and the gear shifts, all the while growling and mowing down unimaginable monsters with the bucket.

At moments like this Peter's love for Andy filled him all the way up. *Linda, you'd be so proud of him.*

While Peter stood there aching with love for the boy, a slender movement out of the corner of his eye caught his attention. From nowhere a curlicue of wind had come, a small dust devil that began spinning across the face of the mound, pirouetting the dead grass and dry leaves. Peter watched the thing rapidly constrict, sucking up the sand and debris until, in a matter of seconds, it was a small dark tornado that cut loops across the mound. It was uncanny with its sudden momentum, and the way it moved—not random, but willful, as if searching for something. It whipped to the far edge of the dome, sweeping along the perimeter. Then in a sudden shift it spun a straight line toward the center where, as if finding the right place, it screwed itself into the ground.

For a long moment Peter just stared at the spot marked by a little circle of dead leaves. He didn't know how long the funnel had lasted in real time, maybe thirty seconds, but it had held his attention for what seemed minutes. Its movement appeared deliberate—as if the thing were sentient. And with its sudden dissipation, the place was utterly still, dead, void of movement. Except for a vague smoky odor, there was no stirring in the air nor the yellow dust. No birds cruised the sky. Even the clouds seemed airbrushed in place. The world had turned to a still life. Even Andy seemed frozen at the wheel.

Then just as Peter glanced at Andy, he felt such a premonition of horror that his body jolted as if he'd been electrocuted. He snapped his head back at the mound half expecting to lay eyes on some hideous demon taking form.

Nothing, just that mute yellow hump of sand, so oddly void of vegetation.

What in God's name was that?

His heart pounded so hard his chest hurt. *What the hell passed through me?* A moment ago he had been enjoying the promise of the dig, high on the thought of spending a few weeks with Andy on the island. Then came a sensation that he'd just glimpsed some unspeakable horror. He rubbed his hands together to relieve the chill in his fingers.

Always a rational explanation, he told himself. A bad combination of sun and subconscious apprehension over the dig. One of those psychic flare-ups the brain sometimes suffers when more than the usual number of synapses fire at the same time. That was it—no ghosts. A purely neurological phenomenon that had all the symptoms of a mystical experience.

That's what Peter told himself as he regarded the mound of sand. Yet, as he let the explanation settle in, he no longer wanted to take a shovel to the dome.

Dig someplace else. It's dangerous here.

Suddenly he did not want to know what the sand contained—as if lying below were secret, sordid things.

"Hey, Dad?"

Like the snap of a magician's fingers, the spell was broken.

"Yeah," Peter called. "Ready to head back?"

Andy was resting his head on his crisscrossed arms over the steering wheel. He was staring out the windshield. He looked tired. It had been a long day for him, too. "Yeah, but you know what?"

"What?" Peter put his hand on the boy's back and kissed him on the top of his head. He was warm and sweaty and smelled like a puppy.

"Who's that man?"

"You know Dan Merritt, honey."

"No, not him." Andy pointed. "Over there in the woods."

Peter looked to the dark patch of woods on a small hill on the other side of the salt marsh. Because of the tilting sun, the area appeared an opaque wall of trees. He saw nothing and decided this was one of Andy's little jokes when, all at once, he spotted something in the brooding patch of woods, barely distinguishable from the senseless background. For a moment he suspected a trick of the light. But, as he shielded his eyes, he felt a small jolt of recognition as a white-faced figure took form like an hallucination—a figure standing perfectly still, half camouflaged by thick, low shrubs, and watching them across the marshes.

"Who is he, Daddy?"

"I don't know." The construction crew was gone, and Merritt said the island was unoccupied. As best Peter could tell, the man was large and dressed fully in black, which didn't make sense on a warm sunny day.

"And you know what, Dad? He's been there for a long time. I waved, but he never waved back," Andy said. "All he does is just watch me."

Peter's heart quickened. He lifted Andy out of the cab and put him down. When he looked back, the figure was gone, as if the trees had snapped shut.

"But, Dad, why was he watching me like that?"

"I really don't know," Peter said.

But he had the prowling suspicion that he'd find out.

chapter
Four

"Yuck! What stinks?" Andy trudged through the cottage door, dragging a duffel bag.

"Beats me," said Peter. "Guess the place has been boarded up a long time."

"Do we have to stay here?"

"I don't think we have a choice."

"Well, I don't like it. It's creepy."

Peter sighed and put down the last of the cartons he'd carried up from the jetty. They had made four trips, and Andy was growing cranky. "It won't be once we get the windows up."

"But I don't want to stay here, Dad."

Peter didn't need this. His head was throbbing from the sun. "Well, it's going to have to do, little man. The Hilton's still a hole in the ground." He followed Andy inside.

Hatcher hadn't understated the condition of the abandoned caretaker's house. In his romantic imaginings Peter had envisioned a large gingerbread cottage with flower boxes. Instead, the place was a dark clapboard saltbox with a wind-slapping screen door and broken windows. It stood alone against a brooding brow of oaks which explained the interior dreariness. And the pungent mustiness suggested the place had been locked up for a long while. Although the yard had recently been mowed, it consisted mostly of weeds and scrub. Its saving grace was the view. The house sat high on the harbor side of a rock cliff, and straight out sat Boston shimmering in blue mist.

From Peter's estimate, the place was old—maybe as much as two hundred and fifty years. The wainscotting that covered three walls of the foyer looked original, its detailing easily eighteenth century. The same with the wide pine floorboards. The closed door, presumably leading to the kitchen in the rear, looked modern. But the front door was ancient and the two small windows on one side were rippled and clouded with tiny bubbles. Most of the right-hand wall was taken up by a huge fireplace, its mantel hewn of the same dark oak trunks that served as ceiling beams. Their surfaces were gummy from dampness. What confirmed the era of the house were the wrought-iron fixtures embedded in the field-stone. They had been forged at least as early as the Revolution. The place was easily one of the earliest houses of the harbor islands.

As a temporary encampment, the place was fine. But it needed considerable work to restore, including jacking up the east end to relieve the floor slant. Looking around, Peter's mind ticked away on the fantasy of having it as his own, reviving its original Colonial charm over slow summer days. Andy would grow up by the sea and far from the madding crowd. It was a nice thought, but it was Hatcher's dream turf; and, in a year, the house would be a pro shop. The nine-hole golf course was already being carved out of the fields behind the trees.

Four weeks had passed since Peter had last been on Kingdom Head. Four weeks of scrambling to finalize excavation plans and paperwork with Dan Merritt and Earthwatch, which was supplying Peter his field volunteers. The good news was that one team member, a Jackie Kelleher, had a hoist license to operate the front-end loader. Peter also signed an agreement that any artifacts or treasure found on Kingdom Head remained the property of Kingdom Associates.

While away, Peter had no more quaking apprehension about the dig. On the contrary, the intensity of preparations, which ordinarily took months, had buoyed his spirits. In fact, he felt a keen sense of expectation—like an actor taking up a role he had long coveted. The project hummed with promise.

He and Andy had arrived that morning in a rented outboard along with excavation tools and a week's supply of food for five.

The three Earthwatch volunteers would be dropped off later that afternoon by water taxi. Meanwhile Andy was hoping to fly his new phoenix bird kite. The steady breeze across the cliff was perfect, but there was a three-story drop-off straight down to the water from the front yard. And no barricade. Peter assembled the kite and instantly the bird was aloft.

Andy squealed with delight as he ran into the open.

"Stay away from the edge," Peter shouted, distracted by one of those nightmare images only parents know: the boy running with his eyes on the kite, heading right for the drop-off. But Andy bounded and yipped about like a puppy. When it was clear he wouldn't listen, Peter said he would have to fly it sitting down until Peter was through unpacking inside.

"But, Daaaad," Andy whined.

"No 'But, Dad.' I said stay in one place."

Andy looked at him. He was burning to run the kite.

"Don't move, or no kite."

Andy made an enraged groan of frustration and stomped his foot. "You're mean. How come?"

Peter felt a flash of irritation. That was Andy's usual strike back, that he was mean. Despite the limitation of a six-year-old's language, that one phrase grated on him. Peter was anything but mean. "Because I don't like that cliff, that's how come. If you get near that edge, I'm going to bring you in the house." Maybe he could find some rope and sticks around back to fashion a fence of sorts.

"I don't wanna go in that dumb house." He started to cry.

"Damn!" Peter mumbled under his breath. Irritation was tightening his chest. He had to get settled, to air out the cottage, check that the stove and refrigerator worked. Then he had to head up to the mound and lay the grids. That would take a couple hours, and he wanted that all done before the Earthwatchers arrived. "Andy, listen to me: It's dangerous. That cliff drops right down to the water. Just stay put until I get back."

"No! You're no fun. You're mean."

"I'm sorry you think so, but I don't want you to go running off the cliff."

"I'm not gonna run off the dumb cliff." He made a face and looked away.

"Fly it from where you are."

"No, I won't." And he turned and stomped his way toward the edge.

Peter saw red. "Damn it!" He leaped off the porch toward the boy. It was irrational he knew, and Linda would have handled it better, she always did. But, Christ! sometimes he would not let up.

When Andy saw Peter barreling down on him, he dropped to ground, the string wrapped around his fingers. Peter jabbed his finger at him. "If you go near the edge I'm going to tan your hide. You got me?"

No response. Just that twisted scowl. From a side pocket of his mind he heard another voice: *Peter, control yourself. You're losing your grip. Something's getting at you.*

Peter felt his hand hum with the urge to backhand Andy across the face. He had never laid a finger on the boy; in fact, the very thought was loathsome to him. But right now he was itching to smack him.

"Do you understand me?"

The boy's lower lip began to quiver.

"Do you?"

"Yes," Andy whimpered. Tears were pouring out of his eyes. "I hate the dumb kite," he said, and threw the string into the air.

Instantly the wind grabbed the kite, and the next moment Peter went bounding after it. Five feet from the edge, he jumped up to catch the end before it blew off. Andy fought to suppress a grin, but Peter saw it and came over to him.

"You think that's funny, do you? Would you like to see Daddy go flying off the cliff? Would you?" he screamed. "Pretty fucking funny, huh?"

Hot blood flooded his head. He wanted to grab Andy by the shirt and shake him until he stopped moving. The boy's face crumpled.

And suddenly the fire was gone.

Whatever had taken possession of him had utterly vanished, leaving Peter standing there stupidly, the kite string a mangled cat's cradle in his hands, and his son sobbing into his fat little fingers.

Peter felt insane.

He's six years old. Six little years old! He still wets the bed. Of course he found it funny—his great big daddy leaping in the air like a Jack-in-the box for the string. It WAS funny, and you didn't laugh like you were supposed to. Nice job of handling your son. A moment ago he was happy as a lark, and now you reduced him to sobs and killed the kite for him. He'd been jumping all day to fly it. Lovely display of parental maturity. And nice how you taught him his first swear word.

Peter's brain felt like a light bulb loose in its socket.

What's happening to me?

How did an innocent little scene get so ugly so fast? And where did all the hot blood come from?

Peter squatted beside Andy, his throat thick with misery. He had ruined everything. Now what? How did he get them back on track?

"Andy, I'm sorry I yelled at you. I just don't want anything to happen to you, okay?"

You wanted to hurt him.

The boy looked up, tears puddling his eyes, and all Peter saw was Linda—the same exotic black Armenian eyes and Cupid bow mouth. The same expression when she cried. How could he want to slap that sweet little face?

He pulled Andy to him. "I'm sorry, little guy. I didn't mean to get upset."

That wasn't your everyday upset, he told himself.

Peter looped the end of the string around Andy's wrist. "I tell you what," he said. The wrist flopped into Andy's lap. "Just sit right here, and when I come back you can run around all you want with the kite. You can even teach Daddy how to fly it. Okay? I'm going to rig up a fence so we'll all be safe. Okay?"

Please don't say "no."

Andy didn't. He just sat there hunch-shouldered with the kite flapping above. When Peter was certain Andy wouldn't budge, he went around to the back of the house.

The remains of a large garden sat in a fenced-in square claimed by weeds. Nearby was a small wooden shed, empty but for some dark boards and bleached lobster traps. With those and porch chairs, he set up a barrier about fifteen feet from the edge. Andy was still sitting in place, but his interest in the kite had picked up, to Peter's relief.

"That's as far as you go, okay?" The barricade was crude, but it would stop him if he got too close. "Okay?"

"Okay." His shoulders drooped in defeat.

"Friends?" Peter asked holding his hand palm up.

"Yeah." He gave him a limp five.

"You can do better than that."

But Andy stood up and walked away without looking back. And Peter headed back inside the cottage.

At the rear of the foyer was a narrow staircase leading to the upstairs, and a passageway into the kitchen in the back. He'd leave that for last. He went through the other rooms, opening the windows so fresh sea air could flush the place out. The cottage was sparsely furnished with pine tables and chairs, army cots, and simple lamps plugged into the walls. Outside sat an old generator near the propane tank, which had a line to the stove in the kitchen. Upstairs was a bathroom with a tub and chain-pull toilet. The walls had recently been whitewashed. With the exception of the lobster pots in the outside shed, nothing in the place hinted at the former inhabitants. No nail holes or shadow marks where pictures had hung. No ashes in the fireplace. The place had been scrubbed clean of its past.

Peter claimed the large front bedroom for Andy and him, then headed down. He was just coming outside when a gust of rotten air swept into his face. He walked around the base of the staircase toward the kitchen door and opened it.

The sweet stench of putrification hit him like a fist. He clamped his nose, fighting down the reflex to vomit.

The room was so dimly lit that at first Peter could not determine the source of the foul air. The whole interior seemed a corrupt ectoplasm exuding pungent rot. But his eyes adjusted, and he spotted it. On the floor in front of the stove. In the dim backlight it appeared to be the body of a large dog, lying in a pool of dark blood under a swarm of flies. He moved closer.

Suddenly Peter's body jolted and his teeth clamped down on

his tongue to stifle a scream that pressed its way up from the pit of his soul.

It was Andy.

His eyes were open and milky and looking directly at Peter. His throat had been slit from ear to ear. His front was black with blood, and in the pool on the floor lay Peter's knife—the six-inch, horn-handled number Linda had given him on their last Father's Day. The one that drove Linda to her death.

The scream in his head stayed with him as he bolted out of the kitchen, as he tripped on the threshold and shot through the foyer and out to the porch.

Andy was there, alive, out on the lawn, in the same white shorts and blue jersey, his back to him. *Oh, dear God, thank you.*

"Hey, Dad, you want to see this?"

Peter staggered against the porch rail. He nodded, knowing if he opened his mouth he would scream.

Dumbly he watched as Andy ran with the string along the barricade. His body cast a shadow as he moved. He was really there. Above the phoenix fluttered happily in the blue air.

Peter scraped his palm against the top of a rusty nail until he bled. Pain coursed through his hand. "Andy." His voice was a rasping whisper.

"Watch this, Dad."

Andy was there like the pain lighting up his nerve endings. "Great," Peter panted.

But the image of Andy, dead in his blood on the floor, seared his brain. He could still see it. He could still smell it. It *too* was real . . . and he didn't understand, but he had no doubt he had seen it . . . and there was no feeling that it was his imagination or that he had been hallucinating.

"Now watch this," Andy called.

"Be right back."

He stumbled back into the house, his head roaring.

Jesus! The place still smelled of death. An egg of nausea swelled in his throat.

He held his breath—*please, God, no*—and pushed open the kitchen door.

Gone. The body, the blood, the swarm of flies. All of it.

God, thank you
No, not all of it.
The knife was still there. So was Lambkin—nailed to the floor through the neck.

chapter
Five

Peter would cut his own throat before he'd raise a finger to Andy.

Murder his son?—the very idea was too repulsive for his mind to hold. But that was the message of his hellish vision: He was capable of slaughtering his own son.

For the next two hours, Peter sat in a porch chair, restuffing and sewing back Lambkin while Andy played in the yard. His mind felt as if it had been stung by hornets. As his fingers worked the needle, he thought about how inexorably close to madness he had come in there—how he had actually sensed the slippage, half anticipating a sickening pop in his skull from that monstrous vision. He had never experienced anything like it before—not even the night Linda died. Then it was profound grief and despair that had taken him over. But never illusions. Something else was going on.

Eventually he worked out a rational explanation: What he saw on the kitchen floor was a bona fide hallucination, replete with visual, auditory, olfactory, and tactile perceptions, but lacking any external stimuli. A waking dream. And, like dreams, it was all symbols. Lambkin was an obvious metaphor for Andy. The knife, Peter reasoned, represented his parental irresponsibility and *not* a murder weapon. Peter was not a violent man. Yes, he had a temper, sometimes shot from the hip, but violence was constitutionally not part of his makeup. Even that night with Linda, that stab at the butcher block was simply dumb macho display—and he knew Linda knew that.

As for the source of the hallucination, he worked out a sound psychological mechanism: guilt over his flare-up about the drop-off. Hot and anxious to set things up, he had overreacted. Somehow guilt and anxiety had projected that nightmare vision in the kitchen—a savage warning that his negligence could be fatal. What he had trouble with was the knife and the lamb. His only explanation was selective amnesia: That he had lapsed into a daze and actually brought Lambkin into the kitchen. Yes, while Andy played outside, he had unpacked it, gone into the kitchen, pulled his knife out of his belt case, and stabbed it as a warning to himself. That he could remember none of it also had a psychological explanation: repression. The notion that his negligence might be dangerous to Andy was too horrific for him to accept. Thus, his rational mind blocked all traces of his behavior, leaving his unbridled subconscious to stage the warning.

A schizoid psychodrama.

As for Andy's reaction—

"Yuck, what stinks?"

—it was just the musty seabreath the boy picked up. Nothing untoward. No *Twilight Zone* stuff. All perfectly rational.

While Andy ran his kite, Peter rocked away, sewing back the stuffing of his son's bedtime companion. But what gnawed at his mind was the thought that he might stumble into another flash abomination.

Worse still, that he might be capable of entranced behavior more awful than taking a knife to his son's toy.

By four-thirty, the cottage was aired out and the lamb was mended. Though his mind was still tender, Peter felt better. From the jetty below, he and Andy watched the water taxi pull up to the mooring with the three Earthwatch volunteers.

Constance Lambert—I'm a math teacher from Stamford, Conn. I'm 32 and enjoy reading and photography. This is my first archaeological expedition. I look forward to the experience.

Virginia "Sparky" Mendota-Kelleher—I'm 27 years old and live in Santa Barbara where I manage a bistro called Scallion's. I don't know anything about archaeology but I'm hoping to have a spiritually uplifting experience getting into ancient cultures. I have lots of interests including astrology, nutrition, and sea otters.

Jackie Kelleher—I'm a 26-year-old business grad student at UC Santa Barbara. I was born and raised in Detroit. I like working outdoors and did construction during high school and college summers. I have never been on an archaeological dig before, but I loved Indiana Jones. I enjoy body building, surfing, and high adventure. This will be our honeymoon.

What a crackerjack expeditionary team! Peter thought. A high school teacher, New Age beachboy, and his bride, a macrobiotic soothsayer. Wonder if Sir Arthur Evans excavated Knossos with such heavy hitters.

He folded the Earthwatch bios and slipped the sheet into his pocket, thinking that a volunteer expeditionary team is better than no expeditionary team. And given the shaky state of his soul, he welcomed adult company.

Jackie was first off the boat. He had a bound-for-glory face: floppy blond hair, a muscular jaw that was working gum furiously, a lot of big white teeth, and mirrored sunglasses. He was dressed in cutoff jeans held up by red suspenders, an open blue workshirt, a red T-shirt, and white high-top sneakers. He looked like Li'l Abner in giant baby shoes. A case of Moosehead beer sat on one shoulder, and with his free hand, he helped off his wife, Sparky, who had magenta-streaked hair and was dressed in loose black pants, an oversized white T-shirt with black footprints all over it, and red vest. She was holding a half-empty beer bottle. She wore round red sunglasses and a ruby nostril stud.

Jackie pumped Peter's hand. "Some heavy-duty construction going on, or what?"

The guy was a breath of fresh air. "They're building a resort."

"That right? I just love big machines."

"Then you'll be in heaven," Peter said. "We've been loaned a Case 580 backhoe. You familiar with it?"

"A 580? Hell, I was raised on one." He grinned. "My ole man

owns a construction outfit in Detroit. I got my hoist license on a 580."

"Good, we're going to need you," said Peter.

From what Earthwatch had told him, Jackie and Sparky had been bumped from the Atlantis Expedition to Santorini, Greece, to dive for Minoan shipwrecks. Likewise, Connie's first choice of Machu Picchu had also been overbooked. Peter could not compete with those, of course. For their $2700 all Peter could offer was three big boulders, twenty eight-hour days of hauling and sifting sand, and a backhoe. And Jackie had been hoping for Nazis and the Temple of Doom.

Connie stepped off in jeans and a white pullover. She had thick hair the color of sunrise, a full and fleshy mouth, and light green eyes that lit up her face. Peter shook her hand and felt his heart slump. Women this attractive intimidated him. He felt better when he noticed the large diamond ring on her engagement finger. At least she was unavailable.

"Is this the island that's got the famous ghost?" Sparky asked. "It was in that Robert Frost book we had to read. The black widow or something."

"I think you mean Edward Rowe Snow," Peter said. *The Islands of the Boston Harbor.*" In addition to materials on field methodology, colonialism, and local Indian history, which he had had Earthwatch forward them, Peter had assigned his team the Snow book. "That was the Lady in Black."

"Oh, yeah," Sparky said. "The Lady in Black." She spoke in such a slow dreamy way that Peter began to wonder if someone had named her "Sparky" as a joke. Up close she was quite striking and not just because of the bird-of-paradise hair and ruby nostril stud. She had a small teardrop face offset with large wondering dark eyes and neat heart-shaped mouth. She looked like somebody who had been raised by fairies.

"Ghost?" Andy sang out. "There's a real ghost here, Dad?"

"No, that's on George's Island, a couple miles south of here. From what I remember," Peter said, "she was the bride of a Civil War prisoner in Fort Warren. She sneaked out there one night to free him, but they got caught and were dispatched."

"But you know what?" Andy said to Connie. He had taken an

instant liking to her. "She came back and spooked everybody. That's the best part."

Connie grimaced in fake terror. "Oh, my. It's a good thing she doesn't live on this island."

Andy nodded.

"Do you believe in ghosts?" Connie asked him.

"No, but I'm ascared of them."

Connie laughed warmly. "That's a safe attitude. Guess that covers how I feel, too."

Peter liked how she talked to Andy, who was beaming from the attention. He started them down the jetty to the wooden stairs. Connie fell behind chatting with Andy. "I saw a ghost once," he said.

"You did? Where?" Connie asked.

"In the trees near Puppet Point." He pointed down the beach.

"How did you know it was a ghost?"

"Because he was creepy, and he disappeared real fast, too."

"What do you think he was doing in the woods?"

He shrugged. "Probably just taking a pee. That's what my dad said. But I think he was spying on us."

"Uh-oh. I hope we don't bump into him."

"I once saw my mom next to my bed, but that was just a dream, because she's dead."

"Oh . . . well, it's nice that you dream about her." Connie started up the stairs behind Andy. Peter and the others followed them.

"I think Snow said something about this island," Connie said to Peter. "Something about an Indian Bride Witch. I don't recall much written about her, just that she was executed for sorcery."

"You mean 1692 and Salem and all that?" Sparky asked.

"Yes, but nothing much was written about it. In fact, the whole island's history is just a paragraph or two."

"Because it's been privately owned for centuries," Peter explained. "And apparently it was never inhabited nor used for commerce. Not until now, that is."

Connie looked down the beach as if trying to reconcile all the construction with the island's virgin past. Offshore a blue fishing boat puttered by. The same one Peter had spotted when they arrived.

"An island with no history," Connie said.

"None we know of."

"Snow discounted the legend," she continued. "He said Indians never occupied the island. Also, there were no court records of a woman executed for pagan worship."

"Maybe they executed her without a trial," Sparky said.

"That's not too likely," Peter said to her. "Cotton Mather and his pals were fairly public about preparing the new world for the Kingdom of God. Dozens of people were prosecuted for witchcraft, and nineteen were executed—all with lots of publicity. It was the story of the century. I think Snow's right about that."

"Just folklore in action," Connie said.

"That would be my guess," Peter said. "Must be hundreds of legends that got passed around these parts. Probably all originated in a tankard of local brew."

They reached the top. "I suppose every island has its ghost," Connie said.

"I suppose," Peter said.

chapter
Six

It took the three Earthwatch volunteers awhile to get settled in; and because a light rain had begun to fall, Peter decided to put off showing them the site until the next day.

After a hearty breakfast the next morning, Peter held a review of local Indian archaeology and field methodology. Sometime around eleven, he led the group down the beach to the site of the stones.

The weather had cleared, leaving a glorious azure sky and white puffs of clouds blown by a warm sea breeze.

Jackie let out a faint whistle as he took in all the construction below Pulpit's Point. "What in hell are they building here?"

"Atlantis, Machu Picchu, Disneyland," Peter said. He smelled smoke, but he could see no signs of burning.

"Jesus, I'll say."

But it was startling how much the machines had altered the land in the three weeks. Some twenty acres between the Point and the salt marshes had been filled in. Just below, a large steam shovel was gouging out a deep trench from the base of the Point inland. At the water's edge, a quarter of a mile down the coast, a high pile driver kept up a steady steam-spitting pounding, as if trying to nail the island to the harbor floor. And in the distance, trucks and bulldozers scrambled to level off a knoll. But what shocked Peter was how in such a short time the once-green hill just opposite Pulpit's Point had been scalped. The whole slope—a thick grove of oaks three weeks ago—was now a raw red incline of exposed granite veins and treeless stumps and two twenty-foot cones of mulch. Of all the machines on the island, it was that chipper that Peter hated the most—a red long-throated monster with insatiable high-velocity grinders that could eat up a tree and spit it out the other end into a neat pile of chips in a matter of minutes. The ultimate symbol of the mindless efficiency that would shear Kingdom Head into one man's dream.

Andy asked if he could play in the front-end loader. Peter glanced at the machine. It sat at the edge of the slope overlooking the outer harbor.

"Sure," Peter said, and watched Andy run off to it.

Peter walked them around the site, ending at the three large stones. He felt a flicker of uneasiness in his gut as he circled the mound. On his first visit the proverbial someone had walked over his grave up here. "There are no public records, but the island's owner claims a chapel once sat here and was blown away in a hurricane in the late seventeenth century."

"Is that what you think?" asked Sparky.

"I'm not sure what to think," he answered. He glanced at the bald dome of sand. Weird. Nothing growing on it—not a twig of scrub nor blade of grass. A mute alien hump. "What's odd is that the stones were under four feet of overburden."

"Why's that odd?"

"There's practically no topsoil on the Point. It's solid granite just a few inches below the surface."

"Meaning what?" Connie asked.

"Meaning the mound isn't natural. The stones were buried."

"Why would someone bury them?" Sparky asked.

"That's what I hope we find out," Peter said. He estimated that more than five hundred tons of beach material had been hauled up the slope. For whatever reason, somebody had wanted to bury the stones.

"It looks like some of the Indian burial mounds I've seen in Nevada," Sparky said.

"Yes, except local Indians didn't bury their dead in mounds. They used flat land, and by Colonial times, even Christian cemeteries. What's odd is that there's no record of Indians ever using

Kingdom Head for anything. In fact, it appears as if they went out of their way to avoid the place."

He looked at the three stones and the mound of sterile earth and felt his spirit sag. Suddenly it all seemed so futile. Even if something were there, he could never do it justice with a backhoe, three amateurs, and a twenty-day deadline.

"In a perfect world what would you like to find under there?" Connie asked.

"In a perfect world . . . an aboriginal temple, and survivors fluent in modern English."

She laughed. "And preferably at this end of the mound."

"God, yes!"

Somewhere the construction crew was burning trees. Had to be, because the odor, more acrid now, cut the air. Funny how he still could not spot the smoke.

Over the next several minutes Peter explained the procedure, how they would be assigned individual tasks on a rotating basis. They would first lay out grids across the mound and set up the sifting screens. Then the digging would begin with sample squares and the material would pass through screens. It was a pathetic way to excavate, in random squares, but they had no choice.

He squatted beside one of the stones to show where it appeared to have been squared off deliberately at one end. "The same with the others . . ."

He was about to continue about the stones when he heard a loud snap like a pistol shot. Movement out of the corner of his eye made the breath catch in his throat.

It was moving.

For a stunned second Peter's mind focused every element from his surroundings like a magnifying glass into a pinpoint of recognition.

The front-end loader Andy was in began to roll backward down hill.

"Daddy. Daddeeeeeeeeeeeee!" Andy was frozen in terror at the wheel.

Peter never remembered his feet making contact with the ground. What he did remember later, as he bolted towards his son, was a flash prayer that the wheels would jam against a rock or drop in a hole or that a gear would suddenly lock before it reached the drop-off. Andy was heading straight for the edge.

A voice screamed in Peter's head!

Not my son, too! God, no!

It all happened so fast—the anguished plea, the sudden sideways tilting of the machine, Andy screaming again for Peter, the sense of others running behind him. Peter made a leaping dive into the open cab. If he missed, those massive black treads would grind him into the dirt. The top of his head exploded in pain as he banged into the levers. His feet curled in behind him. Andy slipped on top of him absurdly to pull him up. Peter's hands hammered the foot brake. Nothing. Like pushing against a stone wall. Jammed, and the machine still kept rolling.

The voice in his head screamed, *"God, stop us!"*

Peter yelled for Andy to hang on to his neck.

Connie and Sparky ran alongside, shouting for him to jump. Jackie hurled a large rock at the back wheels.

Just as the machine tilted toward the edge, with his feet braced against the pedestal of the seat, his legs folded under him, Andy on his back with his legs clamped under his arms, Peter summoned every scrap of energy from his muscles to clear that churning black wheel and made a springing leap out of the cab.

He pancaked against the ground with a violent thud, his face pressed into the dirt.

Through the pain all that counted was Andy on top of him and the solid earth beneath.

Andy was crying, and the others were helping them up. He heard Connie say "Thank God" and Sparky shout to Jackie that he had done it. But it all seemed to come out of a muffling fog. Somebody peeled Andy off him. Peter hurt all over. Sparky helped Peter to his feet.

At the last moment Jackie had tossed a small granite boulder under a rear wheel, catching the machine fast just two feet from the sixty-foot drop-off. It sat at a tipsy angle, exposing its underside.

Peter pressed Andy to him. The boy was sobbing, and Connie was rubbing his back. Peter reached for Jackie's hand to thank him. Jackie smiled and nodded and gave the thumbs-up sign. He seemed more interested in the loader. He went over to it and jammed another rock under the other wheel. Then he checked underneath.

"But, Daddy, y-y-you know what?" Andy said, gasping for breath.

Peter kissed the boy's neck and made a silent thanksgiving. "It's okay, it's okay. I got you now."

"I was ju-just playing with the shifts and it jumped and started to move."

Peter's eyes fell on the red script painted on the engine cover: L'IL BITCH.

"I hate that dummy backhoe." Andy's face crumpled again and he burrowed his face in the crook of Peter's neck and cried. Peter felt his throat thicken.

My God, he thought, I almost lost him. If he went off that cliff, I would have gone after him.

You got a kid—he could get where he shouldn't be.

"Why did it do that, Daddy? I didn't do anything."

It's dangerous here.

Dangerous here.

"It was just an accident, honey. Just an accident," Peter said. "Maybe you bumped the emergency brake. It's okay."

And his bouncing in the seat set it in motion, he thought. Sure. Except the bucket should have anchored it, even on an incline like that. And the bucket was down the way it's supposed to be when not in use. Peter remembered it was down when he watched Andy hop aboard. It was the first thing he had automatically checked for—a safeguard against nightmare possibilities. The hoe was up, but the bucket was down. He was sure of that. He'd bet his life on it.

"Why did it have to roll down like that, huh?"

He squeezed Andy.

Out of the corner of his eye, Peter noticed Jackie. He was climbing out from under the loader and shaking his head.

"What's the matter?" Connie asked.

Jackie said nothing, but Peter noticed the expression on his face.

He came over to Peter, and when Andy put his head down, Jackie made a gesture with two fingers. For a moment Peter's mind was blank. Then recognition passed through like a seismic crack.

The brake lines had been cut.

chapter
Seven

Peter tore down the slope.

A huge truck was making its way to the twin hill across the flats. Jimmy Piscatano was behind the wheel. They had met yesterday. They called him Jimmy P. He stopped the truck and pulled off his headphones when he spotted Peter waving at him.

"Where's Flanagan?" Peter yelled.

"I dunno. Everything all right?"

"No."

Jimmy P. checked his watch. "Try the trailer, he's on lunch break." He pointed toward the high crane.

Peter ran off.

A shiny aluminum trailer with PORO CONST. in red letters on the side sat with a lone pickup truck in front. Flanagan's. Nobody was in sight. The door was closed and the blinds drawn.

Peter climbed the three steps and pushed open the door with a bang. Flanagan was at his desk, reading a newspaper, and eating a sandwich and a bag of cheese puffs. He looked up, startled. "Who the hell you think you are crashing in here?"

"Somebody rigged the backhoe."

"Somebody what?"

"You heard me. Somebody set us up for an accident. My kid was almost killed."

"Nobody rigged nothing, asshole."

Peter felt his body jolt, but he held back. "Flanagan, I'm telling you, the brake line looks melted. It's gone."

"Oh really? Well, Jimmy P. put the thing up there last night, and it had brakes."

In his mind flashed a picture of Flanagan under the machine with a blowtorch. "Then come look for yourself."

"The fuck I will! I'm having my lunch, asshole."

Peter placed his two palms on the desk and leaned his face toward Flanagan's. "Flanagan, my kid nearly got killed because your machine started rolling. You understand?" he said, bearing down on him. "And if you call me that again, I'm going to start banging your face til you don't move."

Flanagan began to work his mouth, but stopped. He was big, maybe six feet two and two hundred and seventy pounds—an inch and eighty pounds over Peter. But it was mostly the fat weight of a fifty-five-year-old man who over-ate and over-smoked. Peter was nearly as solid and quick as he was when he had wrestled in college.

"It can't roll if it was parked against a goddamn wall." The fight was out of his voice.

"All it took was forty-eight pounds."

"Even without brakes, you got the hoe dug in and the bucket on the ground, for chrissakes."

"Then they must have been up."

"They couldn't be up; we don't leave 'em that way."

"Then how'd it start rolling?"

Flanagan's eyes narrowed to shrewd slits. "You tell me." He hoisted himself to his feet. He stood rocking against the edge of his desk, measuring Peter. "We don't park machines in transport position."

"You did this time."

Flanagan squinted as if to confirm something, then shook his head in clever astonishment. "Well, then, it'd be a cold day in hell before I let my kid play on a backhoe with the ends up."

For a long moment Peter stood fixed on Flanagan's accusation like a stuck bug. He was turning the blame around to Peter, the son-of-a-bitch. But, Flanagan was right, Peter told himself. He had never even bothered to check that the hoe and bucket were on the ground. He had just assumed. What he always told his students never to do: Assume. *Ass-u-me.* It got everybody in trouble. He had been too distracted about digging to be certain the machine was safe before letting Andy get on. And now he was trying to pin the rap on Flanagan because he couldn't 'fess up to the message on the kitchen floor, he told himself. The same when he had let Linda fly off on a dangerous night. You're going to kill the thing you love most because you're careless, he told himself.

"I told you the other day you had no business on this island," Flanagan said. "Maybe now you learned your lesson and will get the hell outta here."

For the second time in fifteen minutes Peter's body leaped before he could command it. On one hand he sprang over the desk and grabbed hold of Flanagan by the neck of his shirt.

"We mess up your work schedule so you rig an accident." He pushed Flanagan to the wall.

"I didn't do it, you crazy bastard."

"Then one of your men."

"Nobody did nothing."

"Then explain the melted cables."

Flanagan gasped against Peter's grip. "I dunno, for Chrissakes. It was an accident."

"Hey!" somebody yelled. It was Jimmy P. pushing open the door, two other men behind him and Jackie Kelleher behind them.

"Get this crazy fuck off me." Flanagan's voice sounded like a broken squeeze box.

Peter flung Flanagan into his chair like a sack of flour.

Jimmy P. and the other men pulled Peter back by the arms. "Okay, pal, let's cool it, huh?"

Flanagan stood up, his face drained of color. His shirt was torn. "Crazy bastard comes in here accusing me of trying to kill his kid. Get him the fuck out of here!"

But before they could pull Peter back, Flanagan whacked Peter in the face with the back of his hand. "And that's for the shirt, ass-hole," he said drawing out the syllables.

Peter tried to get at Flanagan, but the men held him back. The third man body-blocked Jackie, who looked stunned.

"A little air'll make you feel better, hah?" Jimmy P. said, pulling Peter toward the door.

Before they stepped out, Peter turned back to Flanagan. "You're the only one on this island who wants us off bad enough," Peter said.

"Wrong again, *asshole*," Flanagan said with more hyper-pronunciation. "We *all* want you off."

Jimmy P. and the other two pressed Peter through the door. The sunlight was brilliant. Outside half a dozen men were leaning against the pickup, with their thick arms folded, glaring at Peter and Jackie from under their silver hats. They looked like a rack of mortar shells.

Nobody said anything, and nobody moved. They just watched. Peter felt their eyes rake them as he and Jackie walked away. Any one of them could have done it to scare them off the island, with or without Flanagan's blessing. Maybe even the good-natured Jimmy P. here, or his brick-faced buddy on Peter's other arm. Maybe it was a grand conspiracy of the whole work crew not wanting their schedule screwed up, or their jobs jeopardized should an important artifact of Colonial history turn up. What pecked at Peter's mind was the thought of being isolated for the next twenty days on an island with sixty hostile construction workers. What else might they pull? Lower a crane on them? Or set off blasting caps a little too close? ("What can I say? It was an accident. The kid got in the way.")

"All's I know," Jimmy said before they left, "is when I parked the thing up there, all pistons were out of transport position. And I pulled the brake. I do it automatically, like parking a car."

"You always leave the keys in the ignition?"

"I left them because they said the kid here's got a hoist license and you're gonna use the thing. Besides, who's gonna steal it on an island?"

Peter didn't say anything.

"You shouldn'ta twisted his tail like that," Jimmy P. said in a half-whisper.

"And somebody shouldn't have rigged the machine."

"It wasn't rigged," Jimmy said. "I checked it myself. The brakes themselves are fine."

"Fine? The thing almost rolled off the cliff."

"I mean the calipers and shoes are fine. It's just the cables are shot."

"That's what I mean. Somebody got a torch to them."

"That's not possible unless they dismantled half the machine, and that didn't happen. Look, I'm not giving you garbage. I really don't know what got to the cables, but nobody tampered with it. And the bucket was anchored down."

"Then how did it start sliding?"

"That's another thing I'm trying to tell you," Jimmy said. "When you said there was a problem, I went up to the Point. Your boy says he felt something buck from underneath. He also said the bucket just jumped up in the air."

"Jumped up in the air? And how do you explain that?"

"I can't, kids imagine things. But all's I know is that last night I dug the bucket into the ground, and the brakes worked. Understand?"

"No."

"Cheezis. I'm saying it's *impossible* for the bucket to go up with the machine off. You got a hunk-a-steel weighing half a ton that can't just jump up by itself. It can't do what he said it did, simple as that."

"Then tell me what caused it to roll."

"He musta turned the engine over to get it up in transport is all."

"The engine never went on," Peter said, and Jackie nodded to confirm the fact.

Jimmy P.'s face was a hard blank. After a moment he shook his head. "I can't explain it," he said. "Maybe I'm superstitious, but it ain't the first time funny things have happened up there."

Peter felt an icy feather wisp across his neck and down his back. "What's that mean?"

But Jimmy just turned and walked away.

chapter
Eight

Peter held the match to the blackened wick of the candle lamp. It sputtered a moment, then bloomed into a teardrop flame.

"But what made you think Flanagan would sabotage us?" Connie asked. She was laying out the flatware at her end of the table.

"We're in the way," he said. "That and a kind of tribal enmity between construction people and archaeologists. We're working on what was, and they're working on what will be. What-will-be pays more."

It was a gorgeous night and they were setting the porch table for dinner. It was nearly eight-thirty, and the afterglow of the sun had turned Boston into a fiery silhouette. The western sky was already an indigo vault fretted with pinpoints of light, and over the northeast horizon the light of a crescent moon marbleized a path that seemed to run clear across the sea.

Andy was sitting on the grass, studying the fireflies he had caught in his bug jar, appearing like miniature stars snatched from above. He looked like an allegory of a young god studying creation.

"But you're convinced it was an accident."

"Now I am," he said. But why the brooding feeling that something's not right? Peter wondered. Why the nagging sensation that there's something out here trying to get my son? Like that premonition three weeks ago on the mound. And that monstrous vision yesterday. And the accident today. Were they connected somehow? And what was Jimmy P.'s last remark all about?

Ain't the first time funny things have happened up there.

A half-glimpsed premonition made him glance at Andy. The boy turned his head toward Peter at the same moment, and their eyes locked. Something seemed to pass between them. A second later, the boy turned back to his fireflies.

Peter placed Andy's mug beside the candle lantern. The glow through the red glass cast a blush across his plate.

"But how are we in the way?" Connie asked.

"While we're scratching in the dirt for arrowheads, they're not building their casino," said Peter. "We're messing up Flanagan's schedule."

"I thought you'd worked that out beforehand."

"I did with Hatcher, but Flanagan never liked the idea."

They headed back inside. Jackie and Sparky were at the counter, working on a dessert of blackberries and whipped cream. Connie went back to finishing the salad, and Peter to the cutting board beside the stove. With his knife he chopped three cloves of garlic for the spaghetti sauce. He scraped the pieces into a pan of hot olive oil. He then sliced the onions, peppers, and mushrooms and scraped them into the skillet. He stirred the vegetables sizzling in the oil, then poured the ground peeled tomatoes. Some hot oil spit on his hand.

"Well, if you ask me," Jackie said, "the way Flanagan was ripping at you, if he didn't do it, he will next time. Or one of his guys."

"I don't like the sound of that," Connie said. Sparky agreed.

"Maybe not, but it's pretty clear where the battle lines fall," Jackie said.

"There are no battle lines," Peter said. "I overreacted and I'm sorry. We had an accident and it's behind us."

"Well, frankly, I don't buy that," Jackie said. "After you took off I checked the brake cables pretty carefully. They were completely fused. But what bothers me is that the housing was still hot to the touch, which means the system couldn't have been messed with before we got there."

"What are you saying?" Connie asked.

"I'm saying it looks like somebody got at it with incendiaries, probably some fancy plastic stuff because there wasn't any magnesium oxide or cordite debris that dynamite leaves. Probably set off on a remote."

"You mean a bomb?"

"Yeah, but without the explosion."

"Nobody set off a bomb for Christ's sake," Peter said.

"Then what's your explanation?"

Peter felt a tiny electric ripple in his midsection. "I don't have one, but it wasn't sabotage." He said it with the conviction of a man who wanted to believe very badly. He could understand their confusion. A few hours ago he had gone flying off the Point screaming bloody murder. But that was the craziness of the moment. His best guess was that there was some freak electrical surge that caused the hoe and bucket to jump up, causing the machine to roll. At the same time, the brake lines had somehow fused. He didn't understand it, but it was the only explanation that made sense. Or that he wanted to make sense.

"Then tell me where all the heat came from?"

"I don't know. I'm not a mechanic."

"Don't have to be a mechanic. Steel melts at sixteen hundred degrees, and it wasn't the sun."

"Then maybe an electrical short."

"Electrical short? Not from the battery of a backhoe. Besides, the brakes don't have an electrical line."

Peter knew that. "I don't have an answer."

"Besides, why would someone try to sabotage a six-year-old boy?" Connie asked.

"Wasn't meant for Andy," Jackie said. "Me or Peter."

"But why?"

Jackie shrugged. "To scare us home," he said. "Most hard hats aren't salaried. They work from one day to the next. If they're sick or there's bad weather, they don't get paid."

"So?" Connie said.

Jackie glanced at Peter. "Well, according to Jimmy, a bunch of guys got laid off once we moved in. Which means there's a dozen guys at home by the phone waiting to the tune of three hundred bucks a day. From my experience hard hats got a real tight support system. If they had a mind to helping laid-off buddies, nothing would stop them. If you pardon my French, they don't fuck around. And the cable looked it."

"Then we better contact the police," Connie said looking at Peter. Her eyes were huge with insistence.

"Yeah," said Sparky. "I'm not crazy about spending three weeks on an island with a bunch of angry hard hats."

Christ, now it's swinging the other way, Peter thought. "We're not going to contact the police," he said.

"Why not?" said Connie.

"Jimmy P. says nobody rigged the backhoe, and I have no reason not to believe him. It was a freak accident, plain and simple and, thankfully, nobody got hurt."

Jackie nodded and sucked down more beer. But the expression on his face said that he knew that Peter knew it had been no accident.

"Then why not report it, just in case?" Connie asked.

"Report it to whom?"

"The police."

Frustration was pressurizing Peter's chest. "It's not a police matter."

"He said it looked as if an incendiary device was set off, Peter. Do we have to wait for another incident just to make sure?"

"Might not be a bad idea," Jackie said. "Just file a report with the authorities. Give us some assurance."

"What harm can it cause?" Connie asked.

"I'll tell you what harm," Peter said at last. "If we contact the police, that would be it for our digging privileges."

"Why's that?"

"Because Hatcher is the Don Corleone of Boston real estate. He avoids bad press like the plague. We cry 'wolf' and he'll yank us out like that."

"So you'd rather take the chance on getting sabotaged again than jeopardize the expedition."

"We weren't sabotaged." Out of the corner of his eye, he saw Sparky shake her head at Jackie to not push it. They were all against him, he thought.

The disapproving set of her mouth told him that Connie was questioning his credibility and wondering why he was denying compelling physical evidence. "Peter," she said, "I can appreciate you not wanting to jeopardize the dig, but it doesn't have to be a criminal complaint. We could notify Hatcher directly, no police."

"And say what: We had a near-fatal accident with the backhoe you gave us, but there's an outside chance it might have been booby-trapped with plastic explosives? And just what do you think he'd do? Revoke our excavation privileges to avoid trouble. Even if he didn't, he might call for an investigation, which could take weeks. And all we've got is three."

"How about Merritt?" she said.

"Merritt works for the state, which means an automatic investigation and work stoppage. We can't afford that."

"So, you're saying we're stuck," Connie said. "If we report it, we risk losing the excavation. If we don't, we risk losing our lives."

"Isn't that a little dramatic?"

"Dramatic? Need I remind you your son nearly got killed this afternoon?"

Peter felt his face flush.

"What if something else happens?"

"If anything else happens, we'll blow the whistle. We'll go to Hatcher, we'll go to the police, we'll call in the National Guard. Okay?"

"I'll buy that," Jackie said. "Flanagan's mean, but he's not stupid."

Connie studied Peter for a long moment, then made a conciliatory nod. She picked up the salad and started out behind Jackie and Sparky.

Peter watched the door swing back. An accident report. It was a reasonable suggestion. The very thought had occurred to him that afternoon, but he had dismissed it immediately. He couldn't risk losing excavation privileges before they even broke the ground. Unassuming as those three boulders may appear, excavating them was better than not excavating them. That was something Connie could not comprehend. None of them could. This dig was much too important for exigencies against risk. He had known that the moment he laid eyes on the mound. The place hummed with promise.

Peter removed the sauce pan from the burner and poured the

contents into a large serving bowl. He found the ladle and sunk it into the sauce. The scent of the tomatoes rose in the air. So did something else.

Smoke.

But it wasn't from the stove. Nor from the window. He wasn't even sure the odor came from the outside—just an awareness in the olfactory lobe of his brain. It passed in a matter of seconds.

He moved to turn off the burner, but his eyes fixed on the jet. A perfect crown of flames. He remembered reading someplace that the hottest part was the blue. Funny, you'd think it was the inner orange or the yellow tips. For a minute, he stared at the perfect points of blue. "Fire without smoke, smoke without fire," he whispered and turned over a dark thought.

It was back—that feeling of disconnectedness. It had hit him three weeks ago up on the Point; then yesterday on this very spot. The knife slit in the floor pressed up like a pebble in his shoe.

He turned off the jet and started for the door with the bowl of sauce.

Ain't the first time funny things have happened up there. Jimmy P.'s words buzzed in his head.

What's going on? Peter thought. What's happening out here? Yesterday he had wondered if he was losing his mind. But not today. They all knew something had happened with the backhoe. Steel just doesn't melt by itself. And if it had been sabotaged, their ears would still be ringing from the explosion. And Andy would have been burned from molten metal.

Peter pushed open the door with his foot. Andy was standing on the other side, his face red from tears. The fireflies in his bug jar were dead.

chapter
Nine

Peter smelled smoke and woke up with a start.

No flames raging throughout the bedroom. The place was dark and perfectly still. His watch said 12:13. Andy was sound asleep in the bunk beside his. Peter got up and checked all the rooms, careful not to wake anybody. Everything was in order. Nothing on fire, nothing smoldering. At least not in the house. The odor came from the outside. He could smell it in the sea breeze. He put on his shorts and Nikes.

Moments later, he was pounding his way down the beach, the sand firm beneath his feet, seashells cracking like eggs. The smoke seemed to be getting stronger as he approached Pulpit's Point, though he could see no firelight ahead. But he didn't let that bother him. He was too distracted by how powerful he felt. His thighs pistoned along and he felt he could run forever. Never could he remember experiencing such animal swiftness, such smooth, effortless strides. It was as if he were being powered by some auxiliary force.

Although it was the same beach they had walked that day—the same shingles and rocks, the same crunch of shells beneath his feet, the same curve of the shore—something about the layout was different. And it took him a few moments to realize that all the heavy machines and construction materials were gone. So were the huge piles of sand, the excavation holes, the pilings, and concrete foundations. Even the floating barge was missing. For some reason they had all been removed. The oddest thing. How did they do it so fast?

Another thing was the darkness. Yes, the stars still burned overhead and a crescent moon made a tipsy grin above the mainland. But the harbor was dark. The Boston skyline was missing. They had removed that, too.

But that didn't bother Peter either. Under the circumstances, it made some odd kind of sense. Besides, he was in a hurry.

He ran on, feeling the perspiration lubricate his joints. The evening was warm with promise. He cut over some dunes and straight up the slopes of Pulpit's Point. He was hardly breathing as he rounded the top. His only concern was that he'd be late.

He wasn't.

The man in the black robe nodded when he saw Peter, then clutched the big book to his chest. Around him the others had gathered in a circle, hunched together and dark but for the flickering yellow light of lanterns. Behind them distorted shadows capered against a backdrop Peter couldn't make out. The smell of smoke was thick.

The robed man raised somber eyes to the congregation.

"Brethren, Satan is among us."

"Satan is among us," the congregation rumbled.

He pointed at the woman with her back against the rock. Peter moved so he could see better. But her face was in shadows, and the only impression he had was of a dark thicket of hair and the occasional firelight reflecting from her eyes.

"Brigid Mocnessa, I accuse you of having committed sundry and pernicious acts of witchcraft against Almighty God and innocent members of this congregation. You have been apprehended to stand trial before this jury on this the fourth day of July in the fourth year of the reign of our sovereign lord and lady, King William and Queen Mary of England, and the year of our Lord sixteen hundred and ninety-two."

Peter felt a little out of place in his shorts and Nikes. All the other men were in waistcoats and wide-brimmed hats.

"Jeremiah Oates, what right have you to stand in judgment over me?" the woman cried.

"What right? You have been accused by sober witnesses assembled here of practicing abominable acts of deviltry, of conjuring engines of malice to torment our people and nature, to inflict our children with fits beyond the scope of any natural distemper. You have been brought before us to confess covenant with the devil in conspiracy to destroy the Kingdom of Jesus Christ our Lord and Savior. What say you to these charges?"

"How can one small woman bring such afflictions to man and nature?"

"How? Because you are possessed of demon powers."

"Were I so possessed, I'd dispel you all from my land."

"Confess," he demanded.

"Aye, aye," somebody cried out.

"Confess, and save your soul," shouted another.

"Yes, confess."

The woman looked around the circle of accusers. "Look at you, good Christian lambs in your white-faced piety, all assembled to hear the abominations of the witch." She spat on the ground. "I'd have you all on a spit before I confess anything."

A roar of protest rose up from the dark huddle.

Peter shifted behind the others for a better look at the accused woman. Her hair hooded her face in deep shadows. All he could make out was the dark dress and shoes. They were absurdly white. But what distracted him was her voice. There was something very familiar about it.

The minister raised his Bible high and quoted, " 'Have I not chosen you twelve and one of you is a devil?' " He pointed the book at her. "You have been brought here to account for the witchcrafts you are conversant in. We await your confession."

"Then you'll wait 'til frost heaves bury Hell."

And again the congregation protested.

Peter was astounded at the defiance in the woman's voice. Why didn't she just give them the confession they wanted?

"You have no right to try me without magistrate or court," she shouted.

"We are the court of God and the congregation of New Jerusalem." Reverend Oates waved the Bible at her. "What higher authority be there on earth?"

"Your god has no authority on my land."

The crowd roared again.

"Then you admit this be a temple of demon spirits."

The congregation held its breath. The woman said nothing. But Peter was certain that in the hush of anticipation, the woman was laughing to herself.

"What, has the Devil no tongue before God's truth?"

Still no answer, but the feather-light chucklings from the woman's throat.

Apparently Reverend Oates heard her, because Peter saw fury light his eyes. "Then bring on the witnesses, Mr. Herrick," he demanded.

A loud shriek startled Peter.

From behind, three boys, their faces white with fright, stumbled toward the circle. They were agitated, cowering. The shorter one with dark curly hair could not look at the woman. He had apparently been told what the eyes of a witch could do. The second boy was braver and stole glances at the woman. The third boy, taller than the others, pressed next to him, frantically scanned the assembly for his mother. When he spotted her, he let out a woeful cry. In the next moment he was on the ground clutching his stomach as if trying to claw out his bowels.

"Dear God, save my child," cried his mother. She broke from the circle of figures, but the minister stopped her with his arm.

"Leave him," he bellowed. "Let the hag see with her own eyes what miseries the poor child endures by her wicked arts."

The boy thrashed in the dust, kicking and writhing and yowling like a crazed animal. The skin across his abdomen was bleeding from where he had gouged himself. The witch looked on with fascination.

Unable to endure the torment of his companion, the second boy let out a howl and threw himself beside his friend, rolling and thrashing in the dirt and pounding the sides of his head with his fists.

Shouts of horror rose from the circle. "God have mercy," screamed a woman.

The first boy had fallen to his knees, tears issuing from his eyes, his mouth jabbering incoherently. Peter moved to get a better look. The boy looked like somebody he had known once.

"Young Worthy Oates is speaking in tongues," someone gasped.

The boy—apparently the minister's own son—was indeed babbling in strange syllables. Suddenly, he began clutching handfuls of dirt and slapping himself in the face. Black tears streamed as if he were ripping his eyes from their sockets. Peter was frozen at the sight of the boy pummeling his own face. Beside him knelt the tall boy, his tongue protruding and his eyes bulging like hens' eggs. The third had hopped to the middle of the circle, where he crouched like a terrified rabbit, grunting at the ground and pounding his temples against some hideous vision behind his eyelids.

People screamed in horror at the spectacle. The minister stepped around the boys toward Brigid Mocnessa. "Do you not see their afflictions?" he shouted over the awful noise. "Do you not think they are bewitched?"

Again the woman remained silent, and her laughter had stopped. She turned toward the Oates boy, whose face was a large dark scab.

"Then it is true, the devil has no tongue in the witness of God's truth."

"God's truth be damned," the woman said.

"Save them," cried a woman tearing at her hair. *"Save them!"*

Others blocked their faces and cried out in pity for the boys.

In the lamplight Peter could see in the minister's face a strange glimmer of elation at the spectacle. His body appeared to swell in his robes to the rising howls as he loomed above the boys like some granite monolith.

"Behold them, witch!" he said to Brigid, half his face in the unsteady yellow light, the other shadowed in black. "Behold your handiwork."

The woman looked on in silence. Her face, in perpetual shadow, was still trained on the Oates boy, who now was pressing his face into the dirt as if trying to burrow into the earth.

In a flashing movement the minister swung around. "Care, care, children," he declared in a heavy voice so all could hear. "No harm shall come to thee." He reached down and touched each of the boys' heads.

In a few moments the boys' shrieks subsided to whimpers and sniffles. The second and third boys pulled themselves to their feet. The boy called Worthy Oates remained collapsed face-first on the ground. A low moan issued from his throat.

"Rise, Worthy Oates," his father said. "She can do you no harm." With one hand he held the Bible in the air above him while Mr. Herrick helped the boy up.

Slowly, the boy's body quivered into motion. He pushed himself up by his hands, his face out of view. His hands were visibly shaking. When he was pulled toward the light, Peter could see his whole body tremble.

The minister put his hand on his son's head. "Worthy Oates, tell us what you have seen. Tell us what you witnessed of her wicked arts."

"You saw nothing." The witch's voice was a low hiss. "Nothing, nothing."

Slowly the boy raised his face, a patchwork of mud and blood. A loud gasp broke from Peter's throat. It was Andy.

Daddy . . . Daddy . . . I didn't mean to kill her.

Peter woke with a start.

Andy was thrashing around in his cot, muttering incoherently.

Peter got up and stroked the boy's head, whispering in his ear that everything was okay, that no harm would come to him.

But Peter felt an edge of petulance. The dream had hooked him, and he was humming with curiosity about where it was going. He tucked the sheet around Andy's neck. His mind suddenly switched to that hallucination from yesterday. Andy was on his side in the same position, but now a dark featureless hump in the cot.

He kissed the boy on top of his head. "You had a bad dream. It's okay now. Daddy's right here."

When Andy was asleep again, Peter crawled back into his own cot. In his mind he could still see the boys, their faces strained with fright, the dark defiant woman refuting the charges of sorcery. Such a strange fascinating dream. Jesus, he hoped he could get back to where he'd left off.

But he couldn't. The rest of his sleep was an irritating blank.

chapter
Ten

He woke up the next morning feeling that he had spent the night in some distant place.

The dream stayed with him for several hours, though he didn't know what to make of it. He had read that dreams were reflections of inner fears and yearnings, often composed from scraps of the conscious day. He had no clue to this inner process, or what was being reflected, but Connie had brought up the Indian Witch Bride yesterday. Apparently, his mind took that and churned out a provocative narrative. But strangely, it had none of the weird non-Euclidian distortions of time or space characteristic of most dreams. It was as if he had watched a movie played on the inside of his forehead. Stranger still was the sensation that somehow the dream was connected to their activity on the island.

They were on Pulpit's Point by eight-fifteen, and already the construction machines were growling full throttle and lacing the air with diesel exhaust. But there was none of the acrid stench of smoke. In fact, Peter would not smell smoke for the rest of the day. What distracted him was the activity just offshore. Divers were working from a barge, setting explosive devices on rock reefs. Throughout the morning the underwater blasts went off, making huge mushroom caps in the water. He wondered if they were using plastics.

Peter carried on as if yesterday hadn't happened, none of it. A bad start, he told himself. Today was for real. He gave an outline of the day's activities and objectives and reviewed the excavation procedures. They would set up two sifting screens and work according to a schedule he had drawn up. With shovels, Peter and Connie would dig designated squares on the grid, and Sparky and Jackie would sift. After lunch, Jackie and he would shovel while the women sifted.

While they worked, Andy dug nearby with his plastic shovel and pail. When he got tired of that, he sailed his kite. And when he had enough of that, he helped shake the screens and push the wheelbarrow. He was enjoying himself and he talked nonstop, swapping stories with Jackie and Sparky.

All seemed so normal and yet, the image of Andy frozen in terror behind the backhoe's wheel glowed in Peter's brain like an ember. He still wondered if somehow he had foreseen the accident three weeks ago.

Around ten, Jimmy P. showed up with two mechanics who worked beyond noon installing new brake cables on the backhoe. When they were through, Jimmy called Peter and Jackie over.

"You operate this okay?" Jimmy asked Jackie.

"If the brakes are working." He was wearing a Hard Rock Cafe-Boston T-shirt and a Lakers' hat. Jimmy handed him a hard hat.

"They're working. Everything's working good. I checked it out myself. The keys are in it, but I gotta take them back for the weekend. You can't use company property unless we're here." He shrugged. "Ain't my rules. What the super says, hah?"

"Okay." It crossed Peter's mind to stop by Flanagan's trailer and apologize for yesterday. It was the honorable thing to do, and a conciliatory gesture might put the bad feelings behind them. Time to start afresh.

Jackie climbed onto the machine and sat behind the controls. He tested the brakes, raised the hoe and bucket, tried the emergency cable. When he was satisfied, he got off and went back to the screens.

Jimmy P. said, "Flanagan ain't too sweet on you folks, you know. I guess you're gonna have to make due with the shovels over the weekend." Then he added, "You need any help, you know where I'll be. And be careful, hah? You're nice people."

Andy wandered over for the pack of bubble gum in Peter's pocket.

"How's the slugger today, hah? You got a little shook up yesterday I hear."

"Yeah," Andy said. "The brakes broke."

"Yeah, I know that. And your dad caught you just in time. Well, it's all fixed now." Jimmy patted Andy on the shoulder and grinned at him like a favorite uncle. "I got one just like you at home. His name's Frankie, 'cept he's twice your size, the way his mother feeds him."

"Jackie says the brake linkage looked fused," Peter said.

Jimmy's face appeared to harden. He nodded. "What can I say?"

"He suggests a small explosion went off, maybe some kind of plastic."

"You hear an explosion?"

"Just a loud snap."

" 'Cuz nobody bombed you is all," he said. "We don't even have plastics on the island. Just dynamite." He nodded toward the barge offshore. "And you know it when you hear it."

One of the other men called for Jimmy to go.

"Jimmy, what happened yesterday?"

Jimmy looked at him, with turbulent thoughts seeming to cross his face. "What happened?"

"You heard me."

"I don't know what happened."

He started to go, but Peter stopped him. "You said it wasn't the first time something funny's happened up here—meaning what?"

Jimmy made a dismissive gesture. "I'm just superstitious is all."

Peter caught him by the sleeve. "Tell me."

Jimmy looked at the guys down the hill and made a signal that he'd be right there. "What can I say? It's crazy, ain't even worth mentioning."

"Try me."

He shrugged. "I don't know," he said then stopped again. A queer kind of grin slid across his mouth. "It's just that every time we started clearing away the stones, something screwy happened, know what I mean?"

"No."

"Like the machine kept going on the fritz. Stalled out every ten minutes. We took the whole engine apart, replaced all the wiring. It does it again. We finally get it working and pull up one stone, then the thing starts to buck like a wild bronco. Stuff like that. We try another machine, the same thing happens—it stalls out soon as we get the hoe under them. What bothers me is we bring the machines down there and they start right up. It's like something up here puts a hex on them."

Peter nodded slowly. "The brakes ever go out?"

Jimmy shook his head. "That's a new one," he said. "I thought all the funny stuff was over with."

"Couldn't it all be coincidence?"

"Yeah, sure it could," he said. "But that's a new machine, and it's doing it, too."

The cold feather brushed across the base of Peter's skull.

From down below Flanagan honked for Jimmy from a pickup truck.

"Gotta go."

Peter's heart was banging again. "One last question. You do any burning yesterday? Wood burning—brush, trees?"

"Unh-uh. Anything we cut goes through the chipper. Why you ask?"

"I thought I smelled smoke."

"Ain't ours." Jimmy headed down the slopes, half running, as if he couldn't get away fast enough.

Peter watched him get into the pickup. Flanagan's large red face glared at him like a stoplight.

Ain't ours.

Peter turned around, and the backhoe filled his vision. The hoe was clawed into the ground, the bucket down and gaping up at him like a mouth.

And he thought all the funny stuff was all over with, the thing seemed to say. *Silly Jimmy P.* The machine stared at him through its twin headlights.

The feather brushed across Peter's testicles. And while everybody is conveniently looking the other way, thought Peter, your big yellow pal here is going to up and do the Funky Chicken. And in his mind it suddenly puffed up into a soft Disney animation, the headlights blinking coquettishly, the hoe waving at him, the bucket a loose, balloony-lipped mouth on stalks. A giant Toon backhoe out of *Roger Rabbit*.

. . . And all of a sudden it jumped up in the air.

"That's right, Buddy boy. Got a real tiger in my tank. Take the boy for another ride one of these days. Wanna come, Big Daddy?"

A moment later, the vision was gone, and the backhoe was just a backhoe. And behind it a small dust devil danced across the mound.

The morning passed without incident. By lunch break, they had cut two squares each about a foot deep. The digging was easy because the material was mostly sand, not the veiny granite bedrock that made up the rest of the island. Under ordinary circumstances, they would have excavated no more than an inch or two in the four hours. But Peter was excavating by shovel and stopwatch. He was committing every violation of field methodology. A blind thrust could shatter an artifact or slice through ancient timbers or even skeletal remains. But it was their only option—to dig random squares for a couple of days, then turn the backhoe on it.

He was still puzzled by the site. If it was the remains of a small round chapel that got blown away in a hurricane, it made no sense why anyone bothered to cover up the foundation with beach sand.

They took lunch down on the beach. Jackie and Sparky stretched out on towels, with CD headphones. Jackie was listening to Creedence Clearwater Revival, and Sparky to Joan Armatrading. Peter sat on a towel beside Connie. Andy was ambling down the shoreline, eating a peanut butter sandwich and looking for hermit crabs.

"He's a sweet little boy," Connie said, watching him.

"Yeah, I think I'll keep him," Peter said, smiling.

"If you change your mind, give me a call."

She had stripped down to a one-piece lavender bathing suit. Peter watched as she withdrew a container of sunblock from her bag and applied the lotion to her arms and legs. He tried not to be distracted by how attractive she was, and how the material clung to her body. He tried not to think of how badly he needed a woman in his life, how much had been missing during the last few years. Also, it occurred to him that he had forgotten how to relate to a woman from scratch. Five years of dating, seven years of marriage, and nearly three years of bereavement had all but robbed him of it. Fifteen monogamous years had also produced a sense of guilt— almost as if by chatting with Connie he was cheating on Linda.

"When's the big day?

Connie peered out from under her visor. "The big day?"

"Your ring."

She held it up so the diamond caught the sun. "Two weeks ago, but I don't think we're talking about the same thing," she said. "I just got divorced."

"But it's on the wrong hand."

She held up her left hand. The knuckle of her ring finger was slightly enlarged. "I broke it skiing when I was a kid. I can't get a ring over it."

Suddenly, Connie did not seem so inaccessible. She, too, had wounds to heal.

"How long were you married?"

"Four years. The national divorce average." To change the subject, she glanced down the beach at Andy. "It must be difficult raising him alone."

"It's easier than it was." Andy had found a dead horseshoe crab and was holding the carapace upside down, testing the legs with his fingers. Even from this distance, Peter could see the boy's raw fascination with death—a fascination void of comprehension and remorse. Andy knew nothing about the circumstances of Linda's death, just that it had happened in a car. An accident.

Accident.

"Does he remember her?"

"Not really. He was only three when she died," he said, and his mind snapped on the scene of three-year-old Andy in a diaper and bare feet waddling penguinlike around the house, calling for Linda. He could still see his eyes large with confusion and the little pink mouth popping the syllables—Mama? Mama? *Mama went bye-bye.* Bye-bye! Jesus, could there be a more vicious metaphor? For several days after the funeral, Andy had asked for her and cried when she didn't come. Then he became frantic with missing her, throwing tantrums, running to the windows, hysterical to see Linda's car come up the drive. For Peter it was a period of dark despair and violent frustration, for he was caught trying to distract the child from a primal void, while averting his own collapse. He managed to maintain a balance, as one cause became therapy for the other. But the weeks passed, and Andy grew to accept the permanence of Linda's loss, but not without lapsing into a sub-dued state of depression until the absence became routine and Linda faded from his toddler universe.

"If you don't mind my asking, how did she die?"

A voice in his head whispered, *Accident.*

But another voice full of smoke said, *He killed her.*

Peter felt his body jolt. Someplace in the center of his brain a node opened. And the thought pistoled out:

HE KILLED HER. Yeah, he did because he wouldn't obey Daddy. Because he had to crawl under the goddamn sink when he was told three times not to.

From across the sand, Andy was staring intensely at Peter, his face blank of expression, as if he had just read his father's mind.

My God, where did that come from? It's not true, honey. IT'S NOT TRUE. I swear I don't think that. Not me.

The boy turned his back to Peter and walked away with the dead creature.

Andy, no! Daddy doesn't think that. No!

"Peter, you okay?" Connie asked.

"Yeah . . . fine." Andy couldn't have picked up his thoughts. "Just woolgathering."

"You look like you've seen a ghost."

"Think I'm getting too much sun."

He wiped the sweat off his brow and put his cap on. His mind swirled with dark currents.

Andy was looking back at him.

A little like lancing a boil, hey, Bunky? One that's been pressing its way up all these years. A little spurt of psychic pus.

The notion astounded him. Never before had he blamed Andy. Never.

Daddy . . . Daddy . . . I didn't mean to kill Mommy.

Such a shudder passed through Peter's body that he had to balance himself with his hands.

"You sure you're okay?"

"Yeah . . . just a little dizzy." The words tumbled out of his mouth like stones.

His mind screamed, *That was only a dream! Only a damn dream!* Suddenly his mind was in a crossfire debate.

And just where do you suppose dreams come from, Sigmund? Your unconscious is where.

No. All blame for Linda's death Peter had assumed himself. In fact, he had flagellated himself with blame—how he had come home that night in a rotten mood and nudged Linda into an argument about the kitchen cabinets that sent her flying out of the house and into a tree.

Then what about the little matter of Andy on the kitchen floor with a throat gash from your knife?

That was simply a reminder to take better care and not some lurid symbol of repressed anger, he told himself. He could not ever imagine blaming Andy, even subconsciously, for Linda's death.

Like the way you didn't try to pin the backhoe accident on Flanagan.

That was different.

My ass, that was different.

"Peter?"

"Mmmm."

Andy dangled the dead horseshoe crab by its tail. Then he fell to his knees to bury it in the sand.

Peter dropped his head to the blanket. His head throbbed so hard his eyeballs ached. A lump of nausea swelled in his throat.

Smoke.

He smelled smoke.

Where there's smoke, there's fire, pal.

What's wrong with me? he thought. What's going on with my mind? That stuff's not coming from me. Those are not my thoughts. NOT . . . MY . . . THOUGHTS.

"Peter, I think you better get in the shade. You're white." She put her hand on his forehead.

"A car accident," he said, and he thought: Maybe I'm having a nervous breakdown.

"What?"

"My wife—she died in a car accident."

"Oh. I'm sorry. What an awful waste. Here, have some lemonade." She handed him the canteen from the cooler. "And let's change the subject."

Peter sat up to take the drink.

He glanced down the beach.

Andy was nowhere in sight.

chapter
Eleven

Peter shot to his feet. *"Andy!"*

Nothing. He called again and again. Nothing. His son was nowhere in sight. Disappeared.

Peter's mind was so scrambled that he had no sense of how much time had passed since he had last seen Andy. Where he had buried the crab sat a small mound of sand—a mini-replica of that cap on the Point, his mind noted on the fly. How long ago was that? A minute? Maybe two? Five at the most.

The beach was empty. And nothing broke the smooth dark surface of the water. And nothing was up on the slopes.

"He's probably just exploring tidal pools," Connie said. She was on her feet beside Peter.

"He was just here," Sparky said.

"Maybe he went back up," Jackie suggested.

But Andy wouldn't have done that. There were more things of interest on the beach. He had wandered off, yet Peter could see nothing but shoreline and construction equipment. The other way—just sand and black shore rocks curling around the base of Pulpit's Point.

They split up. Jackie and Sparky took the beach toward the cottage; Peter and Connie headed around the base of the Point.

"He's probably just around the bend looking for crabs," Connie said.

"Yeah," he heard himself say. His first thought was that they'd round the bend and find Andy facedown in a tidal pool with a split skull. Three minutes is all it would take, three wicked little minutes and a foot of water.

"Andy, Andy!" Peter scrambled over the rocks. He was barely aware of Connie trying to keep up.

No answer. Just waves crashing on rocks. He looked down the coast praying to see Sparky and Jackie coming up the beach hand in hand with him. But it was just the two of them fading into the distance.

Connie took his arm. "Peter, calm down, you're panicking."

He nodded. She didn't know, and he didn't understand, but somehow he felt he had authored this. As if from the subconscious recesses of his mind a rogue beam had shot out, driving Andy off and maybe to his death. It was all part of a master plan laid out just below the skin of his awareness. There had been enough clues, previewed by that vision on the kitchen floor yesterday.

He scrambled around the base rocks of the Point, slipping on the seagrass. The breath bulbed in his throat as he scanned the water, praying he'd not lay eyes on a little body in a blue-and-red suit bobbing in the surf. It all made such vicious sense. From some pocket deep in his psyche a forbidden instinct shoots home—hot rage. Andy picks it up, is stung numb, and wanders off to his death.

But the water was empty.

Those were not my thoughts, Peter told himself. But another voice cut in

Then whose thoughts were they? The kid killed the love of your life, and you can't forgive him, plain and simple.

Peter's mind was a black fugue. You're letting your guilt savage your rational mind. You don't blame him for Linda's death. Nor do you will his death. You couldn't. That's not you. You love him unconditionally.

"Andy?" Why couldn't he hear their shouting? He had been gone no more than a few minutes. Maybe three, maybe four. How far could a kid wander in that time and still be out of earshot?

Halfway around the point, he suddenly stopped. Maybe Andy had gone the other way. Peter began leaping over the rocks he had just climbed.

"Peter."

Connie came toward him. "Let's try the hill."

He hadn't thought of that. Andy could have headed into the woods. He turned and suddenly froze.

"What?" Connie asked.

"Shhhh." He braced himself against her. At first he thought it was a trick of the wind. Or a distant bird cry.

"I hear it," said Connie.

A faint cry.

"Daddeeeee." Very faint, muffled, distant.

"Where's it coming from?"

They looked around in total disorientation. "Where the hell is he?"

It sounded as if it was coming from the air above them. The sun blinded him as he looked up the sandy slope. Nothing.

Then he heard it again. The hill. It sounded as if Andy was calling from inside the hill.

Jesus! Maybe he tried to climb it and pulled down an avalanche of sand.

"Andy, where are you?"

"Daddeeee."

The next moment Peter was leaping over the rocks after the voice around the Point. On their right was an opening to a shelter, partly covered by a sliding corrugated plate. It looked like a concrete garage built into the base of the mound and about twelve feet above the waterline. Because of the contours of the land Peter had never before noticed it.

"Daddy, in here."

Peter climbed over some rocks and up along the edge of a concrete breakwater. Behind it was the opening into the hill. Connie was right behind him.

"Andy, I'm coming," he shouted. "You all right?"

"Daddeee." He was crying.

Peter scrambled up the wall and across a path. The metal cover had been pulled back just enough for Andy to squeeze through. Peter pushed it back to expose the mouth of a black tunnel.

"Andy, we're here." They stepped inside.

"Help me." His voice was coming from deep within the black. They would need lights.

"Are you hurt?"

There was a moment's hesitation, then, "I can't see. And I'm cold."

"We can live with that," Connie said.

Only on a few occasions had Peter heard the high whine of fright in Andy's voice. It was unmistakable.

"We're coming!" shouted Connie. "Just stay where you are and keep talking so we can find you. Okay?"

"Okay," came the trembling voice. "I dropped my flashlight," he shouted. Andy carried one in his backpack wherever he went.

"What is this place?" Connie asked as they moved into the interior.

"Tunnels built during the Civil War." They had once housed cannons to guard the harbor. The nub of the mounts and the circular metal tracks the cannons swiveled on were still in place at the mouth of the cave.

The air within was thick and damp. A black fungoid slime covered cement walls. Small white stalactites hung like icicles in the gray murk. Fresh tire tracks marked the floor, which was scattered with indiscriminate debris.

"I smell gasoline," Connie said.

"Must be where they store their fuel." It was twenty degrees cooler inside.

They moved cautiously, trying to follow Andy's voice. To the right at about thirty feet the tunnel split into two opaque black throats. Andy's voice came from the right-hand one.

Peter took Connie's hand and led her shuffling cautiously across the floor. Behind them, the light from the outside rapidly diminished. When the tunnel turned to the left, their light was gone.

While Peter kept Andy talking—half from relief, half for guidance—they scraped along the walls in total dark. "This is impossible," Peter said. They needed light. Andy's voice was still distant. A sudden drop in front of them or a few more turns could lose them all in the black.

Peter stopped. All light was consumed. Total, unrelenting black. Peter opened and closed his eyes and registered no difference. It was like neurological dysfunction.

"Wait a minute," Connie said. She fumbled around in her shoulder bag. Then a bright orange light from a butane lighter filled their eyes. It was what she had used to fuse the ends of the PVC line they made the grids with. "Forgot I had it."

"Not with all the fumes."

But Connie kept it lit and scurried across the chamber. A moment later, the butane was out, and a flashlight blazed. Andy's Laz-R-Lite. "Here."

"Andy, we found your light." It sprayed a feeble yellow beam against the black.

"This way. Hurry!"

They followed the light into the tunnels, which bisected into blind passageways, some going off in different directions, and one leading to a set of stone steps that seemed to go down forever. The place was a labyrinth.

As they moved inward, the odor of gasoline grew stronger. On the left they came upon two large chambers jammed with hundreds of fifty-gallon steel drums of gasoline and diesel fuel. They had been stored in the safe coolness. Peter tried not to think of the inferno Connie's lighter could have ignited.

Deeper and deeper they followed the small voice down the main tunnel. Suddenly, Peter was stopped by the sound of something barely within range of perception.

Connie took his arm. "What is that?"

Overhead—a thin chittering, almost a fluttery whistle but barely audible. He raised the beam upward. The light fell on what looked like a patch of large black leaves. There were movement and pinpoint red glows: bats. Huge clusters of them. As he swung the torch around, he could see that most of the ceiling in that chamber was covered with bats, their ragged wings making a fretful carpet. In the movement, ratty faces glared at them. Tiny pink mouths gaped in the torch, producing a high twittering protest just at the edge of hearing.

"My God," she whispered, crouching against him. "Must be thousands of them."

Peter pointed the beam downward for fear of filling the air with wings and flashing incisors.

"Daddy, hurry."

They followed his voice down the tunnel to a wall. Andy was crouched in the corner like an animal. His face was distorted from crying. "Why did you take so long?"

"We didn't know where you went," Peter said.

He reached down for him, but Andy slapped his hand away. His fright had turned into anger. "You didn't want to find me."

"What are you talking about? Of course, we wanted to find you."

"No, sir. You let me almost get killed!" Andy screamed. "You did it on purpose. You wanted me to get killed, I know it."

Peter didn't know what seized him, but his mind filled with hot smoke in a snap. He reached down and yanked Andy off the ground. "Let you get killed?" he growled. *"Let you get killed?"*

"Peter!" cried Connie.

"Why the hell did you wander off?" He shook the boy violently.

"But, Daddy . . ."

"No 'but, Daddy,' goddamn you!" He barely registered Connie pulling at his arms to stop him, the stunned look of fright in Andy's face. "You never obey me. Never! And I'm sick of it. You understand? I'm sick of you going where you don't belong. I'm sick of you making trouble for me."

"Peter, you're hurting him."

"I don't fucking care!" he screamed.

"Daddeeeeee!"

"You think it's funny, do you? A big joke. Just like with Mommy, right?"

"Peter, leave him alone."

"Answer me!"

"Peter!" Connie tore Andy out of his arms.

At the sight of her shielding him, Andy's face wild with terror, gasping screams reverberating throughout the tunnels, Peter suddenly snapped back. His body slumped against the wall. "Oh, God, Andy," he said, tears burning his eyes. "What am I doing?" he pleaded. "I'm sorry, I'm sorry. I . . . I was just so scared, so scared." He held out his arms.

But Connie put her back to him and moved with Andy toward the exit.

"I'm all right now," Peter said, with his hand out. "I just lost it, please. I'm okay."

Connie looked back at him.

"Really I am," he said.

She put Andy down. He was gasping to catch his breath. Peter held out his arms, but Andy didn't go to him. "I thought it was a pirate's cave," he said to Connie through his sobs.

She nodded and took his hand. Peter shuffled behind them, feeling sick with confusion.

They followed the light beam toward the opening. Andy cried most of the way. They were maybe twenty feet from the mouth of the tunnel when the air turned warm again.

"Let's go home," she said.

"No." Andy's back was up against the wall. He was struggling to talk. "I'm trying to tell you something. There was someone in here."

"There was?" Connie said.

"Yes."

"Might have been one of the construction men."

"It's Saturday," Peter said.

"Maybe a fisherman."

"*No!* It was the man in the woods."

"What man?"

"The man in the woods. The ghost," he shouted. "He knocked the flashlight out of my hands and chased me . . ."

Connie looked at Peter.

". . . and he said if he catches me again, he's going to cut my throat."

From someplace deep in the tunnels a loud rasping sound sang out—like metal on stone.

"It's him," Andy said. He began to whimper again.

Peter stood up. "Who's there?" he shouted.

Then the sound of footsteps. They were fading into the tunnels.

"Stay here," Peter said.

"Peter, no! Don't go."

But he ran down the tunnel with the flashlight. Within a few feet, the temperature dropped fifteen degrees and the air turned to black fur. He shot down the main throat after the sounds. Some-body was running from him. Somebody who had just threatened to slash the throat of his six-year-old son. What kind of a man would say that to a kid?

A loud scraping sound again. But with all the chambers and blind alleys, it was almost impossible to get a direction. He shot to the left at the juncture, keeping the beam low so he wouldn't fall in a hole or stumble over a fuel barrel. He also didn't want to rouse the bats.

The echo effect was maddening, and every few feet, he had to stop to determine if he was chasing other sounds or those of his own feet. At another turn, the smell of gasoline and fuel oil filled his head.

Suddenly the clang of something on his right stopped him dead. A small side corridor opened up. He aimed the light beam. It happened in just a split second, but way down he caught a flash of movement. The door clunked shut.

He wasn't certain if it were real or imagined, but his mind had clicked on that same implacable white-faced man in the oaks.

Peter ran down the corridor to the end. There was a small metal door with a little barred gap and slide shutter. A prisoner's cell.

For a moment he held his breath. The silence was so com-plete, he could actually hear his eardrums clicking to the pound-ing of his heart. He gripped the flash tightly like a bludgeon and put his hand on the heavy metal pull.

Better brace yourself, man, because soon as you swing open that door, a great hairy id thing right out of Tales of the Crypt *is going to swipe your face clean off.*

Peter braced himself and pushed it open.

"Jesus!"

The light fell on a small four-walled crypt—no door, no win-dow, no trap, no escape hatch in the ceiling. A cubicle of ancient stone.

And as vacant as death.

chapter
Twelve

"Dad, I don't like this island."

"We had a rough day."

"No. I want to go home."

"Well, we can't go home, not for three more weeks. We still have a lot of digging to do."

"How many days is three weeks?"

"About nineteen."

"Nineteen? That's too long. I want to go home tomorrow."

"Well, we can't. You just got a little scared today. We both got scared. And I'm sorry for getting so upset, okay? We pals again?"

"Yeah."

He gave him a kiss on the forehead. "I want you to promise you won't wander off like that anymore, okay?"

"Okay."

"Never again."

"Okay, okay."

"You get to sleep, now."

"But, Dad, I want you to sleep with me."

"There isn't enough room on your cot. But I'll be right next to you."

"Pull yours closer."

"Sure. How's that?"

"Okay."

Peter kissed him on the forehead again. He also kissed Lamb-kin.

"Sweet dreams."

"Sweet dreams."

"Sleep tipe."

"Sleep tipe."

"See you in the morning."

"See you in the morning."

"Good night, Pooch."

"Good night, Dad."

"I love you, Andy boy."

"I love you, Daddy boy."

"You silly goose."

"You silly goose." Andy gave Peter a giant hug around the neck.

It was their nightly ritual—the little bedtime litany, including "sleep tipe," a carryover from Andy's babyhood and one which Peter just could not let go of. Nor would Andy let him. Even the order was important; if anything was left out or switched around, Andy would protest and make them start all over again, from the top. Even at his age, he was a creature of habit.

The same with the bedtime stories. Two each night. Tonight Peter read him *Amos and Boris,* a story about the friendship between a mouse and a whale; then *Where the Wild Things Are.* Andy loved to announce, "Let the wild rumpus start."

Peter thought Andy was asleep, but then he said, "Dad, you wouldn't hurt me, would you?"

The question sent a nugget of ice through Peter's heart. "Hurt you? Of course not. I love you, I'm crazy about you," Peter said. "I just got scared."

"That's not what I'm talking about." Andy hesitated for a moment. Then he said, "I had this funny feeling on the beach, that you were angry at me and wanted to kill me."

A bigger nugget pushed through. He went back to Andy's cot and knelt beside him. "That's a terrible thought. Terrible. Don't think that again. I love you, Andy. I love you more than anything. I'd never let anything happen to you. Never, never." He pressed his face against his son's. "Not true," he whispered.

After a silent minute, Andy said, "Dad, I really did see a pirate today."

"I'm sure you did, Pooch, and if I get my hands on him, I'll tan his hide for scaring you like that."

"What's 'tan his hide' mean? You said that to me the other day."

Peter felt his heart sink. "It means make him sorry he did that."

Andy pulled Peter close and kissed him. Thank God, children are so forgiving, Peter thought.

"Did he say anything else to you?"

"No," Andy whispered.

"Did you see his face?"

"I told you, it was the man in the trees we saw."

"Oh, yeah."

"Least he's not a ghost."

"I'll say." Peter's guess was that it was a local fisherman who had stopped by to relieve himself in the tunnels when Andy happened by. He got startled and bolted down the tunnels so he wouldn't get caught trespassing on private land. How he managed to elude Peter was a mystery. There was simply no way out of that cell. Of course, it was possible Peter only thought he saw the guy slip into that cell—that his mind was playing tricks on him again. It seemed to be a mounting condition. But what bothered him was how the guy had threatened to cut his son's throat. Peter thought again of his first hellish vision of Andy on the kitchen floor.

Andy turned over and closed his eyes. "Dad, do you like Connie?"

The question surprised him. "Yes, she's very nice. Why do you ask?"

"I don't know. Do you love her like you loved Mommy?"

"No, but I like her. She's very nice."

"Are you going to fall in love with her?"

"I'm not planning on it."

"Was Mommy like her?"

"A little. She's very nice and very pretty like Mommy was."

"Would you like to marry her?"

"No, nor would she want to marry me. We just met the other day, so we don't know each other very well."

He rolled over. "Maybe I'll marry her. She's neat, and she saved my life." Then he added, "With you."

"She might be a little tall for you."

"Not when I'm seven or eight." A minute later, he was making light snoring sounds.

Peter got into his own cot. For a long time, he just stared into the black, trying to compose his mind to sleep. The events of the afternoon had wracked him. He had lost his temper in a way that was alien to him. He had screamed at Andy. But what scared him was how he had grabbed and shook him. It was the first time in his life he had ever physically touched him in anger. He had crossed a barrier—a high tangle of wire barbed with taboos.

As he lay there thinking back on the moment, he recalled the sensation that something from the outside had entered him—like the first day in the yard with the kite. Some alien sentience.

Peter closed his eyes. I need rest, he told himself. Lots of rest. Peace of mind . . . peace of mind . . . peace . . .

The next thing he knew he was back on Pulpit's Point, and the smell of smoke was thicker than ever.

Everybody was still there and waiting for him.

"Let us continue," Reverend Jeremiah Oates said.

The same small boy, his face in the shadows, stood cowering in the circle near the accused woman.

"Worthy Oates, tell us what you saw of her wicked arts, child," Reverend Oates said.

The boy wiped his face against the back of his hand. He fought for a time for his breath. His eyes flashed to Brigid, then back to his father. To Peter's relief, the boy looked less like Andy this time. There was a strong resemblance in the curly black hair and shape of his head, but he was not his son.

"You are a witch," he declared with his finger extended toward her. "I saw with my own eyes."

"How do you know what a witch is, boy?" the woman asked. The woman's voice had a menacing tolerance in it. To Peter it seemed as if she was paying special attention to him. He still could not see her face for all the wild hair, but he was certain he knew this woman.

"I . . . I saw what you did on the night of the Sabbath. It was a fortnight ago, and the three of us were fishing late off the Point, sire. We saw light of fire from these stones."

"And you climbed this hill, the three of you," said the Reverend.

"Yes, sire."

The other boys nodded.

"And the fires make me a witch?" the woman asked.

The boy was suddenly at a loss for words.

"Continue," demanded the minister.

The boy stammered a little. "Well, sire, we saw her in this circle, and . . . and . . ."

The boy tried to look away, but the minister took his chin and raised it to him. "You must tell us, son."

Trying not to look at the witch, he said, "Sire, she was wearing those devil beads and a headdress of antlers most frightening. And . . . and she was communing with specters."

"Communing with specters," shouted Oates, amazed.

"I was paying homage to ancestral dead," the woman shouted.

"No, sire," continued the boy. "As sure as I live I heard her sing chants to the dead. I heard her talk to them as if receiving their words."

He stole a glance at the woman, but she did not protest, leaving Peter wondering at the validity of the boy's claims.

"She conversed with the dead," Oates said. "What else did you see?"

"Oh, sire, so horrible, I witnessed her conjure a demon."

The woman's body lurched forward. "You little worm." Her voice spit fire at him. "You saw no such thing. You lie!"

"Never mind the hag," shouted the reverend. "Go on."

"Father," whimpered the boy. And around him the implacable faces glowed like so many moons in the firelight. "I saw her at that very stone, and above her hovered a demon thing made of fire. It had horns and great wings." He threw his hands to his face. "It was most horrible!" he shrieked. "I saw her raise her arms in supplication."

"In supplication?"

"Yes, sire. She was asking for the power of its fire, but I know not what she meant."

"And you, Simon Hubbard?"

The boy hunched and faced the circle. His voice was thin. "I saw the fire demon, too, sire. It stood on that same white stone. And she made exchange with the creature, and that's when I knew she was a witch. Because I saw her open her dress, and the demon handed her a little thing like a cat, but it had no hair on it but hands and ears like a man's. . . ."

"He's lying," shouted the witch.

But Oates cut her off. "Go on, child."

"And she brought it up to her . . . to her . . . teat and made it suckle."

Appalled gasps shook the circle.

"The Imp!" shouted someone.

"Yes, yes," Oates said. "You saw Brigid Mocnessa give suckle to the Demon Imp."

"I saw it, too," the other boy, Joshua Biddle, said.

"And I," declared Worthy Oates, turning his head toward the circle. "When she saw us, she ran to us with the Imp still at her breast. And that's when I saw the third nipple under the others, where she gave it suck." He pressed a finger to his middle. "The devil's teat. She said she would slash my throat if I told."

The phrase flared in Peter's head like a bulb blowing its filament.

The boy screamed as the woman lurched toward him. And that was when Peter realized she was tied by one leg to the high stone.

"Worthy Oates, hear me!" she screamed. The boy buried his face in his father's robe. "That was no demon imp, that was my own babe of my flesh, Isaac. You defile me and my child," she said. She yanked against her chain. "Had I had you in my hands I would most surely slash your throat."

Shouts of protest rose up again.

"I told you, Father," Worthy Oates cried. "She means evil."

"She *is* evil," declared the minister.

"You don't know evil." The woman's words spat out like flames.

Suddenly the boy turned brave. "I'm telling the truth." he cried. He shot a finger toward her breast. "It's there, the devil's teat."

"The proof," someone demanded.

And the circle picked up the chant.

Fury nearly choking her words, Brigid said, "The proof?" In the next moment she tore open the front of her dress for all to see. "There's your bloody proof."

At the sight of her exposed breasts, people shrieked.

Peter woke with a jolt.

chapter
Thirteen

The humidity was so low the next morning that the Boston skyline stood out with stereoscopic clarity. It was also one of those days when the moon was visible, hanging in the blue like a wan ghost.

Peter was back in that dream again, and this time it left him rattled. He remembered having had dreams that repeated themselves, but never two in a continuing narrative. Or on consecutive nights. This one had picked up where the other left off. It was uncanny. So was the luridness of details. He woke up feeling less like he had emerged from a dream and more like returning from the event itself. But even though subliminal flashes passed through him all day, he refused to let it occupy his mind. Just one of those quirky things of the psyche.

Nonetheless, it seemed that since arriving he'd spent more time trying to rationalize the inexplicable than analyze the explicable. Today was a new day, he told himself, and time to get on with archaeology. They had only nineteen left, and so much mound to excavate.

They were up on the Point a little before eight. The day passed uneventfully. No more accidents, no lost Andy. And no more funny visions or voices. Peter told himself that all that was behind him now like a twenty-four-hour grippe.

By five they had dug two more sample squares, this time on the far side of the mound. Andy never left Peter's sight. With his red plastic pail and shovel, he helped sift the overburden. He also built a sand castle with Sparky and Jackie. Not once did he say he wanted to go home. As the hours passed, Peter felt himself become centered again. Sheer physical labor had brought him back.

The digging was the same story as yesterday—a covering of beach sand, shell fragments, and pebbles. That was the configuration so far, and probably for the rest of the sixty-foot dome.

Peter had little doubt the mound had been fashioned as a cap. But claims of a chapel still baffled him, since nothing seemed to have survived except those foundation boulders—if that's what they were. Had the original chapel been constructed of stone, there was little evidence: half a dozen small fieldstones. The other possibility was a structure of wood—not the best choice given the location: the highest, most easterly point on the island and, thus, most vulnerable to hurricanes and nor'easters. It was possible locals had carted away what was left using the timbers for firewood and fieldstones for walls. Such was common practice. But what still nagged him was why the three boulders had been buried.

For three more days, they would continue taking sample squares, and if nothing unusual turned up, they would use the backhoe to clear away the cap down to the three stones.

By five o'clock, Andy was hot and tired and covered with dirt. Jackie and Sparky took him back to the cottage, while Connie helped Peter put the tools away and cover the squares with plastic in case of rain. At first Peter felt uneasy letting Andy out of his range, but the Kellehers swore that he would not leave their side.

When Peter and Connie had secured the site, they sat on one of the stones facing the open sea and shared lemonade from a canteen. Connie's face glistened with sunscreen. She had worked half the day on hands and knees, and the other half sifting debris through the screens. Her jeans and T-shirt were covered with dust. She untied her hair and let it fluff out in the sea breeze. "I never knew archaeology was such a blast."

"Two percent inspiration, a hundred-fourteen sweat."

"But, you know, there's something quite satisfying about digging and getting dirty. It's like being a kid again." He handed her the canteen. "It must be wonderful when you find something."

"You go through three tons of sterile dirt, and an old button looks like the Holy Grail."

Connie laughed. "I'm glad I signed on."

"So am I." The words fluttered in the air like butterflies.

"I almost changed my mind about it." She took off her sunglasses, and her green eyes blazed. "It was here or three weeks of Jamaican hedonism."

Peter nodded at the piles of dirt. "And miss all this?"

She smiled. "It was the disarming appeal of the Earthwatch write-up that convinced me: 'Excavating the remains of a Colonialist chapel eight hours a day under a hot sun.' Wow."

"Were you looking for a vacation or penance?"

"I guess a little of each," she said and slipped her sunglasses back on. "This was my starting over, and I liked the idea of doing something I'd not done before. Besides, hedonism gets old fast."

Peter wanted to ask her about her divorce, but couldn't think of delicate phrasing. So he said, "Why did you divorce?"

She peered at him over her sunglasses. "Why do I want to say 'Such a bold question'?"

"I dig dirt for a living."

"Ho-ho-ho." She thought a moment. "How do I answer that? We fell out of love. Our poem stopped rhyming. Our Mars and Venus didn't conjunct." She chuckled to herself. Sparky had done natal charts for her that afternoon. Connie was a Virgo with a lot of funny planetary alignments that said she was analytical and discriminating. Peter's hadn't been completed yet, but he was a Leo. He could have been a kangaroo for all he cared. "When you get married, you're so full of flowers and bells that you believe you can conquer anything, including those little bugs of incompatibility. Then the years pass, and unless you've worked them out, made compromises, those bugs can grow big. By then it was too late. He wanted me to change in ways I couldn't. And I couldn't change his wanting me to change. By then the bugs were demons that tore us apart." She took a drink from the canteen and handed it back to him. "In every relationship there's a victim and an executioner."

Her words rose little prickles at the base of his skull.

"But, the funny thing is," she said, "sometimes it's hard to tell them apart. The roles swap. Victim becomes executioner." Connie picked up a handful of sand and let it pour through her fingers. "I wonder what we'll find."

"Probably more of the same."

The mound was gilded by the late afternoon sun. "It looks like the roof of a buried temple."

"Yes it does," Peter said. He looked away to the water. Several sailboats floated in the distant mist like phantoms. Peter thought about how nice it would be to go sailing. Maybe when this was all over. He and Andy. Maybe Connie.

As they sat there, it occurred to him that this was the first time he'd been alone with her. They had been near each other nearly every waking hour of the last three days, but never out of sight of the others. In fact, Connie was the first woman other than Linda he'd been alone with for fifteen years. The realization produced a warm surge. They were side-by-side, high above the sea in sultry air, all alone. The construction crew had left for the weekend half an hour ago, and the others were back at the cottage. He did not believe in karma, but the moment started humming with rightness. He wondered if she felt it, or the tension in the closeness of their bodies. Or the ritual of the canteen—the fact that their lips were drinking from the same spout. Probably not. Besides, the last thing on Connie's mind was starting up with a man again. Yet, the moment produced in him a giddy lightness he hadn't experienced since his first date with Linda.

While Connie studied the mound, Peter studied her profile. It was an elegant, intelligent face. Those green firestone eyes were flecked with motion that seemed to pull you in. But what held his attention was her mouth. It was full and fleshy and so warm looking in the sun. More than anything he wanted to kiss her lips. But he talked the urge down. It would be very stupid, for one, it was totally out of place. As principal investigator, his job was to head up his expedition, not put the make on his volunteers. Secondly, what if she objected? Not only would he destroy a lovely moment, but for the next eighteen days there would be this dumb awkward thing between them. She had come traveling light and wanted to go home that way.

After a long moment, Connie said, "I wonder how long they've been buried." She was looking at the stones.

"I don't know. They've been tugging at my mind since I got here."

He didn't tell her that since early morning he had had flashcard images of the stones in odd formations—a colonnade or some sort of wall. From the dream. But his mind couldn't hold them long enough to grasp. The image flicked away just before they composed themselves. He also didn't tell her of his vague sense of connection to those stones and that mound. A weird, nearly proprietary connection, that underscored the premonition on the first day he was out here. He couldn't explain it, nor did he understand it, but he was beginning to believe that it was not accident that he was here to excavate, but fate. Or, more exactly, by design. But it was too crazy to put into words.

"I don't believe they're part of a colonial foundation," he said.

"You don't?"

"No. They didn't need foundation stones. The hill is solid granite right down to the tunnels."

"What about an Indian site?"

"Possibly."

"That's not exactly the voice of conviction."

"Well, there are other possibilities."

"Like Mystery Hill?"

Peter felt a flush. "Now who's digging dirt?"

She put her hand on his arm. "Peter, I didn't mean it tit-for-tat. I looked up some of your articles and stumbled upon the interview in *The Durham Ledger*."

"And the refutations?"

She nodded. "Does that bother you?"

He laughed. "What, being a professional leper?"

"But you made it quite clear that you were merely speculating. I also thought all the refutations were arrogant and shrill."

"Only because archaeology is uneasy about not being an exact science," he said. "You're not supposed to speculate and not supposed to assume things, and I did. It was my one concession to romance."

"I guess you took some heat."

"*Goddamn it, Peter, that's imposition not discovery, and you know it.*"

It had been the only time he had ever known Dan Merritt to be capable of emotional display.

"Yeah, I took heat. One statement in *The Durham Ledger* about the possibility of prehistoric migrations, and I was up there with the lunatic fringe insisting ancient Egyptians had settled the Mississippi Valley and Atlantis lay off the Jersey coast. So much for out-loud speculation."

She gave his arm a small squeeze. "I'm sorry I brought it up," she said. Her eyes pulled him in. "Maybe this will make up for it."

"Maybe."

He put his hand over hers. She smiled and gracefully slipped free. "I think we better head back," she said getting up.

Out in the water a small blue fishing boat puttered by. The same one they had seen yesterday. And the day before. A small part of Peter's brain wondered about that. With the rest, he thought about how pointless his life suddenly seemed—a life of forever pushing stones up hills.

chapter
Fourteen

"Dad, how many more days before we can go home?"

"Eighteen."

"Eighteen?" He counted from one to eighteen. "That's wicked long."

"It'll pass soon enough. We still have a lot of excavating to do."

"Yeah, but . . ."

"No more 'yeah-buts' "—which he rhymed with rabbits—"Go to sleep."

"But, Dad, I want to tell you something."

"What's that?"

"I had a funny dream last night. It was about Mommy. And you know what? She was all on fire."

Peter's arms broke out in gooseflesh. He had never specified Linda's death, just that she had had a car accident, leaving Andy to surmise that "accident" meant when a car hit another car or a tree, and people simply went directly to God. Nor had he described the mangled, severed limbs, crushed skull and chest, her body pinned in place while burning gasoline reduced it to charred stalks. Just a nice neat transubstantiation.

"But she wasn't all burned up. And she wasn't in a car either."

"Where was she?"

"I don't know. She was just kind of standing there. But she called me."

"She did? And what did she say?"

"She said, 'Hi, Andy.' "

"That's nice. It's because she misses you."

"Yeah, and because she watches over me, too."

"That's right, hon. She's a guardian angel for both of us. She say anything else?"

"Yeah. She asked if I wanted to visit her."

Another cold flash up his back. "Visit her?"

"Yeah, but I told her I had to die first, and I wasn't ready. I still had to grow up."

"That was a good answer. Someday we'll all be together in heaven." He turned off the light. "She say anything else?"

"Yeah."

"What's that?" Peter tucked the blanket around him and put the book on the night table. Tonight it was Susan Jeffers' illustrated version of *Hansel and Gretel* by the brothers Grimm.

"She said . . . she wanted me to come to her. Now."

"What bothers me is that he's contemplating dying."

"It might be he's experiencing a kind of survivor's guilt," Connie said.

It was a little after ten, and they were walking down the beach.

"I also don't understand why he's having scary dreams of her all of a sudden. Before this, he mentioned only one other dream of Linda, and that was pleasant."

"Maybe because this is his first trip from home," she said. "And being so far, he feels insecure. Since his memories of Linda were back home, this sudden displacement might be a kind of second separation from her."

Peter thought about that. It sounded plausible. And he felt a little better, although it didn't explain the flames and Linda's demand. But, he told himself, he was not going to bog himself down with any more psychoanalysis. It was too fine a night. The tide was lapping its way in, and a gentle breeze caressed the shore. The sky was a clear black-velvet vault crowded with stars. And he couldn't remember the last time he strolled a night beach with a woman.

After Andy went down, the four of them played cards. Then about ten, Sparky and Jackie went off to bed to catch up on their honeymoon. Peter and Connie sat on the porch for a while and chatted until Peter suggested they take a walk. She said that sounded good, and they left a note on the table in case of an emergency. They headed for the Point.

As they walked along chatting, Peter thought about how much he had deprived himself.

For a spell lasting two years he had convinced himself that Linda had made other women impossible for him. So he had resisted all impulses to date. Instead, he locked himself away with memories: Linda humming while she brushed her thick black hair in the mirror; Linda radiant when she learned she was pregnant; Linda at the kitchen counter teaching him to cook with paper-thin dough, goat cheese, and exotic herbs; Linda beaming as Andy took his first steps; and Linda with volcanic passion that belied her serene beauty.

Linda, with her half-mystical yearnings, had in the drowsy warmth of their bed one night made Peter swear that if he died before she did, he would return to her. His heart still pounding from lovemaking, the thought of one of them dying jolted his mind. As the family rationalist, he had reminded her, he entertained no belief in the afterlife or gods and ghosts. But Linda was a religious woman who had been deadly serious. "There's nothing crueler in the universe than the death of a mother," she had said. The thought of no longer being with them was just too monstrous for her to accept. "So help me God, Peter, if something happens to me, I'll find a way to come back. I will." For a long moment Peter lay in the dark with Linda's vow humming in his head, half convinced that the sheer potency of her will could reanimate her.

Linda, whose presence filled any room she entered. How, it seemed, that in marrying her Peter had pulled off a major coup— winning the living component of western man's romantic dreams: Shakespeare's Dark Lady, Homer's Helen, Scheherazade. Linda had made all other women seem gauche and dull.

As he and Connie walked down the shoreline, he thought how much nicer this was than self-mortification. So much healthier than marriage to a ghost.

Peter had no idea where it would lead if anywhere, but over the last couple of days he had spent more time thinking about Connie than Linda. The black era was coming to a close, he decided. Finally. He wanted to tell Connie how he enjoyed being with her. But he guessed she knew that. Besides, such things were best left unsaid.

"You all right?" she said, catching him gazing at her.

"Sure." He cleared his throat. "Why do you ask?"

She raised the small penlight to his face. His forehead was beaded with sweat. She produced a tissue from her shoulder bag and wiped his brow. "You look like you're having a heatstroke again."

He liked the gesture. "I think I am."

"In the middle of the night?"

"Warm thoughts."

"Uh-oh." And she took his hand.

When they reached the base of Pulpit's Point, he said, "You know, this is the first time I've held a woman's hand in nearly three years."

"You did *very* well." Her laughter sounded like wind chimes. "In case you're interested, it's my first time in almost as long."

They walked up the slope to the stones.

The sea spread before them like a dream. The only sound was the hush of the tide against the rocks. In the eastern sky a half moon rocked between the stars.

" 'An infinite moment,' " he said.

"Shelley?"

"Wordsworth."

"Why bicker?"

Before he thought about it, he pulled her to him. There was no sign of surprise on her face, just an amused half-grin. He leaned over and kissed her mouth. The next moment, she was pushing him away.

"Never like the movies," he said.

"You're not kidding."

He was standing on her foot.

"Like I said, it's been awhile."

In movements emulating a mother with an awkward child, she positioned him properly. When his feet were straight, she whispered, "Roll 'em."

In the next moment his mouth was against hers, and her arms encircled his neck.

And in a flash it all came back—the sweet sensation of lips against his mouth, that special leaping of his heart, the giddiness in his loins. Connie's mouth made small teasing kisses like phantom nibblings across his lips. He pressed his body close to hers, feeling her respond ever so slightly. When her hand slid up his back and caressed his neck, he thought he would faint with pleasure.

They were both breathing heavily, but when he started to lower her to the ground, she stopped him.

"Okay," he said holding up his palms. "I still respect you."

"Then not in a hole," she said. They were standing at the edge of one of their sample squares.

She reached into her canvas bag for a thick beach towel. "Be prepared."

"Yikes, it's Girl Scout of the Year."

Connie laughed and took his hand. She led him to a sandy plot near the box of excavation tools. She spread the towel.

"Here?" he asked, sitting on the towel. He felt his heart thump with expectation.

She lay back on the towel and took his hand. *"In situ."*

Peter grinned with delight. Thanks, God, he thought.

She flicked off the penlight and took his hand. He did not know how far this would go, but he would follow wherever she led. It had been a long, long time.

In the scant light of the sky, he could see her smiling at him.

"What are you thinking?" she asked.

"I don't know. It's mostly in hormone." She smiled and pulled his face to hers and held him in another long kiss.

Soon they were moving in half-conscious rhythm against each other. They were making love in their clothes. He had met her just four days ago, and although they had shared polite interaction, he never suspected that she had found him desirable. He slipped his hands under her top, kissing her, and telling himself that it was really happening. He had so long resigned himself to a life of gray celibacy that he had held out little possibility of making love to a woman again. He opened his eyes, and the moon grinned down on them.

In short breaths Peter said, "Is-is this *it?* I mean, are we . . . ?"

"I think so," she gasped. "Unless you'd rather talk."

He wanted to laugh and cry at the same time. "You know," he whispered, "it's been a long time since I've done this kind of thing. Is it still done the same way?"

"Mmmm, but now we take our shoes off."

"Nothing's sacred anymore," Peter said.

She laughed and squeezed him warmly. "Long time for me, too."

"Bet it comes back to us."

"Bet."

Their lips came together again. Hers parted and he felt the tip of her tongue tease him. In synchronization with their kissing, she gently pressed herself against him. When they were naked, Connie lay back against the towel. A vague urgency lit up her eyes. She was breathing heavily. "Not bad for a couple of retreads."

He lowered his face to hers and she slipped her hand around the back of his head and pulled him toward her. Tenderly, they kissed. When her lips parted, she drew him in again, and her hands slid down his back urging him into motion.

In a small pocket of his brain, Peter registered smoke. Then it was gone.

Gently they rocked and caressed each other with their hands and lips. Peter explored the contours of her body. He touched her breasts and ran his hand down her long flanks and across her belly. His hand stopped. In a phantom moment he touched the corrugated scar of Andy's birth. Then it was gone.

At last, Connie reached down and slipped him into her.

"Oh, God," she whispered in his ear.

And deep in his head another voice whispered

Hurt her.

His stomach spasmed as if he'd just spit something up.

He slipped his mouth off hers, burying his face in her hair. He felt woozy, detached, as if he were losing himself, falling down a shaft.

Full of smoke. He could smell the acridness.

He pulled back and looked at her. Her eyes were closed. He gave a sudden thrust, and they snapped open.

HURT HER.

The voice was louder, more insistent.

He did it again, and suddenly she looked startled. One more thrust and she winced in pain.

"What are you doing? Take it easy."

But he didn't say anything.

HURT HER.

He rammed himself in her again.

"Peter, what the hell are you doing?"

But he just stared at her face and pounded himself into her again.

"I said stop it, for Christ's sake. Stop!"

A wild roar filled his head—voices in rage and agony, of fire winds, of screeching brakes and crashing metal, of things exploding and exploding and exploding—

MORE HURT MORE.

He locked her fingers in his and stretched her arms out so she was spread-eagled. Her eyes were huge.

"You're hurting me."

MAKE HER PAY.

She opened her mouth again to protest, but this time he clamped his down on it, pressing hard. She began to struggle, but he held her fast and pushed hard into her.

"Stop it!" she said.

But he could not stop himself—his will was extinguished, overridden by directives he could not define nor contain nor dismiss. His rational mind had given way to a lunatic stroboscope of flesh burning, melting, charred and splitting open in running fissures— and beneath it all was the command to punish Connie.

"Goddamn it, get off me!"

But he wouldn't. He had retreated into himself, oblivious to Connie, to himself, to the outside world. His eyes rolled into his head so that only the whites were showing, his face like a fist—and he was panting through clenched teeth and moving in and out of her like some crazed animal. He looked possessed.

A sudden thrust with her knee to his groin and it was over.

With a loud groan Peter folded in the middle, and Connie pushed him away.

When he opened his eyes again, he found himself lying naked on his back staring at the stars. His groin ached, and the inside of his head felt scalded.

A few feet away Connie was pulling her clothes on. He didn't understand, but she looked upset, angry.

"What happened?"

"What happened?"

"Did you kick me?" His mind was a dark whirlpool.

"Yeah, I kicked you," she said. Her voice was rough.

"But why?"

"Because I didn't like what you were doing to me."

"What was I doing?" He really could not recall anything, just swirling hot fog and screaming voices.

She struggled to pull her clothes on as if she couldn't get dressed fast enough. "I don't know what you're used to, but I'm not into S&M or wham-bam sex, or whatever the hell that was."

"What are you talking about?"

She stared at him in disbelief. "How the hell could you not remember?"

His head hummed in agony. Nothing came back. "I think I blacked out."

While she slipped on her clothes, she glanced at him, wondering how that could happen or if he was lying.

"Connie, tell me what I did? All I remember is kissing you."

She stood to leave.

"Connie, please tell me."

She flashed around toward him. "You spread me with your arms and legs and pounded me like a goddamn jackhammer, like I was just some slab of meat. And when I told you to stop, you wouldn't. So I stopped you. That's what happened!"

He looked down at himself. He was tumescent and wet. A slight pressure inside told him he was just short of orgasm. But what distracted him was the general discomfort of his genitals. His pubic bone was aching and his flesh felt ragged. He made a move to get up, but his head spun and he flopped back down on the dirt.

"Jesus, no. I don't remember any of it. Nothing. I guess I got carried away. I don't understand, but I'm sorry."

For all his effort, he could not recall what she described, nor could he identify with the violence. But as he lay there, he was certain of the fact that he was not capable of hurting a woman. Nor had he ever entertained sadistic sexual fantasies or yearnings for leather or fists. Though they had their stormy moments, he had never raised a hand to Linda. In fact, the thought was loathsome to him. Peter was not a violent man. He could not abuse a woman.

And, yet, shadowy images came flickering past his mind's eye—savage shapes in hot light. A woman on fire. A child screaming. And grumbling beneath the surface of it all was the urge to hurt Connie.

"Christ, I feel like I'm losing my mind," he whispered. It had begun the first day he stepped on the island with that awful premonition, then three days ago in the kitchen. He wanted to tell her, if for nothing else but to get it out—like lancing a boil—but he couldn't. "Connie, I'm sorry."

"So am I," she said.

As he began to get dressed, he suddenly felt a ripple of raw fear. Suddenly he wanted to get far away—off the mound, off the island, to be miles away from the place. He didn't understand, but he could not shake the feeling that the place was soured with a bad presence.

As he stood up and moved toward the drop-off, the surge of blood to his head made him stumble blindly. In a split instant, Connie caught his arm and pulled him back, but not before he had the realization that he had nearly gone tumbling over the edge—a prospect not totally unwelcomed by him.

chapter
Fifteen

"Does this mean you're going home?"

"I don't know what it means."

"I don't want you to leave."

"Frankly, I don't give a shit what you want, Peter."

It was some time later, and they were walking on the beach back to the cottage. Connie led the way with the penlight, walking briskly and keeping her distance.

Words didn't come strong enough to capture how Peter felt. He wanted to ask for her forgiveness, but what had happened was not exactly a product of his will. It would be like asking forgiveness for having an epileptic seizure. They moved down the waterline— the same patch they had strolled just an hour ago, laughing and holding hands and thinking about being lovers. Now she marched ahead of him wondering just what kind of a sexual creep she had taken up with.

"Connie, please, believe me—that wasn't me up there. I don't know how else to put it, but it was like I was possessed."

The instant he uttered the word, he felt its rightness. *Possessed.* Yes, as if somebody else—or some thing—had tenanted his body.

Connie stopped abruptly in her tracks and turned to him. "Peter, I don't know what happened to you, but at the moment I really don't care, nor do I want to talk about it. Period."

That was it. And they walked in silence down the shoreline, Connie several paces ahead of him.

She's thinking you're a first-class psycho, he told himself. *She's thinking that beneath the just-regular-guy exterior lurks a real-life Freddie Krueger. And who can blame her?*

As they moved away from the Point, Peter's mind firmed up. While he felt sick with remorse, he could not remember doing what she had described. Yet, given the images that had scalded his brain and the flashes of Connie's wide-eyed horror, he was certain that those savage urges came from outside. It did not make sense, but he felt used.

He moved toward her. "Connie, all I ask is that you give me a second chance."

"A second chance? Sure, I'll disrobe right here, and if you don't go nutty again, maybe we can pick up where we left off."

"That's not what I meant."

His eyes dropped when he noticed that in her other hand she was holding one of the ice picks from the site. While he had gotten dressed, she apparently had taken it for protection. "Christ, you don't need that," he said, nodding at the thing. "I'm not dangerous."

But she did not look convinced.

Across the black of the harbor, the amber beacon of Graves Light pulsed like the eye of a waking ogre.

"What happened was just . . ." But he drew a blank.

His mind slipped back to the beach yesterday and that hideous psychic assault that sent Andy running into the tunnels. And how he had nearly shaken the life out of him for not obeying. He had gone crazy again. More autopilot maneuvers. More selective amnesia. But tonight the spell had been total, beyond his will. He could still taste the greasy coating of smoke at the back of his throat. He could still hear the awful command: *Hurt her! Make her pay!* And he could still feel a little of the dark urge to fulfill it. Had she not stopped him with her knee, he had no idea what he might have done. Maybe, in fact, he *was* dangerous.

He shook away the thought. "Connie, I don't want you to leave."

She didn't say anything, but marched down the beach, the light in one hand, the ice pick in the other.

He wanted to tell her that he was a good man, that he had

never in years felt such joy as when they kissed. "I know how this sounds, but that wasn't me."

"Then who the hell was it?"

"I don't know . . . I don't understand it either. Something took me over. Something I can't explain, some kind of momentary fugue. Who knows, but I just want a second chance to redeem myself." He touched her arm to stop her. "Please."

She stopped and looked at him for a moment.

"Will you stay?"

"I don't know." Then she continued to move down the beach toward the cottage. The evening for her was over.

Peter fell behind. Shells cracked under his feet like small skulls.

As he moved across the black sand, he knew deep down that he wasn't crazy. Yet he wondered if crazy people actually knew they were crazy, if they looked in the bathroom mirror and said *Hello, I am a crazy person, a goddamn blithering lunatic—I think I'll brush my teeth with my shoe.* The only other explanation was that accumulated frustration, guilt, remorse, and all the other swill in his soul had backed up against the dike until it burst. And for whatever reason, it all happened while making love to Connie Lambert.

When Connie reached the stairs, Peter stopped her before she rushed up to the house.

"One last question," he said. "Up on the Point did you smell any smoke, like something was burning?"

"No."

"Just curious."

Then she hustled up the stairs. He watched her go. Slowly he climbed to the top.

The cottage was dark but for a small nightlight. The lamp in Connie's bedroom went on. Then the bathroom light. A few minutes later, the upstairs went to black.

Peter took to the porch, and for several minutes he sat in the dark, staring at the pulsing light of the Graves and thinking how he wished life were a strip of tape he could edit, if only once. He wondered which cut he'd make: the night Linda died, or tonight. He knew, of course, it would be that November two and a half years ago, but this was a close second.

chapter
Sixteen

"You're *very* Leo," Sparky said. "And that's good. Leo's the king of beasts, the most vital sign in the Zodiac. They're natural-born leaders, very ambitious, and determined to achieve."

Yeah, and they make love like werewolves, Peter thought.

It was Saturday, and for the next two days Kingdom Head was theirs.

An eerie calm hung over the island. No pile-driver, no high-whining grinders, no growl of trucks. Just the antediluvian squawking of the gulls. And nothing moved. It was as if the place had slipped into a time warp of millennia past. The way the island had been before man.

Except for what the machines had done to it: The landscape resembled those antivivisection photos of some pathetic lab animal left etherized and wired on a table, its fur shaven, chest clamped open, hide stretched, and organs exposed. The machines had savaged the place.

All day Connie worked with Jackie on a fourth square near the middle of the circle. Her mood was sullen, although she never let on what had happened. She had said very little to Peter, and he went about his work trying to avoid her. In a private moment during lunch he asked her if she'd made up her mind about staying. She said she hadn't, that she was taking it one hour at a time. For the rest of the day nothing else was said.

During a short break, Sparky had done a natal chart on Peter, as she had on all of them over the days. Peter was not in the mood, but he didn't want to be rude.

"In fact, you have the same astrological signature of many great leaders—Haile Selasse, Napoleon, Benito Mussolini."

"One deposed, one exiled, and one hanged by his feet by his own people," he said. "Dynamite sign, Leo."

"There you are," she said turning the chart toward him. The diagram consisted of a circle divided into twelve equal pie sectors transected with triangles and astrological scribblings and number notations done in a tiny hand.

"Gee, I feel better already," he said.

"Don't get smart, mister. That's the kind of crap he gives me." She nodded toward Jackie. Her T-shirt, a birthday gift from her husband, read ASTROLOGERS DO IT WITH STARS.

Jackie didn't brook with her astrology any more than Peter did, but there was considerable affection between them. Peter spotted them kissing several times when they thought nobody was looking. They always held hands when they walked. Even in their bantering, the strength of their bond was apparent, like opposite ends of a magnet—the young, beefy, blond, no-nonsense man-boy and this pink-tipped pixie who did natal charts and cooked macrobiotic tacos and dreamed of Atlantis. The original odd couple. Hard to believe they had survived their first date.

Probably because they didn't nearly rape each other.

He envied their togetherness.

But he wished she would drop the subject. He didn't want to know how natal charts worked.

But she continued. "Being Leo, you have energy and drive . . ."

And up here on the slope you're known as the Velvet Jackhammer. Wham-wham-wham-wham—drive the ladies wild. Why, just ask Missy Lambert there.

". . . and you're determined to succeed no matter what the risks."

Connie caught Peter looking at her and turned away.

"You listening?" Sparky asked.

"Mmmm."

He fought to concentrate on her explanations, but he grew

weary of the effort. What were natal charts but another version of fortune cookie aphorisms—those little strips of bullshine that applied to all five billion people on the planet: *You're a dynamite person but, at times, you tend to be a tad selfish. Try to control your impulses and life's a goddamn bowl of cherries.*

He was hot and gritty and not in the mood. He wished he could clear his head of Connie.

Now let's get this straight, old sport: You're isolated on an abandoned island with a first-class woman, who's recently divorced and available. And it's miles from the nearest singles bar and the guys in the red Porsches. And the only other competition is a honeymooner and your six-year-old kid, and you're both up here under the stars, naked and happy and pressed against each other when suddenly you go Rambo on her. Way to go!

My God, what did I do?

He inhaled a deep breath and tried to lose himself in Sparky's chart.

She took her calculations very seriously. Her nostril stud, a diamond chip today, looking like an incandescent zit. She drew some lines, made more scratchings, then checked a pocket ephemeris. As he watched, he began to feel sorry for her—how could an intelligent woman at the end of the twentieth century seriously indulge herself in such nonsense? All those earnest little calculations held no more truth than a Ouija board, or those foundation stones for that matter. Pathetic.

"There's a predominance of Pluto and Neptune in your aspects. Pluto's the planet of change and upheaval. People with strong Plutos are individuals given to great personal transformations, and that's good."

Yeah, and I got a libido with a fifty-megaton warhead, probably transform all of womankind.

"You also have a Mars signature which helps you direct your energy toward important discoveries." She made more calculations as he tried to be patient. "Your Neptune influence indicates a personality that's very independent and impatient, sometimes unpredictable. Strong Neptune aspects almost always indicate people given to anxiety and guilt."

She's got your number, pal.

"But the upside is that Neptunes are also visionaries, idealists, mystical people."

"I've never thought of myself as mystical," he said. "Just the opposite." He wanted to get back to his screen.

Sparky shrugged. "I'm telling you what it says. Also, your moon squares Saturn."

He looked at her blankly.

"You linger in the past, which explains why you probably chose archaeology as a profession. You won't let go ties to earlier times. You have a romantic yearning for days gone by."

"Gee, that stuff really *does* work."

"Now you're making fun. Forget it." She slapped the pad closed. She shrugged again. "It's okay, I'm used to it. He's the same way, Jackie. Thinks it's all crap. Everything's cut-and-dry rational with him, too." Then she looked at him with those dreamy eyes. "It's just that I find it kind of strange, Peter. I mean, if you were just a regular kind of scientist, you know a physicist or chemist or rocket scientist, then I'd understand. But you're an archaeologist."

"An archaeologist *is* a scientist."

"Yeah, but not in the ordinary sense—you know, formulas and computers and all."

"We use formulas and computers."

"Do you reject spiritualism, too?"

Peter wasn't too sure what she meant, but he nodded for fear she'd explain.

"You've never discovered anything you couldn't explain scientifically?"

"Not really."

She looked disappointed. "Never find a skull too big or an alien artifact or something made of stuff you never saw before . . . ?"

No, but I saw a beautiful woman violated last night—face-to-face.

". . . Nothing really strange?" She was dying for him to say "Yes."

"Not really," Peter answered.

"Well, I read somewhere how they found an electric battery in a Greek tomb and drawings of spaceships in Mayan ruins. Remember that movie *Stargate?* No? Well, they're digging in ancient Egypt and they find a large ring thing which turns out to be a portal to another world. Now that would be something."

"Guess so."

Peter was fond of Sparky, but she was one more graduate of the Shirley MacLaine School of Archaeology—someone who hankered for Martians and magic rather than human history.

Peter's own mind had firmed up against such mystical yearnings early—back in his high school days. He stopped going to church, feeling a little sorry for those who stayed behind. Ironically, Linda had been a religious person, and although he hadn't shared her beliefs, the inner peace she found made him suspect that believing was better than not believing. There was a time, however, back in college when over a few six-packs he and fraternity brothers would get into heavy-duty rap sessions about some of the notorious, unexplained phenomena such as the Sasquatch and the Loch Ness monster and extraterrestrial life. And there was always somebody in the house who had seen dead relatives or who had come face-to-face with UFOs. Back then such speculations were fun, made all the more credible by the fourth can of Coors. But by the time he finished graduate school, he had little tolerance for such tabloid foolishness. His studies had exposed him so thoroughly to the workings of the primitive mind, of the myth-making apparatus, that it finished off any doubts he had about the universe. Man had created the gods in his image, as well as Satan, Beelzebub, Dracula, Jeffrey Dahmer, and Adolf Hitler.

As for aliens, he had little reason to doubt life existed elsewhere in the galaxy, maybe even intelligent life. But UFOs were another story. How come a crashed saucer was never found? Or a truly inexplicable machine? How come close encounters always took place on some deserted midnight road in Barnstead, New Hampshire? And why was it Peter Jennings never reported on the eleven-year-old girl—always from places like Bhutan or Paraguay—giving birth to a space baby? or the *New York Times* never splashed its front page with headlines of the swamp monster carrying off the girl scout? It never ceased to amaze Peter how people living in an age of space shuttles and gene splicing could still embrace such absurdities—like the guy who argued blue in the face with the mechanic about the knocking under his hood, but who wouldn't question the claim that Martians helped build the pyramids. Maybe it had to do with the individual's feeling of powerlessness in a culture where cold science ruled. What did Mark Twain say? "When the scientists explained the rainbow, we lost more than we gained"? Maybe all the irrationalism was a desperate attempt to recapture the magic.

Then tell us, dear professor, a little voice whispered, *just how would you explain away last night or Andy with his throat slashed?*

He shook his head clear.

"I just find it kinda funny you don't believe," Sparky said.

"I also don't eat eggs."

Sparky looked a little nonplussed. "I don't see the connection."

"That's my point—there is no connection," Peter said. "Because an archaeologist excavates an ancient temple, say, doesn't mean he's required to share in the religion."

"No, but don't you feel some spiritual connection? I couldn't imagine digging up a talisman or some icon and not feeling a sense of . . . I don't know, a sense of awe or something."

"Awe is different," Peter said. "I've felt awe. I've also felt a connectedness to the people whose baskets I've excavated. But I've never felt anything mystical. And I've never found anything that didn't make scientific sense."

Bullshit! whispered the voice.

"So you don't believe in the spiritual realm either?"

The feather of ice was back and brushed the length of his back.

"No I don't."

"But I'm ascared of them."

"So, you really think the material realm is the only realm—that once we die, that's it? No transcendent spirit?"

"Yes," he said weakly.

"Hey, you guys! Get a load of this." It was Jackie waving them over. He was on his knees beside Connie. They were hanging over their square.

Peter was sweating. He got to his feet and followed Sparky.

In the hole, almost eighteen inches down was an amorphous

lump of dark fur. Peter's first thought was that it was the remains of some pelt clothing, possibly aboriginal. He took the trowel, and in a few minutes he exposed the hindquarters of an animal, its right leg putrefied to bone, its torso dessicated, and humming with insect larvae like so much boiled rice.

"Gross!" Andy exclaimed.

Peter watched as Jackie cleared away more debris until he exposed the flank of the animal. A foul odor rose out of the pit.

Smell familiar, does it, pal? Recent kitchen odors, perhaps?

"Doesn't look too ancient," Jackie said, spotting a bright red collar.

"My God, it's a dog," Sparky said.

"That or a hobbit," Jackie said. "The tag says 'Bilbo.'" A license number and a New Jersey address were stamped on the reverse side.

"Pretty much eliminates any of the workers," Jackie said. "Besides, who'd bring a dog on an island with a lot of machines rolling around?"

"How long you think he's been buried?" asked Sparky.

It was not completely skeletalized. "From the looks of all the parasites," Peter said, "not too long. A couple months."

The eye sockets were plugged with decay and the jaw bone visible. The fur was relatively fresh looking, but it appeared to have been pulled back off the snout, as if the dog was forced nose first into the sand. Larvae foamed in its mouth.

With trowels and brushes, they cleared away the debris until the animal was exposed in full profile.

"Strange," Connie said softly. "It was buried on an angle."

"Yeah," Sparky said. "When Sheena died, we dug a hole in the backyard, wrapped her up in her blanket and laid her flat."

"We also didn't leave her leash on," said Jackie.

With an ice pick he probed the carcass. "I don't know," he said and stepped back with Peter to get a better perspective. "The body's upright and in a straight line," he said. "What's weird are the front paws. They're both broken clean through. The head looks crushed, and look how the skin's been pushed back. Beats me."

"Maybe it fell off the cliff, and somebody buried it up here," Sparky suggested.

"Looks more like the thing died in place."

"As if it dug itself in," Connie added.

"Or got sucked in."

"How do you explain that?" Sparky asked everyone. Her diamond flickered in Peter's eye.

But Peter didn't have an answer.

chapter
Seventeen

Peter was back on the beach that night. But this time things were different.

The smell of smoke was cut with the sweet stench of death. And the source of it was all the seaweed washed in by the night tide. The stuff stretched down the length of the beach in long black humps, looking like the flotsam from a massacre at sea.

The smoky decay he could taste in the air, and it turned his stomach. Worse still, he had to watch his footing lest his feet get caught in the tangle of weeds and rotting jellyfish.

It was dark, but he managed to keep to the sand as he hustled along. His breath came hard, and his heart felt heavy. He really didn't want to go up there again. In fact, he was afraid to go up, but something pulled him along. Also, he was chasing somebody— an obscure but swiftly moving figure.

In the scant moonlight, he couldn't tell if his quarry was human or animal. He also wasn't sure why he was in pursuit. Something just drove him on. He was on autopilot again.

He told himself that if he could only run faster he'd catch up. Yet he was afraid to do so.

By the time he reached the slope, he realized it was a dog, and that gave him relief. The animal paused for a moment at the base of the Point. It looked back at him. Something in its demeanor made Peter feel very sad. Suddenly it charged up the incline, its feet moving with amazing speed.

Peter bounded after it, but by the time he reached the top, the dog had vanished. So had the stench of putrefaction. He smelled smoke. Wood smoke, and something else.

He thought about looking for the dog, but everybody was waiting for him, standing in a circle, looking like a scene out of Madame Tussaud's Wax Museum.

Yellow light flickered from lanterns, making dancing shadows against the wall of stone.

In an instant, the scene came to life.

"Look, look what proof you see," the witch shouted in defiance. "A simple blemish, and which of you has come into this world without one?"

She was in the center of the circle of people, naked from the waist up and tethered by the feet to a tall white stone. Before her stood the three boys and the Reverend Jeremiah Oates. The minister's son was covering his face with his fingers. All around him women were screaming at the sight of the witch's breasts.

The voice of Reverend Jeremiah Oates rocked across the harbor. "You still deny the charges?"

"I gave suck to no demons!" Her eyes blazed at him.

He nodded and two men came up behind her and held her arms back. Her breasts bulged fully.

Peter noticed the reverend's distraction caused by two pink nipples staring at him. Peter moved closer, yet he still could not make out the witch's face nor the third teat. But he saw Oates reach under his robe and pull out a long metal needle. He held it up so the circle could approve. It glinted wickedly like a filament of light.

Brigid saw it, too. "What are you doing?" she cried.

The men restrained her arms against the white pillar.

Like a cat, Peter moved silently behind the others for a better view.

"The third teat gives nourishment to devils," the minister said to the congregation. A strange grin lit up his face. "The devil has placed his mark upon the witch so its imps might suckle." He lowered his face to Brigid. "This shall be your test, woman."

She looked at the needle as it approached her flesh. "No," she protested. "You have no right to do this to me."

But the needle moved closer.

Peter watched with the others in hushed anticipation. The woman held her head cocked at an angle that obscured her face in the thicket of her hair. Yet, he could tell from the tenseness of her body that she was straining with every ounce of will to hold firm.

As the minister lowered the needle, Peter heard the woman suck in her breath. Gooseflesh made her nipples pucker.

Oates looked to Brigid's face; then he stabbed her in the right nipple.

She let out a loud yelp.

Peter felt a sliver of pain rebound from his skull to the soles of his feet. He was horrified at the barbarity of what was happening. He had the urge to burst into the circle and demand Oates stop this torture. But a side awareness also told him he was dreaming the whole kangaroo-court drama.

Besides, he was darkly eager to see where it would go.

Oates nodded. Then in a sudden move, he pricked the left nipple.

The woman screamed out again. She had been taken by surprise.

Peter could see tiny beads of blood rise and trickle down the white skin.

Oates then lowered the needle to the dark floweret of flesh. The woman looked down at the mole beneath the milkful mounds of her breasts. She heaved deeply. Her head went back with a groan as she held her breath.

The large, flat-joweled face of Jeremiah Oates hung over her breasts like a moon. Beside him, men he addressed as William Biddle and Caleb Herrick looked on like twin satellites.

They want her to scream in pain, Peter thought. That's it. They want that mark to be as sensitive as her nipples. But he was sure the woman would hold tight, that she would not cry out, no matter how deeply Oates pushed in the point. She would not give them the satisfaction they desired.

The muscles of her body clenched in waiting.

"Make her hurt," some woman shouted. "Make her pay."

"Hurt her," cried another. *"Hurt her!"*

Their words were dim echoes in Peter's head and he tried to grab them, but the needle jabbed Brigid then. The woman's body twitched under the prick, but she made no sound. Oates jabbed her again and again and again. Yet she held back.

"You feel no pain?" Reverend Jeremiah Oates looked dismayed.

The same woman's voice shouted disgust. She wanted Brigid to suffer. They all did.

"You feel no pain?"

Brigid's breath exploded from her lungs. "No," she said. The skin on her chest glistened with perspiration. Small rivulets of blood forked down her torso like claw marks. She shook her head with defiant pride. "I felt nothing."

The men let go of her arms. William Biddle glowered at her.

Brigid covered her breasts with her arms. She looked directly at Reverend Oates, her eyes burning defiantly.

The minister's face was flat. "She feels no discomfort," he announced to the crowd.

The woman's head proudly rose up to face the congregation. The crowd made a loud sound of dismay.

"Brigid Mocnessa feels no pain from the needle," he declared again.

Peter suddenly felt confused. Jeremiah Oates's face was beaming with gratification. He looked positively radiant, as if he had just glimpsed the Promised Land.

Suddenly a bolt of realization crashed through the woman. "No!" she bellowed.

The Reverend Oates swung around toward the circle of faces. "The devil's mark is cold. Cold! It kills the flesh to touch." He thumped the Bible with a hand. "She is a witch," he shouted. "Most assuredly *she is a witch!*"

And the circle echoed the litany. *"She is a witch. She is a witch. She is a witch."*

"You tricked me!" Brigid screamed.

"Nay, Hag Mocnessa, 'tis you who tricked the Lord."

"Expiation!" Caleb Herrick shouted. *"Expiation!"*

"Expiation!" someone else cried, and in an instant the chant rang out from the circle.

The minister gloated at Brigid, who shook her head at the

voices raised against her. He let the chant ring for nearly a minute; then with a grand sweep of his hand he silenced the circle.

For a final time he raised his finger to her.

He stabbed out the words: "Brigid Mocnessa, The Lord saith, 'Suffer no witch to live.' God's will be done!" He clapped his palm against the Bible.

And from some place three men came with wood and torches. A fourth bore a naked squirming baby.

The woman let out a hideous scream into the night. "My baby!" Her arms thrust out to it. The baby began to cry from all the commotion. "My Isaac."

"Yes, flesh of your flesh, blood of your blood," said Oates, his eyes wide. He took the child from the bearer.

The baby looked deformed not demonic. Peter could clearly see its small mongoloid face. Down's Syndrome, Peter told himself.

"Your imp of abomination," Oates called out. Then he tossed the infant to the woman like a bag of garbage.

She caught the child and clutched it to her breasts. "You bloody bastard, I curse you, Jeremiah Oates. I curse you," she screamed, and the men dumped the wood about her feet. "I curse you all!" she screamed, and the men set the torches.

"Waaaaaaah!" Wordless rage filled the harbor basin, and the flames circled around her feet and the tether.

Peter watched in horror as the fire rose up around the woman and her naked infant. He fought to wake himself up. He punched his hip as hard as he could, but he could not get out. He scratched his nails across his chest, but he was trapped in the dream.

With vicious ferocity the flames crackled up the woman's dress and enveloped her arms. The smoke lashed Peter in the face like a whip. He could smell her burning hair. He could smell her flesh as it split and sizzled in the torrents. Greasy foul smoke—he'd been smelling it for days.

For a long savage moment the baby shrieked. It would be a sound that would score Peter's mind for life.

With blackened arms still clutching the child and half dead with agony, Brigid Mocnessa raised her head to Reverend Oates and his son for her final moment. Her hair was a blazing cloud; her voice, one with the roar of fire. "*Vengeance.*"

Peter looked away. All he could think of was comforting the boy who stood before the brilliant pyre, with his hands to his face. But as he forced his way through, Peter glanced at the witch. In the full light of her immolation he recognized the face of Linda.

chapter
Eighteen

He bolted upright.

The room was a gaping silence. The neck of his T-shirt was cold with perspiration. The blanket was on the floor, and the cot under him was damp. He could feel his heart accelerating.

Andy was in a deep sleep beside him, his face pressed against Lambkin.

The only sound was the steady chirping of crickets.

His watch said one-twenty.

He got up and replaced his T-shirt with a dry sweatshirt.

The dream had left him alert. Too alert. He shuffled to the window. His mind was raw from the image of that woman and her baby. He could taste the smoke, and their screams still echoed in his ears. The same roar of agony that had filled his ears with Connie. The witch had Linda's face. And her dying words were a curse directed at a boy who was Andy. Linda on fire and swearing vengeance on Andy!

In all of his adult life he could not recall a worse nightmare, nor one that had left him so limp. He felt as if he'd been forced to witness an atrocity. He didn't want to think about it, to analyze it, to rationalize it. He didn't want to touch it. For a long while he stood at the window, laboring to purge his brain.

He tried to concentrate on other things. The night. The stars had slipped behind a gauzy apron of clouds. A heavy storm bank was advancing from the east. There would be rain tomorrow. Digging would be messy. Maybe they could set up makeshift tents with plastic.

Then his mind drifted to that dog carcass. Glad they discovered it while the sand was dry. The rain would only have accelerated the putrefaction. It had smelled bad enough as they shoveled it out and reburied it on the beach. As for how it got there, the best guess was that it had died and somebody buried it on a funny angle. Probably broke its legs in an accident.

It was an island of accidents. It was an island of rotting things.

He parted the curtains farther. Hanging over the water to the left was a fat half moon that silver-washed the old harbor. The same moon in the dream, he thought to himself. The only other light came from yellow pinpoints on the adjacent islands and the light of Graves Rocks. He watched the red eye blink and blink and blink and blink and . . .

Suddenly there was a cold shock in the center of his chest.

Something had dashed across the open plot just below his line of sight. It was too fast for his mind to catch, but he had the sense of something large—not a rabbit or a dog. And moving quickly.

Peter slipped into his jeans and sneakers. It might have been one of the others—maybe Jackie walking off Sparky's Big Sur Chili and beers. But this figure moved too fast.

He found his silver flashlight and left the bedroom with Andy still asleep. The other two bedroom doors were closed. It wasn't Jackie. He could hear him snoring.

Peter wanted to check for Sparky and Connie, but the house was old and a squeaking door might startle them. And certainly Connie wouldn't appreciate him creeping into her bedroom.

He cut down the stairs, through the living room, and out onto the porch. He gripped the flash, but decided against turning it on.

Nothing moved, and the only sound was the electric chittering of crickets.

He stepped onto the lawn, wondering if he had imagined the movement after all. Maybe it had been a combination of tired eyes, tricky night light, and a wavy old window badly in need of Windex.

Peter rounded the side of the house. His heart was making a tympanic rhythm in his ears. He felt fear and didn't know why. The dark behind the house was all the more dense because of the oaks.

He heard nothing, just the crickets. He crossed the back to the other side feeling relief and thinking about crawling back into bed.

A dry cracking sound behind him made the skin of his skull contract. A sound like flesh on fire, he thought and turned, gripping the flash like a club.

A figure was standing in the bushes maybe ten feet from him. A figure of a woman standing perfectly still, her hair missing. Burned away. And she had no face. She had no face.

No face.

Jesus, just a black hole.

A charred eyeless skull.

Light blasted his eyes.

Connie held an axe up ready to split his head.

"No!"

"Peter," she said and lowered the axe. "Sorry I startled you."

"Jesus Christ, Connie!" His organs dropped back into place. Bright yellow balloons floated across his vision. " 'Startled' doesn't come close." He took a deep breath. "I think we're even."

She didn't laugh. "I didn't know it was you."

He took another deep breath and let it out. "Seems we've been chasing each other in the dark for the last ten minutes."

"It wasn't you," she whispered.

"Huh?"

"Someone was in the house. I heard him. You were still in bed."

"Maybe Jackie or Sparky. They had seven beers between them."

He could feel her shaking. "They're both in bed."

"Did you actually see somebody?"

"Not at first. I heard a noise downstairs. I came down into the kitchen and saw somebody run out the front. A man. A big man."

"Flanagan big?"

"I don't know. It was all too fast. He heard me and ran out. And when I got outside, he was gone. Who else is on the island?"

"No one."

Peter turned on his flashlight and led her to the front. "But lots of people have boats." Just some curious boater stopping by to check the place out.

They were standing at the top of the stairs leading down to the beach. The house and yard were dark, silent. And the water was a moon-glazed black ruffle. Below, their boat sat alone against the dock. No other boat, no dark figure running down the beach. Nobody crouched on the stairs below. If, in fact, there had been somebody snooping around, he was gone the way he had come, because everything was as it should be—the house, the yard, the beach, the water. Everything. Even the stars—all fixed in their usual places.

All but one. Above the nearly opaque crest of Pulpit's Point was a flickering yellow light.

At first glance Peter thought it was the midsummer star. But this star was too yellow. Too low. And it was moving.

"Somebody's up there," Connie said.

The light was bobbing from side to side. "Could be campers, people out fishing all day and decided to overnight instead of heading home." The thought brought some relief. But Peter didn't like the idea that maybe Flanagan or his men were tampering with their equipment again. Or maybe destroying the site to get them off the island for good.

"But would they break into the cottage?"

"It's supposed to be an abandoned island. Maybe they were exploring."

"Maybe."

"Whatever, he scared the hell out of me," Connie said.

"Imagine his surprise when you show up axe in hand like the Indian Bride Witch."

Peter watched the yellow light move slowly. He didn't mind visitors. He just didn't like the thought of them camping on their dig. They could make a mess of things. Besides, the backhoe was there, with the key in the ignition. "I think I'll take a look."

"Then take this," she said. She held out the axe.

"Sure you trust me with it?"

"I've got another one under my pillow."

He gave it back. "If he turns aggressive, maybe I'll kiss him."

"Peter, that's not funny."

He raised the flashlight. "Probably just a couple of kids."

"Be careful," she said.

Before he left, he said, "Please don't go home. I don't know what happened, but I'm really not a whacko. Really I'm not."

"We'll see."

The quickest and most direct route to the Point was the beach. Peter jogged down the sand, feeling a strange kind of *déjà vu*. The Boston skyline gave him comfort. So did the row of concrete mixers just over the dunes. It was the first time he'd ever been glad to see construction equipment. The last time he'd jogged the beach, he was on his way to a seventeenth-century execution of his wife.

Then like a seed beginning to sprout, something occurred to him. What if up there . . . ?

No! That was just a dream.

It took him less than ten minutes to get within range of the Point. The light at the top was not a campfire but some kind of lamp. And not electric. It flickered. And it moved from right to left, bobbing oddly over the ground. If it was a camper, what the hell was he doing hopping around the mound like that?

Peter kept the flash off. He wished he'd brought the axe.

Because the tide was high, the footing became more difficult. Pebbles clinked beneath his shoes like broken glass. He cut up over the dunes. The flats behind them were black, but he could make out the shapes of heavy equipment. The main truck path was solid. He passed a large concrete pit that marked the edge of a complex called Pilgrim's Pride on the map Hatcher had given him.

He stopped. The light at the top had slipped below the crest. In a strange way it had been his beacon. Now it was gone. So were the stars behind the clouds. The only lights visible were those of the next island . . . the next island.

Shepherd's Island.

That's a damn prison out there, he reminded himself. And on top of the Point could be a couple of escaped convicts, armed and desperate. It all began to make terrible sense. A couple of escapees float in on a makeshift raft, check out the house, leave when they realize people were inside. *They could have murdered us while we slept.* What the hell was he doing sneaking up on them? He should go back to try to contact somebody.

But there was no telephone on the island.

There was the boat radio. He could go back and call the Coast Guard. But another thought crossed over that one. If they were convicts, why hole out on the highest point on the island, waving a lantern? Unless they were signaling others. But that was even more unlikely. Why risk discovery after escape just to let your buddies know where you are?

Think *campers,* Peter told himself. *Campers*—nice, ordinary people in their Docksiders and Eddie Bauer windbreakers, who have boated up for an overnight.

The huge chipper stood near the top of the slope, rearing its neck like an iguanadon. He climbed up it to see the Point, his blood throbbing at his temples. He pulled himself onto the top of the grinding chamber.

Suddenly he heard something that made every joint lock in place. A high-pitched ululating warble from the top of Pulpit's Point.

It was too big a sound to be a loon or some other animal. He steadied himself against the throat of the chipper. Then Peter saw it.

There in the dim yellow light, its shadow capering insanely over the ground, the excavated squares gaping like open graves at the night sky—stood a large solitary figure in black, wearing what appeared to be a ragged cape that flared widely in the wind like the wings of a monstrous bat. A large creature that Peter's brain would have been accepted as a human being but for the fact its head was antlered. And it was producing a hideous cry that re-peated itself over and over like some awful incantation. It strutted in jerks across the mound, with its arms extended in a wide *V* of supplication.

Suddenly the chipper chute began to slip against his weight. It moved a few inches with a metal-on-metal groan. That set the di-rectional hood over his head in motion. By reflex, Peter made a wide leap from the machine, fearing the hood would come down on top of him. He hit the ground and rolled. The hood sang out a loud, rusty-throated protest.

When he pulled himself to his knees, the top of Pulpit's Point was black. No light, no creature—just the implacable backdrop of the blank night sky.

He scrambled on the ground for his flashlight. He would need it to get back to the house in time, for the only thought that echoed in his brain was that Andy lay asleep back there and someplace in the black was a large lunatic thing enraged at its discovery.

Peter found the flash.

It was smashed dead.

chapter
Nineteen

He stumbled down the dunes onto the beach. He gripped the dead flash like a bludgeon. God, that it were the axe! he thought.

The beach was empty, and the sky was now opaque gloom. Nothing moved—nothing but the dim night waves raking the pebbles. He stood at the water's edge, dazed, disoriented by the image of that thing up there—an image so preternaturally horrible that it took the strongest reflex of his mind to convince himself that what he had glimpsed was a verifiable human being, born of man and woman, and wearing a deer headdress and not some eldritch thing that defied creation.

Then something occurred to him that stopped his breath. From the other night, that dream. *She wore a headdress of antlers most frightening.* Worthy Oates's claim. *Jesus Christ!* That was just a dream. This is real. Coincidence, he tried to tell himself. Coincidence.

But nothing held.

He turned toward the cottage when a peripheral movement made him glance back at the Point. A light was moving down the far end of the slope. The creature was going down the truck road in the direction of the cottage.

He stumbled back up the dunes. The image of Andy asleep in his cot filled his mind. And Connie on the porch. He would try to cut it off. He could not let it get there before him.

As he ran, it occurred to him that everything that was happening had a weird inevitability. Call it superstition or psychic perception or telepathy, but for the last five days Peter had kept pushing aside the dark suspicion that something bad was going to happen to Andy. The hallucination, the backhoe, the dreams, even Flanagan's ominous warning. More than that: He had a low grumbling premonition that there was something on this island that wanted Andy. Something sentient, something evil.

Ain't the first time . . .

Maybe it even explained last night with Connie.

He could not let that light disappear. All that he held dear in the universe depended on it. And he raced after it, not thinking what he'd do if he caught up. But the creature moved fast, as if gliding over the ground without contact.

Peter crossed the ruts to the edge of the salt marsh. If it *was* heading toward the cottage, it was taking a different route. He raced along the fill, then up a slope toward the wall of dark oaks. Never before had Peter wished so much for daylight. The black night was oppressive.

By the time he reached the ridge of trees at the top, a light rain was falling. Wind stirred the trees. Moving with animal swiftness, the light flickered deep in the woods.

Peter had not explored that part of the island. He had meant to, but it was cut off by the machines. He wished he knew how far the trees went. It couldn't be more than a few hundred yards at most. He moved inside along a vague path, his feet cracking branches. Trees rose all around him like giant aliens. The overhead canopy of leaves was so thick that barely any rain fell through. The air was still and moist and tangy with wood rot. Smoke laced the air. The only sound was the crickets. Millions of them making a metallic twittering as if something were about to happen.

He moved in deeper, trying not to catch his feet on fallen branches or lose sight of that flicker ahead of him. He kept telling himself that this was crazy, that he should head back to the house and keep vigil with the axe—that the thing out there could suddenly turn on him. But he couldn't go back. He had come too far and taken turns he couldn't duplicate in reverse, not in this muzzy dark. Without a light of his own, he could stumble around in circles for hours.

Suddenly, out of the black came a high-pitched shriek.

Then another, this time so piercing that it was impossible to determine its direction, as if whatever produced it was right on top of him. Peter crouched with his arms up to protect his face. Something passed over his head with a soft fluttering.

A screech owl, he told himself. That's all, just three pounds of feather and bone simply exercising its biological imperative. Probably out there someplace picking apart a poor stunned mouse. A little night drama, all perfectly natural, he told himself.

He stumbled on.

Despite the coolness of the wood, his face was an aspic of cold sweat. The flash felt greased in his palm. It was the only comfort against the fear that was beginning to wrack his bowels. The black was total everywhere but in the direction of the light. If that lamp were suddenly extinguished, he would be lost, helpless. . . . And the illustration from Andy's Lewis Carroll book pushed its way to his mind.

"And the Jabberwock with eyes of flame came wiffling through the Tulgey wood and burbled as it came."

What if that thing out there blew out the flame? What if it decided they were deep enough in the woods for the kill? This could all be a trap. And any second now that antlered phantasm would suddenly come screaming down on him out of the black. But nothing came at him.

He stumbled on for another few minutes, the lunatic song of the crickets filling his head. Suddenly, he became aware of something out of the corner of his eye. The ground to his right was beginning to burn with a weird green fire. He could see it distinctly—a hard, bright-green glow, as if the ground cover had become incandescent. He turned around. It was all around him, seeping out of the ground like lava. The path in front of him had disappeared in the glow. He was surrounded. He stumbled toward the direction of the lamp. The stuff was sticking to his running shoes and the bottoms of his jeans like phosphorescent mites. Millions of them. The place was aglow.

"Jesus!" he growled and stomped his feet against the unreason threatening to reduce him to chin-drooling panic.

What's happened to the ordinary world? he thought. What the Christ kind of place is this? Premonitions of horror, hallucinations from hell, backhoes fire-popping their brakes for a deadly plunge, fits of rapine madness, broken buried dogs, and those goddamn witch dreams. What's happening with this island?

Maybe he had somehow slipped through a fissure in the time-space continuum and into a parallel universe. A little pit stop with Rod Serling.

The thick moist air closed around him like a sponge. The glands under his jaw were swollen hard with tension, and his tongue had that metallic taste of raw fright.

Let the wild rumpus start.

No. Stop it! This is a natural phenomenon, a well-documented occurrence of known chemical reactions that take place in fungus, rotted punk. Fox fire, friar's lantern, will-o'-the-wisp. Your basic *ignis fatuus.* Goddamn it, man, you're a scientist! he screamed to himself. There's a rational explanation. He looked back—his footsteps left a green trail as if he were walking in shoes wet with radium.

Sweet Jesus!

Peter was not a religious man. He did not believe in any realm beyond the visible world. He had no reason to fear the supernatural simply because he did not believe in it. The universe was a phenomenological reality, perfectly testable and knowable through rational scrutiny. There were no such things as ghosts, demons, or half-humans. And, yet, these woods were making him doubt the world as he knew it. The skin of reality was peeling away. He felt the same shuddering apprehension that had struck him on the first visit to the mound: That he was in the presence of some preternatural power. An Evil.

Perhaps the Indians had felt it, too, otherwise why was this island the only one of the thirty-three they never occupied? Everything about the island would have made it a perfect outpost—the size, proximity to the mainland, the fishing. But not an aboriginal scrap in the records. Maybe the Indians knew better. Maybe it was a great Wrong Place. A place soured with curse.

A tang of smoke.

And just below the surface of his mind something began to take voice, muffled syllables. Then it was gone.

Peter began to run.

The light ahead of him had disappeared. But the fox fire was still there. As he moved, it moved, silhouetting hummocks and saplings and fallen limbs, and splashing up with each footfall, as if just below the surface was a thin lake of liquid green light.

For a moment he thought it was his imagination, but the stuff was growing in intensity, as if somebody had turned up the rheostat. What was worse, it seemed to anticipate his moves. He made a turn to the right and the stuff lit up the ground before his foot. He dodged left, and the stuff dodged with him, but just a little bit faster. How could it do that? Phosphorescence was a chemical reaction activated by impact. *This stuff's glowing before I hit. Like it's sentient. It's not following me, I'm being led.*

God, make this stop!

Peter stumbled against an oak, gasping. Another tang of smoke, and he heard a tiny voice in the breeze.

This way.

"Whaaaat?" He looked around expecting to clap eyes on somebody. An electric rocket shot up from his testes and exploded in his head. The whole floor of woods behind him was brilliant green fire as far as he could see. Trees, scrub, deadfall, saplings, rocks were all in silhouette—a black-and-green neon jungle.

Wheeeeeeeee! He bit down on his tongue to stifle a scream.

I refuse to believe this. I do not accept what I'm seeing.

He squeezed his eyes shut and pressed his fists against them. For a long moment he held his breath, his knuckles pressing painfully into his face.

"Please, God," he whispered. He opened his eyes again.

Nothing. Total black.

Of course, the nightmare was over. You just woke up. Which explained the cool wet feeling around his neck. Sleep sweat—I'm in bed he told himself. Asleep. That explains it. But it didn't explain the oak tree he was pressed against.

He was in the woods—the same mad woods—but now photon free. Without the phosphorescence, Peter was blind. He put his hand in front of his face and opened and closed his eyes. No difference. And no relief from above. The tree cover made an impenetrable roof. Nothing. This was worse: The air had turned to stone.

He fumbled with his hands, feeling his mind straining to assemble again. He felt his way along, concentrating on not impaling himself on low branches and telling himself that in six hours these same woods would be alive with chipmunks and sparrows and black-eyed Susans. It was the same earth, the same familiar biosphere—except in the thick of the night. And all that other stuff was in his head. Just a little pocket of anxiety. That thing out there gave you a fright, he told himself, and his imagination took it and ran. That's all. Just another momentary hallucination. All the anxiety about the dig and Connie and Andy and the shit with Flanagan and your ragtag career. You just got scared and your mind began to slip. Happens to the best of us.

He shuffled along the ground, testing with his hands for obstacles. Several times he stumbled and fell onto mud and woodrot. There was only scant growth because so little sunlight penetrated the canopy. He had no sense of how long he had been in the woods. Time and distance had become meaningless. He also had no idea how long he could last before disorientation would absorb his little candle glow of sanity. He had all but dismissed the creature, concentrating on the mechanics of moving through the black without hurting himself.

As he groped along, he became aware that the place had become perfectly still. Not a sound. A few moments ago the air had been shrill with insects. Now it was dead, as if he had just recovered from a severe case of tinnitus. Dead quiet. Nothing but the rasping of his breath.

This way.

This time he heard it clearly. He took a step toward it. He knew that voice.

No, Peter, here.

That voice. His name.

He turned again. And suddenly the world beneath his feet snapped away.

chapter
Twenty

The next moment he was tumbling down a steep slope of sand. The forest had ended abruptly at the top of a bluff, which dropped to flat ground. Peter rolled head over heels and came to a rest at the bottom.

He lay still for maybe a minute. He was breaded with sand. A steady rain was falling. He moved his arms and legs to check for broken bones. He was still intact.

Though he was scuffed and soaked, Peter felt a strange serenity. He was out of the woods. That metaphor had never made greater sense.

And it was because of Linda. She had led him out.

Peter found himself standing on flat ground, though soft and a little squishy. In the iron-gray gloom of the sky, it appeared as if he were at the edge of a field of tall reedlike grass. He moved away from the bluff. Up top he could see the high black fortress of oaks. He couldn't get far enough away from it.

As he stood there feeling the rain against his body, things rapidly began to make sense. He didn't know how or why, but as sure as day follows night he knew he had had a mystical experience. Maybe even religious. He had gotten lost in those awful woods, and she showed him the way to safety. It was her voice, loud and clear. He'd recognize it under any circumstance. It was not something one forgot, the voice of someone you loved, no matter how long they had been dead. She had spoken to him from the other side. Linda had come back as promised.

Peter was amazed at his calm acceptance. Perhaps it was because of the odd pitch of his mind, tenderized from all the night's wildness. But it made good sense. And he hadn't imagined it, otherwise how did he end up here, alive and safe? Linda had been watching over him. His guardian angel, as Andy said. And Peter had heard her. His Linda. He did not understand it and never would, but there *was* such a thing as life after death, and Linda's voice was proof. I'll never not believe again, he told himself.

He started to walk, his mind a tranquil pool—the serenity he imagined saints felt following an epiphany.

After a stretch, he realized the ground was getting softer underfoot. Obviously, it was from all the rain. It had been falling since he'd entered the woods.

He wondered what had happened to the thing with the light. It seemed almost an experience of another lifetime. And now it was gone and with it the debilitating fear.

Peter, here.

"Linda, is that you?"

I have something for you, Peter. Something very important.

They weren't real words, intelligible to the outer ear, just shadowy impressions of words audible only to the mind.

"What is it? Where are you?"

There was no response, but that was okay, because now he was certain. And he moved into the high grass, feeling a ripple of elation. She was still there, Linda, watching over him.

Thank you, dear God.

The fact that there was no light was okay, too, because a low translucence in the clouds helped him to make his way. And in the distance there was the soundless flickering of lightning.

He pushed on, and water seeped into his shoes. Warm water. Warmer than the rain—water that had been sitting without movement all day in the sun. He took a few more steps, his feet slithering on muddy clumps of growth. He looked back, and when his eyes adjusted to the sky's glow, he became aware of tall grass all around him. He took a few more steps when it occurred to him that tall reedy grass and muddy ground were the stuff of marshes.

He could turn around. He had probably sloshed only twenty or thirty feet. But then what? Try to scale a wet sand slope? And what if you made it up? Back home through Wonder Woods? No way, José, as Andy would say.

Andy.

His heart took a hard swallow. *God, let him be asleep.* If he woke up before Peter got back, at least Connie would be there.

Connie.

Suddenly it all began to make wicked sense. The other night it was Linda, not dementia that took him over. Linda. Yes, it was she who had possessed him, mind and body. Linda. But, he told himself, it was best not to think of Connie at the moment. Linda always was a jealous woman. Besides, he had to get back.

He wondered how long he had been gone. Maybe an hour, maybe two. Strange how he had lost all sense of time. "Linda, help me," he whispered.

He moved on, trying to put away the thought that he might be wandering into the depths of a salt marsh filling with rain. He turned in another direction, but the ground was still mushy. He turned another way, spreading the reeds.

This way.

His foot landed on some rocks. Footing. Cool relief flushed through him. "Thank you," he whispered.

Yes, Peter . . . this way, this way, this way.

The voice was louder, like the low distant thunder. It was Linda, all right. *I've been waiting for you.*

Her voice, but with none of her music in it.

Maybe the rocks formed a vein, like a natural walkway out to the beach. He moved along, but after the fourth rock, there were no others. And warm fecal matter began to ooze into his shoes.

The place stank of soft decay, and he imagined himself standing on the upper layer of a bottomless chasm of sludge, the decayed matter of all the things that had ever lived, died, and putrefied here—a black pudding of swamp rot straight down to Cenozoic dregs.

If it is Linda, where is she leading me? he thought. He was still on the edge of the marsh. He could backtrack maybe to the bluff and wait out the dawn. In a few hours the place would be crawling with workers.

No. It was Sunday. The Sabbath, and nobody worked.

To his right there was a flurry of movement and some raucous chattering. Birds. There were nests all around him—probably red-wing blackbirds. He took a few more steps. Mush oozed over his ankles, and the rain whipped his eyes. He pulled his feet out of the ground with deep sucking sounds. The sharp sour odor was burning his nose. With each step, his feet seemed to sink a little farther into the revolting stuff. It was like slogging through excrement. But what bothered him more was that each step took greater effort to retract his foot.

"Help me."

Peter, Peter. Your fulfillment.

"What?"

Turn here.

He lunged toward the voice, flailing against the high serrated grass. He touched long rigid reeds, his fingers sliding up to the spongy cylinders at the end. Cattails. He remembered once cutting some by a roadside with Linda. Furry brown sausages, she had called them. Now he was surrounded with thousands of them in the middle of a perfect little bird sanctuary—an Audubon's delight by day—a killing swamp by night.

"Linda!" he cried. "You tricked me." He was stuck.

The sky flared green through the cover, and three seconds later thunder exploded overhead. Rain beat dismally against his face.

Peter had heard stories of people being lost in marshes, disappearing in pools of quicksand. But that was always in faraway places like Africa or Asia. This was the Boston Harbor. Suddenly, it occurred to him that maybe this was the real thing. That this was quicksand but made of mud. A soft foul fudge that with excess water could suck him down full body.

It all became brutally clear: Linda had led him here. She had been doing it all night. That was her up there. That was her presence last night on the mound.

Linda: She had attacked Connie with his body.

Linda: She was getting back for her death.

Linda: This was her revenge.

In a sudden panic he wrenched one foot free. Then he yanked out the other, placing it down on a clump of cattails. He lunged forward, reeds cracking under him. He had to keep moving like this or sink in place. He stumbled a few more steps, when his right foot suddenly plunged into a watery chamber. There was a thick gurgling sound, and he found his leg covered to the knee. Then in an instant, the ground under the other foot gave way with a bubbly belch.

"It was an accident," he pleaded. "A goddamn accident."

He grasped a bundle of reeds like a lifeline. He steadied himself, not daring to move a muscle lest he thrust himself farther down. For several minutes he held still, breathing in quick shallow pants—the kind they had practiced in Linda's Lamaze class. He struggled to get hold of his mind. Cold rain pelted his face like birdshot.

The image of Linda's face that night rose up—the last he had seen her, full of venom and hate. It bloomed in his mind in brilliant green light.

Leave me! his mind shouted.

He had to get centered again. He had to get back to saving himself. He was probably at the edge of a large well of quick mud. If he could make a hundred-and-eighty-degree turn, slide along on his belly—maybe he would reach the slopes again. And no matter what, he'd wait until daybreak. Andy hysterical for a few hours was better than Andy orphaned.

Clutching the reeds, he raised one leg. But as he did, the other sank—he was being slowly sucked down. By reflex, he sat down. The mud made a warm pocket under him. He grabbed his right pant leg with both hands and pulled his leg out. He rolled half onto his side, his other leg twisting under him. The mud crept over his left knee and very slowly up his thigh like a warm hand. He lowered his face onto the mat of reeds. He could taste the salt. Rainwater streamed down his head. He felt his elbows being drawn under and the mud rise up his side, reeds sticking into his flesh like so many spikes. The cesspool smell filled his head. For one long exhausted moment he lay perfectly still while he mustered a last effort to free himself.

He recalled those photos of bog people flawlessly preserved for two thousand years with garrotes still tight around their necks, their flesh like bronzed leather. They had been executed for some unknown crimes and dumped into the muck. Just as he was. For killing Linda. He closed his eyes and told himself: My fulfillment? This is my death. She came back to lead me to my death in this cesspool.

Peter let out a long cry of agony—the final outrage of a man who knew he was about to die. Then, in a surge, he made a huge scissor kick against inevitability.

But the effort only opened a liquidy subchamber, and the mud sucked him in to his waist. In a moment it would rise to his chest, paralyzing his legs and torso, then up his neck, filling his mouth and nose. Then in the blink of a bubble, it would close over him forever. And for three long wicked minutes, Peter would thrash and sink, and his diaphragm would heave for air, but suck hot mud.

Will I go to see God?

Those were Peter Van Zandt's last thoughts before a blinding light filled his face.

chapter
Twenty-one

Light.

"Linda?"

A large dark figure hung over him. He couldn't determine the face. There was a sharp poke in his shoulder. The whittled head of a spear wagged in his face. Without thought he grabbed it with both hands. Then in a telescoping moment, he felt himself being dragged powerfully out of the warm sucking mud toward the light.

The light—a flame flickering in an old lantern sitting at face level with him. He kept his eyes fixed on it and thought how that flame was the most wonderful thing in the universe.

He gave hard porpoise kicks and in a moment was lying on a narrow plankway that cut through the marshes. He had nearly drowned just five feet from it.

He rolled to his side and looked up. A large human figure with the antlered head of a deer stood above him, holding in its hands a Y-shaped wooden spear aimed at his chest. He stared up at it stupidly. Nothing registered. Then, like a Polaroid photo developing, everything came back with bright clarity—the whole Lewis Carroll revue.

He pulled himself to his feet, his clothes heavy with foul mud. He found himself looking at two faces. One, a black-snouted buck with hollow eye sockets and a large rack of horns. The other, partly hidden by the headdress, was human—white and puffy, with shaded inset eyes that regarded him like the eye sockets of a skeleton. The bad light and driving rain made it impossible to compose a face, and before Peter could try, it turned away. But it was not Linda. It was a man.

The figure moved down the plankway, swinging the lantern for him to follow. And like a hatchling after a mother duck, Peter cut through the reeds after it.

The rain lashed against him. In the light he was able to make out some features of the figure. The rack of buck horns connected to a full dark skin that covered the entire body in front and back. On its feet were high rubber boots, the old-fashioned galoshes, snap-fasteners up the front, what his mother called "gaities." It was the only sign that the thing he followed belonged to the ordinary world. Yet, he wasn't quite certain the ordinary world still existed, or that he was in it. The overwhelming sense of Linda's presence was gone.

They moved through the swamp while dozens of questions flashed through his mind.

Daddy, who's that man over there in the woods?

The same flat, featureless face.

He said he'd cut my throat.

None of it was making any sense. And, for the time being, Peter did not care, for what he told himself over and over again as he slogged along like a mummy was that he was alive. Outrageously alive. He had been spared. Linda had spared him. That swamp had been his atonement.

Never before in his life could he remember such exhilaration, such a sensation of body-lightness, of rising up within himself—as if he were full of helium and might at any moment become airborne. Perhaps it was the sheer physical relief of being out of that mud—what somebody might feel having a lower-body cast removed. Despite his cold mud-packed clothes, warm sensations coursed through his loins. It felt magnificent to walk again. The only term that came to mind was *high*—but not like the cocaine rush from college days. This was more like the high after a stiff seven-mile run. A high of well-being, naturally generated—probably a special brand reserved for those who've clapped eyes on the Grim Reaper and walked away. A born-again euphoria.

No, something greater than euphoria. Rapture. That exquisite joy known only to mystics and saints.

Everything around him appeared to have an exaggerated reality—the cattails, the reeds, the fast flickering shadows, the darkened silhouette leading him out. Even the pelting rain looked like a school of incandescent minnows in the light. It was as if the whole physical world had taken on a strange exaggeration, as if he were seeing everything in hologram. As if he were seeing it for the first time.

What the mystics meant by spiritualism.

Peter's sweatshirt, heavy with mud and water, hung from his shoulders like an old skin. He pulled it off and tied it around his waist. The rain beat against him. It felt gloriously cool and clean. It washed the mud and salt off his skin. He held up his face and caught the peltings on his tongue. Cool sweet new water. He rubbed his arms and chest—not because of chill, but because his skin felt electric with sensitivity, like a Geiger counter registering each micro scintillation.

Peter felt reborn.

Reborn, and for some great purpose. Knowledge lay ahead. And new wonders.

Peter blanked his mind with ease, savoring the sheer physical pleasure of walking back out into life.

The figure neither looked back nor uttered a word. Instead he led them to the end of plankway and across a flat expanse of sand. Not too far away Peter could hear the ocean, the first time in hours. The rain had subsided and the wind was now a gentle zephyr. In the distance were broken clouds and stars glinting through thin gauze. In the eastern sky, the moon had again appeared and set the sky in motion again. The universe looked familiar and friendly again.

Peter's exhilaration slowly faded as they walked along. In a short while, he began to feel normal, even chilled. He rubbed his arms to stimulate circulation. He was not certain exactly where they were. Long ago he had lost orientation. But he sensed they were on the western coast, the other side from the cottage and heading in the opposite direction.

"Excuse me." He felt a little silly addressing the rack of horns.

Either the man did not hear, or pretended not to, because

there was no acknowledgment. He just kept walking and swinging the lantern. Peter decided not to pursue the question.

They cut into another patch of woods at the edge of the flats. Peter felt a quickening in his chest, half expecting the ground to light up and a screech owl to attack his face. But there was none of that. His mind felt whole and focused. He had no idea of the time. His watch was on the table beside his cot and his internal body clock had blown a circuit back in the swamp. How many hours had passed since he had left the cottage? Two? Three? It seemed several nights' worth. He wondered if Linda was still nearby.

He thought about Andy waking up and Connie trying to comfort him. Andy would not accept any excuse for Peter's absence. He would want to go looking for him. Andy was like that. Wouldn't take no for an answer.

Suddenly Peter felt anxious to get back. He had no idea where he was being led. Several times he wanted to tell the man to point him back to the cottage, but he could not make himself do it. The figure still did not seem a being you made ordinary requests of. Besides, Peter's curiosity was mounting.

He had not gotten a good look at the face under the snout, but he sensed age. And yet the man was stepping along with a youthful suppleness. He also moved with an uncanny radar sense through the woods, never hesitating to determine direction. From what Peter could tell, there was no path beneath them, no trampled growth or bare ground. They wound through the trees and brush and down into a deep ravine, through a stream and up hills, and all along a wall of tall oaks and birches and pines.

The sound of waves grew louder as they came to a clearing in the trees. A small dark shack sat at one edge of the clearing, an amber light glowing inside. Against the wall was a stack of lobster traps, and on the ground colored floats and line. The place stank of sea matter.

The man pushed open the door, and the light fell on the half-flayed carcass of a seal sitting on a plank between two barrels. It was frosted with salt. Before Peter stepped inside, he caught a glimpse of a small blue fishing boat moored just offshore—one he had seen several times before.

The man led the way inside. Peter followed and closed the

door. A rope of iron-colored hair tumbled down the side of the man's head.

The man was a woman.

That did not shock Peter. He was simply relieved she was human.

The interior was damp and fishy. A kerosene lamp burned on an oil drum along the side wall. The shack was a small boathouse, filled mostly with a small wooden outboard sitting right side up on wooden horses. Some blankets were balled up in the bow. Along the walls were oars, rope, other marine paraphernalia, and hand tools.

"If you hadn't come back, I'd still be sinking in that mud." He had wanted to ask if Linda had sent her, but he didn't know if the woman had felt Linda's presence, too. The shack was dull and ordinary, not the haven of a supernatural entity.

The woman glanced at him without response, then moved to the shadows in the rear. She placed the headdress on a form made from a float on a stick. The hides she untied and folded with care and placed them on a shelf against the back wall. It was a ritual she had performed before. Probably like her activity on the mound. It all seemed so anticlimactic now.

When she moved back into the light Peter had no doubt—it was the same face that had watched them from the trees, probably for days. The same broad, implacable face. A face made for staring. What gave the woman her startling appearance were her eyes—they were askew. Her right eye, large and alert, stared intensely at him, while the left—probably from a weak muscle—had permanently defected to the corner to squint into the dark. The appearance was of two faces: one fixed straight ahead, the other gazing off to the side. Two faces superimposed—one in this world, the other someplace else. The eyes were blue-gray and didn't match her vaguely Asian features.

She was a large woman, nearly as tall and wide as Peter, and powerful looking. She was dressed in black bib overalls and a dark sweatshirt. Her hair, wet from the rain, was slicked back behind her ears. Except for the gray, there was no way to fix her age. She could be fifty or seventy. Her skin in the yellow light appeared dark and oily. On one cheek was a velvety mole looking like a bug that had crawled out of her mouth.

"I have to thank you for saving my life."

She said nothing, just glared at him like a Cyclops.

She reached into a hip pocket and produced a long thin knife. With a thumb she examined its sharpness, then began to scrape the mud from the tip of the double-handled spear, silently rolling the stick in one hand while scraping with the other and occasionally wiping the blade on her pants. While she worked the knife, she glared at him with that weird reptilian eye.

"That's a divining rod."

Again nothing. She eyed him suspiciously and scraped the point. There was no indication the question had any meaning to her. Her lips were pressed tightly together, yet moving as if an inner conversation was going on.

"Who are you?" he asked. The question drifted lazily in the air for a long moment like a smoke ring. Alice addressing the caterpillar.

No response. He began to wonder if she understood English or was capable of language. That granite silence, along with that impossible glare and robotic whittling, was beginning to unsettle him. "I had an uncle who made a livelihood dousing artesian wells up in Maine."

Nothing.

"I've got a feeling you weren't looking for water up there."

More nothing. More big eye. More scrape, wipe, scrape. Maybe she was one of the "boat people" he had read about—island-hopping scavengers who steal what they can from beach houses and boats to fence on the mainland. But that didn't explain the antlers and divining rod. "Maybe you can tell me what you were doing on our site in that headdress?"

Her face rose like a half moon. *"Your* site, is it?"

Her voice was rough from disuse. Despite her tone it was a relief to hear ordinary English from her. He had begun to suspect that she was from a distant century.

"No offense. What I mean is we're excavating up there, you know, digging for things."

She wiped the knife on her pants and continued to whittle. "I know everything that happens on this island," she said in a low voice. Her teeth were gapped and yellow like an aged dog's. "You're no different from the others." The long slender blade flickered menacingly.

"We're not part of the construction business, if that's what you mean."

"You *have* no business on this island. You come and dig it all up."

"I think you've got us all wrong. We're just archaeologists looking for clues to the island's history."

He wasn't sure she knew the word or cared. Nothing he said had much impact on her.

"Violators is what you are. All of you."

"We're not violating anything."

No response.

"You came through our cottage tonight."

Her good eye flared at him. "Your cottage?"

In the next instant the honed head of the divining rod was just inches from the center of his chest.

"Know something, Mr. Archaeologist, I was born in that cottage. So was my mother and her mother and her mother all the way back. You're in *my* cottage, mister, *my* cottage."

"You were the caretaker."

"I *am* the caretaker," she growled. "I'll always be the caretaker. You can tell that to your Mr. Shit and his fancy lawyers." She raised the point to his face. "Maybe I shoulda let you die. Maybe I should let you all die."

He wasn't too sure what she meant, but in the orange light the woman looked deranged and capable of violence. She no doubt hated Hatcher for evicting her. What crowded his mind was the thought that the night's wild rumpus might not yet be over—that maybe he was being saved for this half-crazed Baba Yaga with a killing rod. Who would ever know? She could skewer him through the heart in a second, and in half an hour he'd be at the bottom of the harbor, weighted down with an anchor and swarmed over by crabs. In her mind he was one of Hatcher's men.

"That was you in the tunnels."

No response, but the spear head floated just inches from his solar plexus like a snake.

"And you rigged our backhoe. It was you. My son nearly went off the cliff." He wondered how she had done it. She knew boat engines and generators, but Jimmy said only Superman could have done that to the cable. And how did she pop the bucket?

"You think everything has a simple answer."

"I don't know what you're talking about."

"Don't you, Mr. Archaeologist?"

"No, I don't."

The vague rumbling in Peter's head again picked up, and he fought it. He was not going to let unreason tyrannize him again.

"And I know nothing about your business with Fane Hatcher. I have nothing to do with him, his lawyers, or the construction out here. And, for what it's worth, I don't like what they're doing out here any more than you do. But I have no say. I'm just a simple archaeologist excavating Pulpit's Point for a few weeks with my assistants. I would hope you don't tamper with any of our equipment, because one way or the other it's not going to stop what they're doing here, and innocent people will get hurt."

While she weighed his words, Peter thought about making a grab for the stick, and in his mind he rehearsed the moves—a swing with his right and a chop at her forearm with his left. Except he couldn't pull back because he was against the wall. He tried not to think of that point piercing through his organs.

And in a crazy side thought, he wondered if he had died and gone to the Hell for men who sexually violate women. *Peter Van Zandt, meet Lady Beelzebub, who's gonna show you what HER dowser can do.*

The spike was just above his navel. "What do you want with me?" he asked.

"Why are you digging up there?" The intensity of her expression was palpable.

"I told you, we're here to excavate the mound. I'm an archaeologist."

"You're digging up the stones for Mr. Shit." The tip of the spear dimpled his skin, sending an electric shock from the top of his head to his genitals.

"Half an hour ago you saved my life, now you're holding me hostage. What the hell do you want?"

Her bad eye squinted to a glassy slit while the other filled her face. "The stones."

"What about them?"

"What's your business with them?"

"I have no business with them. I'm just clearing them away."

"You're lying."

"Goddamn it, I'm not lying." The point pressed deeper. And his back was flat against the wall. If he breathed any harder his skin would be pierced.

"What do you know about them?"

"Nothing. Maybe part of an old church. Maybe something the Indians set up. That's what I came to find out."

She glared at him for several seconds, then pulled the stick back.

Peter's breath exploded from him.

"An old church?" she said. She seemed vaguely amused.

"That's what I've been told."

"And what do *you* think about them, Mr. Archaeologist?"

He shook his head. "They're nothing I've seen before."

"They're sacred."

"They're sacred," he repeated as if taking an oath. And in his mind's eye she shuffled and chanted across the mound with her divining rod and antlers.

"This island is sacred."

"I see."

"No, you don't see, Mr. Archaeologist. You're just here to dig. And when you're through, they'll break 'em up for fill."

"Maybe they are sacred, and maybe that's what I'll find out. It's what I do for a living—dig in the dirt and hope for the truth."

"The *truth*," she said, as if testing the word. "And what happens when you learn the truth?"

"I don't follow you."

She raised her voice. "What do you do with them, Mr. Archaeologist?" She pronounced the words with the same contempt as "Mr. Shit." "What happens to the stones when you're through digging 'em up? What happens when you go back to the mainland with all your money?"

"I'm not getting paid, and I have no say in what happens to the stones or anything else we find. If they're of archaeological value I will do what I can to preserve them. But I doubt it, because it's private land. Even the president can't prevent them from breaking them up or whatever, sacred or not. If you want to know, put that thing on Hatcher, goddamn it. It's his island and his stones."

He wished he hadn't let the adrenaline talk again. Defiance under the circumstances was dumb. But he was shivering and weary and wanted to be back in a dry, warm bed.

For half a minute she said nothing, evaluating him according to whatever strange criteria she measured the world by. Her face settled into a hard neutrality. The blaze from her eye seemed to dull as her facial muscles relaxed. Then she took a deep breath and let it out in an audible groan. She apparently believed him because she lowered the rod. "It's not his stones."

From the inside of the boat she pulled out a blanket and handed it to him. While he wrapped it around his shoulders, he noticed her put a pill into her mouth from a small vial. She winced a little from pain and stuck the bottle into her bib pocket. "You have a name?" she asked.

"Peter Van Zandt."

"Let me tell you something, Peter Van Zandt. They came one day, Mr. Shit and all his fancy-pants lawyers. They came with papers what said I had to move, they were gonna rebuild the place. They said my acres were just leased to us to farm and it was up and I had to find another place to live." She spat on the ground.

"I'm sorry to hear that." The menace in her had passed. "Did you check with a lawyer?"

"Didn't do no good. I even checked with the Indian Office. His papers said the place was his and I had to go."

"You're Indian?"

She nodded. "They sent me a big check to find some other place. That's the way it always is. They buy your right to be what you are." She wiped the knife, slipped it back into its case, and plunged it into her hip pocket.

"Did you find another place?"

"I been here seventy-two years. There is no other place."

"You're living here now?"

She shook her head. But it was clear that maybe on occasion she had used the outboard as a bed. She lived on that boat bobbing offshore.

She stepped out of the light to the rear of the shack and returned with something in her hand. In the light she removed a frame that had been wrapped in animal skins. She draped the hides on the side of the boat and handed him a glass-covered picture. He lowered it to the light.

An engraving, done in sepia and a gray wash, the paper blotchy with discoloration as if from considerable age. Yet the central drawing was clear and meticulous and expertly done—a bald hill rising out of a violent sea, waves exploding on large shore rocks, and against a heavily smoldering sky at the top, like hundreds scattered across the British Isles, sat a ring of boulders.

A stone circle.

Figures were drawn in and around the circle—males in long waistcoats, leggings, and wide-brimmed hats. And within the circle was a female in long robes and an antlered headdress. She was standing before a crude pillar against which a terrified child was bound and awaiting the sacrificial dagger quivering high in her hand.

There was an inscription in flowing script along the margin: "Sacrifice of Innocents at the Stone Temple on Druid's Head." In the lower right-hand corner was the signature of the engraver, Ezra Bodwell. And the date—1692.

"That's Pulpit's Point?"

"What they call it now."

The scale of the engraving was off, as was the style of old cuts. The waves were too high and the hill was too low. But everything else was exact—the contours of the Point, the rock line, the shadow of the forested peak behind it, the skyline of Colonial Boston in the distance. Even the sharp pinnacle of rock just offshore. It was the eastern end of Kingdom Head. And on top of the Point were several stones—he counted thirteen in a perfect ring, another toward the center—all a little taller than the figure of the priestess.

"There's your old church, Mr. Archaeologist."

A thought floated through his mind. I'm still dreaming. All of it—everything that's happened tonight is pillow cinema: the trip through the woods, Linda guiding me, sinking in the swamp rot, this googly-eyed grimalkin, the engraving, a stone circle on Pulpit's Point. It's all inside my head. It had happened before—the last few nights, in fact. This was just an extension of that with a few more plot twists thrown in. Still roller-coastering down the old Mobius strip of dreams.

He fingered the chain around his neck, the one Linda had given him. Cold slender metal. It felt real. So did the glass over the engraving.

"The date says 1692."

"The year they pulled down the stones and burned her."

"Burned who?"

She thumped the glass with her finger. "Brigid. My poor Brigid Mocnessa."

chapter
Twenty-two

"Brigid Mocnessa?"

"Her real name before they made her Mac Ness. It's what they did."

For a long inert moment Peter stared at the engraving.

Brigid Mocnessa. The syllables clanged in his brain. He rubbed his forehead as if trying to massage his prefrontal lobe back to life. Yes, I'm dreaming all this.

Then a second thought floated up like a lazy bubble. *NOT a dream. I've lost my mind. I am someplace physically, but my real essence is dead. Synaptic blowout of the first order. I'm probably rolling in my corn flakes this very moment, sucking my big toe.*

The woman moved to the rear of the shack again. It was all still there. She was still there. Peter was still there. The engraving still in his hand.

He had seen it all in the dreams—the woman, the trial, the stones. *"Then you confess this be a temple of demon spirits."*

A stone circle.

Even if it were some kind of autosuggestion—snatches from historical records of witch trials crossed with local details, recent implications coming together in a grand coincidence—he could never have come up with Brigid Mocnessa. There was no such name in the records. He had never heard the name in his life. The others, maybe. But not that one. He couldn't imagine even putting it together.

The woman shuffled back from the shadows. In her hand was

a black ledgerlike book wrapped in clear plastic. She opened it on a marker and showed him in the light.

The pages were covered with small thin writing in rusty sepia on discolored paper. The ink was blotchy in places and the hand a little shaky. But Peter could make it out. It was a letter addressed to "Dearest Cousin." The date was July 17, 1692. The letter went on for three pages. It was signed Lydia Mocnessa.

"Her only child, Brigid's, after they killed her son. She was fourteen years when they killed them."

"What about her son?"

"She had a baby, Isaac. They burned him, too. Go ahead, read it yourself."

His eyes rolled across the words.

It must have been past midnight when I was awakened by the sounds of men pounding at the door and my mother's screaming. I remember it was Caleb Herrick who first came into the house, followed by Abel Badger and William Biddle, when my mother opened the door and asked them their purpose for disturbing the peace of our home with such horrid noise. Caleb Herrick made no imediate answer but seized upon my mother's arm as did Abel Badger and marched her out of our house into the night, and I could hear her protesting that she had done no wrong. I neede not tell you, dearest Cousin, how greatly frightened I was by the men and how they had seized upon my mother and had taken her into the night with no explanation. But as I chased after them, Caleb Herrick did turn to me and said that Goodwife Oates, Wife of Reverend Jerimiah Oates of Boston, would look after my person and tend my soule.

A small alarm went off in his skull: Jeremiah Oates, William Biddle, Caleb Herrick. More names from the dream:

It was then Caleb Herrick said my Mother was a Wytch and that she was the engine of unatural Wickness and Devilry in New England. I started back to the house only to see William Biddle stealing poor baby Isaac into the night. He was

crying woefully and naked of his swaddlings. I implored him
to leave my brother, that he was innocent and not right. But
my Pleas were not heeded, and in a state of Confusion and
Fear, I followed them in the night. It is almost too horrible to
put before your eyes, but then most fiendishly they did take my
mother to Druid's Head and the Stone Circle where in most
hideous circumstance I did witness as the Congregation of
villagers bore Witnesse against my mother for certaine
forbidden Arts, felloniously Practiced within the Stone Circle on
Devill's Finger. They tore from her neck the Sacred Moonstone
Torc. And with my heart breaking I did witnesse as Reverend
Jerimiah Oates did administer the Trial and call for the
execution by burning of my Mother and innocent baby brother
Isaac in the Druid Temple and the pulling down of the dear
Stones to be buried with the ashes of them both on the 4th of
July 1692. . . .

The letter continued, but the woman pulled it away. She said
something about how the good reverend's wife felt sorry for Lydia
and took her in and how she later went to live with her cousin,
then married an Indian named Moses, who was so good with his
hands that he and Lydia were allowed to move back to the island as
tenant farmers.

But Peter barely heard her. "I don't understand," he whispered to himself. "None of it."

"Their ashes was still warm when they buried them."

Peter raised the lantern to the drawing again. The priestess
was wearing long Druidic robes, her hair flowing down from under
the antlered headdress, a knife raised high in the air, her mouth
pressed implacably shut. "She's sacrificing a child."

"That's Ezra Bodwell's knife, not Brigid Mocnessa's." She
scowled. "She never killed nobody. That's what they wanted everybody to think."

"Then why did they execute her?"

"Because they were stupid and afraid."

"Afraid of what?"

"She was different. She chose the power of those stones to
their God."

"They said she was a witch? They accused her of conjuring engines of malice, of sorcery, of suckling Satan's Imp."

The woman cocked her head. "How do you know these things?"

"I dreamt it, all of it, I don't understand how."

"That place up there has power. It gets into your head and makes you see things."

Peter nodded. "In the dream she was executed because witnesses saw her commune with the dead."

"She was the keeper of the flame," the woman said, then she took the lantern and moved to the dark rear of the shack to refill it from a large kerosene can.

Keeper of the flame.

The contents of his dreams, he thought, were no less real than her claims, that engraving or that diary. They shared the same reality—a reality he had no rational explanation for. He had run out of them.

That meant the foundation of Hatcher's little mariner chapel on Pulpit's Point was really part of a Celtic stone temple where three centuries ago this woman's ancestral grandmother was executed for witchcraft by local Colonialists. From all the records of Colonial life, Peter knew that nobody convicted of witchcraft was ever burned. Any such accounts had confused the Salem witch trials with earlier European practices. During the mad purge of 1692, nineteen Massachusetts residents convicted of witchcraft were put to death, eighteen by hanging, one man pressed. But nobody was burned, that was certain. If there was a Brigid Mocnessa who was torched for witchcraft, it was done without sanction of the Commonwealth court system. And without record.

The woman lit a match and the lantern flared up, filling his head with the dim firelight image of her in antlers and divining rod. She's as crazy as a coot, Peter told himself. And he was just as crazy because he saw it all in dreams.

But there was nothing crazy about Linda's presence in that swamp. He had felt it. He had heard her. She was there as sure as he breathed. He had no explanation for how it had occurred— perhaps the sheer exercise of her will, but Linda had come from the other side and led him through atonement into new life. It was nothing less than a bona fide supernatural experience, the kind reserved for prophets and saints. Perhaps this was his destiny, his *karma*. And the more he wondered, the more certain he became. Yes, his karma—hinted at through premonitions and dreams and teasing moments of awareness. All beckoning him for the last few days—maybe throughout his professional life. His own private Troy. The vindication of a life of digging dirt.

Your fulfillment, she had said.

He moved closer to the lantern. The engraving looked real. But even supposing it were a fake, who would have bothered? And to what end? None he could see. Eliminate fraud, and that left a late seventeenth-century original engraving of a stone circle. Rough as it was, it exhibited the topography of Pulpit's Point. And the three recumbent boulders appeared the same shape and relative size as the three uprights in the foreground of the engraving, including one with a slanted right shoulder. Which meant that as early as 1692 a Celtic ring of stones had sat up on Pulpit's Point, which once had been called "Druid's Head." And a woman named Brigid Mocnessa was burned up there for witchcraft, her baby as well, its genetic malformation construed as Satanic.

"Who put up the stones?"

"My people did."

"Your people. You mean your family?"

"Yes."

"Do you know when?"

She made a weak shrug of her shoulders. "Brigid tells Lydia a thousand years before the first white men."

"A thousand years. You're talking the sixth century."

"Do you really believe everything came over on the *Mayflower?*"

Peter swallowed dry spit. His heart pounded. Go easy, he told himself. Move too fast, reason crumbles, and more goddamn white rabbits come pirouetting through the room. "Where did your people come from?"

"The Abnakis, came from up north."

The Abnakis were New England's northernmost tribe of Indians. Unlike most other tribes, they had not been obliterated by epidemics or wars with Europeans. "So, the Abnakis built the stone circle."

"Not what I said, Mister. I have white man's blood, too. The Mocnessa blood's from Ireland."

"Ireland. How do you know that?"

"What Lydia learned from Brigid. She put it all in here." She tapped the bound volume. "She says that our people came over when the Christian priests began converting everybody and driving out the old gods."

"The old gods."

"The Celts worshipped spirits in oak trees and ancient gods who ruled long before Christ."

"So, they escaped."

"That or be killed."

"And you're saying your ancestors, ancient Celts, sailed across the Atlantic and ended up here?"

"Yes. They came across the sea and put up the stones in the right place, like they did in the old world. That's all that's left, the stones."

In the light Peter studied her face for some clue, some indication of falsehood. But he saw none. She believed everything she said.

So did Peter.

Suddenly everything came clear, like a photograph rapidly developing. It was all part of the master plan—that weird sensation on the mound last month—what he had thought was some kind of warning. It wasn't a warning but a premonition. Yes, a premonition of some great purpose that had been pulling him along for months, beginning right back with the cancellation of his dig in New Hampshire. It all made perfect sense when he put it together. Everything that had transpired over the last several weeks was some kind of master plan. And it all had to do with what lay under that mound on Pulpit's Point.

He held the engraving to the light. A stone circle erected by pilgrims from Celtic Ireland a thousand years before the *Mayflower*. His hands began to shake. He had to get back up there, to start clearing the sand. He only had seventeen days left. Seventeen days to confirm what might be the greatest archaeological find in the

Western hemisphere. He had to get back to those stones. Their implication was stupendous.

The woman started wrapping the diary in its skins.

"I'd like to take another look at that if you don't mind."

But she put it back in the bag.

He'd have to get it from her later. The damn thing was probably an historical gold mine.

"They burned her to death," she said. "The good Christians of Boston. They burned her, her baby, and all her belongings, everything. They said they were relics of the devil. They even killed her animals. The only reason they spared Lydia was the minister's wife."

"Was Brigid a witch?"

"What's a witch? Lydia says she knew the secret of the stones, had the old magic to call up the dead. If that's a witch, then so was their Jesus."

"Are you descended from Brigid?"

She nodded. "She was a caretaker, too."

"A caretaker."

"She kept the flame. She kept the magic of the old spirits alive."

"I see."

She looked out the window for a moment. Gray light silhouetted the small fishing boat in the water. "Some things don't die," she said. "Those stones, they still got fire in them." Her eyes were jelly slits. "You know what I'm talking about. You felt it."

His heart surged. He had felt it. *Oh, yeah. I felt the fire. Like the Fourth of July.*

"There's great power up there, mister. Great power, and it gets into your head, talks to you, shows you things. You know what I'm saying. She gets into you like smoke."

Smoke. He nodded. Like the other night with Connie. And when he had that vision of Andy, and when the backhoe suddenly started to roll. And all those other times smoke had laced the air, but only for him. Yes, he knew what the old woman was saying. But she had it wrong.

"They tore the stones down, but they didn't put out the fire.

It's been getting stronger," she said. "You felt it tonight. It told you things."

His eyes were fixed on the engraving, half in shadow. He could make out the fore of the circle with the figure of the priestess sacrificing a child. "I heard something in the marsh," he said. "A voice."

"Tonight's the strongest it's ever been."

"My wife."

She looked at him blankfaced.

"It was my wife."

"Your wife?"

"Linda. She died two and a half years ago, but I heard her in the woods, then in the marsh. She was guiding me out . . . I think to this."

The woman made a hiss of derision. "You heard Brigid."

"No, it was Linda, her voice," he insisted. "I heard her clearly."

"You heard Brigid, I'm telling you. She's coming to you because you're special. You have the machines and can do something. They catch me, they'll call the cops. It's Brigid I'm telling you. She wants you to save the stones."

He nodded. To save the stones, yes. "I'll do what I can." There was no point in arguing with her.

"You dig them up, you'll be a bigshot."

He said nothing. He was ten steps ahead of her. He watched her wrap the engraving and put it away. As she picked up the lantern, Peter noticed she was wearing a necklace of some sort. Small beads with larger metallic discs on either side of a central crescent.

"That necklace." He raised his hand toward it.

The woman exposed it in the light. The three small discs contained spirals in a dark, worked metal, maybe bronze. The central crescent appeared to be silver foil set against a bronze plate, the whole surface of which was whirling and spinning designs in relief. He held the crescent in his fingers.

"It's a Celtic lunula," Peter said. He studied it, and from all appearance it did not look like a reproduction. The silver was worn with great age.

"I don't know what you call it," the woman said. "It was my mother's." She didn't seem to want to talk anymore. But the necklace sent a little thrill through him. What discoveries lay ahead, God only knew.

She opened the door. Dull gray light illuminated the eastern sky. He stepped out. He gave her back the blanket. He didn't need it. Anticipation had raised his body temperature. The sea air smelled fresh and clean. Somewhere a gull squawked, and through the morning mist he saw the blush of dawn enamel the sea in burnt gold.

"You know, I don't even know your name."

"Hannah," she said. "Hannah Mac Ness." As Peter stepped outside, she caught him by the arm. "Be careful, mister. That fire is full of wrath. You have a son. You watch him good."

"What do you mean?"

"The dead are always jealous of the living," she said, her eye intense. "She'll get inside your head, make you do things you'll be sorry for. She wants to get back for what they did."

Peter nodded. "We'll be fine," he said, but he thought: Poor woman, she was stuck in some quaint delusions that prevented her from understanding what was *really* going on. But, how could she understand? How could this pathetic, lonely old creature comprehend a love so intense that it transcended the mortal plane?

But Peter knew. Linda had led him to the stones as a confirmation of her forgiveness. She had even brought him those dreams in preparation for what was to come. In fact, since the first day he'd stepped foot on Kingdom Head, she had been guiding him on, like Beatrice leading Dante through the levels of Hell. She apparently was somewhat rough with Connie the other night, but Linda always was a jealous woman and, like the lady said, some things don't die. His only problem had been his thick-headedness. He'd simply missed the meaning of the signs—all by dint of his scientist's mind. Worse still, he had nearly misinterpreted them, attributing evil motivations. How wrong he had been.

The realization was like an epiphany. No, it *was* an epiphany. Dreams do come true. Those stones were reward for the guilt he'd borne these two and a half years. And the expiation of his guilt was in their excavation.

Of course. So simple and clear. It wasn't some dead witch's spirit talking to him, showing him strange things. It was Linda. She was back.

She was back, and hot.

He nodded good-bye and headed toward the dawn.

chapter
Twenty-three

"The *sixth* century? That can't be possible," Connie said.

"I'm starting to believe anything's possible on this island."

Peter had told them about last night—about Hannah Mac Ness chanting on the mound, the chase through the oaks, the salt marsh rescue, the engraving and diary—all of it. All, that is, but the wild stuff. Of course, nobody at first believed the woman's claim, but the more Peter went over the details the more they bought his conviction.

"You mean," Sparky asked, "her ancestors packed up ten-ton boulders and sailed across the Atlantic?"

"She didn't say that. The stones are local granite, probably quarried right over there." He pointed south toward Quincy where granite had been quarried for centuries. "She said Lydia's diary put the migration a thousand years earlier. Apparently her ancestors came to escape the forces of Christian conversion."

"That would mean the era of St. Patrick," Connie said.

"That's right," Peter said. "He died around four-fifty, four-sixty, which would jibe with the transition of Ireland from paganism to Christianity."

"And not a very smooth transition from what I recall."

"Hardly. The island was heavily tribal and still under Roman rule. To the oppressed, Christianity was a salvation, a kind of democracy they instantly latched on to. But not the Celtic aristocracy and Druid priests. They resisted conversion, and that led to upheaval." Peter's mind felt lucid and strong.

"So, she claims they set sail and ended up here and put up a stone circle in the tradition of their ancestors."

"Yes, and to escape persecution by the Romans. A witch hunt, if you will." He chuckled to himself.

"Sounds like the photographic negative of the pilgrims: born-again pagans."

Peter laughed. "I like that." Like me, he said to himself.

"Still sounds unbelieveable," Connie said.

"I know. But you didn't see that engraving. It looked genuine. So did the diary."

"But sixth-century Celts migrating to America?"

"I hear you," Peter said, "but for the lack of evidence, which will be the focus of our second mission."

"What's our first?"

"Finding more stones."

It was a little after seven when Peter marched them down the beach. Andy rode on his shoulders, scanning the ocean for seals and whales through field glasses. He had slept through the night and never known Peter was gone. Peter, on the other hand, had not slept a wink. And his eyes felt it, as if the lids were full of sand. There was also a dull buzz in his head. His hands and face were scratched from stumbling through the woods, and his knees and right hip were bruised from falls. But none of it bothered him. He was above pain. His metabolism raced as if his heart were pumping jet fuel. He could barely keep from running ahead.

"But couldn't the engraving and diary be fakes?" asked Jackie. "I mean, you catch her up there dressed like J. Bullwinkle and hopping around with a divining rod. Kind of raises questions of her credibility."

Another little swipe at Peter's chalice hand. But he deflected that, too. "We'll no doubt determine that, also."

In all fairness, he'd tossed around that very possibility just two hours before—that he was the victim of a well-labored hoax: That maybe the engraving was a depiction of another locale, some Neolithic site in England or Ireland. Or, that it was of Pulpit's Point, but the results of the artist's allegorical speculation on the earlier name, "Druid's Head." He had even considered the possibility that Hannah had made up the story of Brigid and her daughter to dramatize her plight—the last-ditch stand of an old woman exiled from her island home.

But he knew none of that was true.

And the expectation over the last two hours had produced such a surge of will that he would shudder to repress it. The only other time he remembered wanting something so badly was that night two and a half years ago, when Mount Auburn Hospital called. And then he was shuddering for something monstrous *not* to be true. Against all that, he still recognized the importance of appearing speculative. It would be madness to tell the group how he'd been brought to the truth. They would simply not understand, including Sparky whose spiritual hankerings would reduce it to the vulgar stuff of tabloid journalism. Besides, there was more hanging on the discovery than personal glory. It was the final confirmation of Linda's return.

Yes, he must appear cool and rational.

"If the engraving is accurate and there *is* a stone circle up there," he said, "we'll have to assume it's recent, at best Colonial. You can't carbon date stone, so we'll have to look for other evidence such as organics in the soil, artifacts. We find an old sandal or piece of garment or even a bone we can date to A.D. 500 then we'll have something."

"What about the name Druid's Head?" asked Sparky.

"That's tantalizing," he said. "But there's a Babylon, New York, a Bethlehem, Pennsylvania, and an Athens, Georgia. We can't take much stock in a place name." He was the voice of academic reason. "And for the record, you should know that the Druids didn't build stone circles. They just used them for their own rituals. It's a common mistake, but the fact is that the original Druids didn't emerge until about the time of Christ, some twelve centuries after the last stone circle went up."

"They just took them over," said Connie.

"That's right, by succession. The best guess is that they recognized the circles as ancient power centers"—

There's still fire in those stones, Hannah's voice echoed in his head—

—"and claimed them for their own purposes. But they wrongly got credit for them."

"Then who built Stonehenge and all those other stone circles?" Sparky asked.

"Bronze Age tribes. They started about four thousand years ago and continued for the next thousand years all over England, Ireland, and Brittany. About nine hundred sites are still standing. God knows how many they built."

"But nothing like them in this country," Sparky said.

"Nothing."

"Hell, what if we find the real thing?" Jackie asked.

"Upset the Knights of Columbus something awful."

By the time they reached the top of the Point, the sun was bright and the air clear. The last of the storm clouds had faded into the ocean sky. The rain left puddles on the mound and the incline was etched in runny brown rills.

The three exposed stones were drying in the sun. The rain had washed some of the dirt from them, leaving a yellow film that blazed in the sun like a golden patina. They looked like ancient kings in repose.

In his mind Peter composed the stone circle of the engraving against the delft-blue sky and sea—an image that created a fluttering in his belly.

Let it be so.

"Where do we begin?" Jackie asked.

"If you wanted to pull down a circle of thirteen stones, how would you do it?"

Jackie looked around for a moment. "Pull 'em down toward the middle."

"Or away from it," Connie said.

"Right," Peter said, "just so they didn't fall on each other."

"How big did the circle look in the drawing?" Jackie asked.

"Wasn't much of a scale except for the figures. I measured about six of them across—about thirty-five, forty feet."

"That'd about do it."

The mound roughly measured between forty-seven to fifty feet in diameter. Peter looked into the cab of the backhoe. The keys were gone. *Damn!* He'd forgotten it was Sunday.

"Can you hot-wire this thing?"

Jackie gave a glance at the machine sitting near one edge of the mound. His mouth expanded into a cagey grin. "A requirement for growing up in Detroit," he said. "But how you gonna explain to Flanagan tomorrow all the dirt we moved?"

"Exuberance," Peter said.

"Exuberance." Jackie nodded, still grinning. "He's not going to like us exuberating his equipment without permission." Jackie was right. The deal was he could operate the machine as a special employee of Poro Construction, but only on scheduled work days.

"We'll worry about that tomorrow," Peter said.

"Peter, aren't you taking a big chance?" Connie asked him. "It's all he needs to get Hatcher to revoke our permit. He'd jump at the chance."

"Yeah, man, another day wouldn't kill us," Jackie added leaning on a shovel.

"Besides we could clear away a lot of stuff on our own," Sparky agreed.

"It's rain soaked," Peter said. "We'd break our backs."

"I don't think we should risk it," Connie said.

He felt his face flush. They were against him again. They were thinking that what he was proposing was irresponsible and unbefitting a professional scientist. But they didn't know, goddamn them! They didn't know how important this was. How this was the vindication of his life. Or how he had been guided here.

"Remember the forms we signed?" Jackie said. "If we're held to them, we're screwed."

Peter's chest tightened. He looked at that mound of dirt. It was within touching distance. Right there under the sand: the American Stonehenge. His Stonehenge.

But his rational mind said that Jackie might be right. Their only trump card was Hatcher. He wanted that touch of historical character, and Peter was hired to dig it up. But just how badly was another question. Hatcher had squelched Flanagan's protests the first day. But how would he regard an infraction in the name of eagerness?

"We'll take our chances," Peter said.

"I'm sorry, Peter," said Connie. "But I don't like the idea."

She was talking as if she'd decided to stay on, he thought, but why was she standing in the way?

"We'd be violating our agreement, and if they tell us to go, we lose everything. And just because we couldn't wait a day."

Jackie and Sparky nodded.

Jesus! They were unified against him. They couldn't do this.

"Peter, I want to see what's under there as much as you do," Connie said.

"Bullshit."

Connie's face froze. "I beg your pardon?"

"Why are you fighting me?"

"I'm not fighting you. I'm saying you're taking a hell of a chance with our expedition and our money." She emphasized *our*.

Peter felt as if she had slapped his face. Again. He trembled with anger, hating how those big right-reasoning eyes bore down on him, trying to extinguish his will—that same damning stare she had given him the other night. Jackie could probably be swayed. Maybe even Sparky. But not tight-ass Connie Lambert. Deep down, of course, he knew she was right in the straight-and-narrow pursuit of things, the way Linda always was. Like putting on those damn child-proof locks. But, at the moment he just didn't give a shit about the straight-and-narrow. He had been waiting too long for this. Too long. He took a deep breath for control. "If there's something of archaeological importance under there, Hatcher will stop the world for us to bring it up."

"Then why not wait another day just to be on the safe side?" Connie asked.

"Because I can't." He turned to Jackie. "If you won't run that damn backhoe, I'll do it myself."

Jackie made a *humpfing* sound. "You know how?"

"Watch me learn."

"Forget it, man, you'll kill us all swinging that thing around." Jackie tossed the shovel down and headed for the backhoe.

"Jackie!" Sparky's voice was braised with warning.

"Sorry, babe," he said. Then to Peter, "I don't remember

anything about stealing backhoes in the Earthwatch field manuals."

"You also didn't read anything about stone circles in the Boston Harbor."

Jackie hopped up onto the fender. He opened the cover over the engine. In a minute he had it roaring. Peter felt the elephant's foot lift off his chest. Jackie tested the brakes and the hydraulics of the bucket and the hoe. They were in working order.

Peter directed him to the edge of the mound where the most northerly of the boulders lay. If a toppled stone circle was beneath, they would have to work from the outside, dragging off the overburden with the bucket to avoid crushing whatever lay buried. The hoe arm could extend nearly twenty feet—a good distance into the mound without entering it.

For two hours Jackie carefully scooped off the sand. Meanwhile Peter worked with Sparky and Connie with shovels to clear away the three original stones. Sparky seemed to have come around about the backhoe, but Connie had not. She went about her work like a mute. Peter could feel her brooding. A small part of him was bugged by that. She just didn't understand. It was his only option. Great discovery always meant risks. It was the lesson of the salt marsh. Sinking in the maw of Death had been a message to seize the day while he still had a chance, and sweat the consequences as they came. It was something Connie Lambert could not appreciate.

By eleven-thirty it really didn't matter. They hit stone.

Jackie had removed two feet of overburden leaving a trough five feet wide and ten feet long into the mound. With metal rods Peter poked through the trough. At about fourteen inches he hit something solid. He tapped the rod in dozens of spots and came up with a consistent depth. Something large and solid was just a foot below the top. With shovels, the four of them dug a clearing at the edge of an imaginary arc connecting the three recumbent stones. It took little time to expose it. The end of a gray granite block. Like the others.

Peter's temples pounded as he ran his hands down the flanks. Only about two feet of the end were exposed, but the surface was clearly mauled and dressed flat—intentionally shaped by human hand—leaving him no doubt about what lay hidden.

Triumph pulsed through him.

Jackie pulled the machine back and scooped away another two feet. The stone went on like the spoke of a great granite wheel.

A megalith lay as if it had once been toppled from its place. The bottom third was permanently discolored from centuries of sitting in a ground socket.

"My God!" Peter said. And as he watched the stone emerge from the sand, he felt a momentary shuddering not unlike fright. The kind of fright you feel at those rare moments in life when you realize you're straddling a cusp in your own history—like first sex, marriage, birth of a child, the death of a loved one. A moment from which you date the calendar. His resurrection.

The four stones lay in a quarter arc.

"It's happening," he whispered.

chapter
Twenty-four

By late afternoon there was no doubt.

They uncovered four more stones along the perimeter of the site—four roughly squared granite boulders that lay flat near the others along a three-quarter arc where they had once formed a ring of pillars. As in the engraving. There was still a hump of over-burden to be cleared away, but he knew its contents completed the picture.

In his mind the eight stones rose to attention.

"Did we find something? Or did we find something?" squealed Sparky. She threw her arms around Peter's neck.

"I'm almost too afraid to say it." He pulled a Moosehead out of the cooler and popped the cap. He could barely steady his hand. He took a swig and drained half the bottle.

Jackie climbed off the backhoe and gave a high five to Andy. His hard muscular body, slicked with sweat, glistened in the sun like a bronze statue. "Hey, man," he said approaching Peter. He was wearing his million-watt smile. "This expedition's getting better by the minute."

Peter handed him a beer and one to Sparky and Connie. "No regrets about getting bumped from Atlantis."

"Really!" Jackie said, his face looking like a polished apple. He guzzled some beer. "Maybe the old lady's not as loony as she sounds."

"Maybe not." Peter took another swig of beer. It was beginning to calm him down. He sat on the cooler while the others used a stone as a bench. Andy had wandered off to the screen where throughout the afternoon he had sat trying to build a castle from the sifted sand. He seemed a little sullen, but Peter guessed he was just tired. It had been one hell of a day. "If I may be cautious, it appears we've found a collection of once-standing stones," he announced. He stood up because he could not sit still for the excitement. His mind was suddenly lucid, and as he talked it seemed as if he were watching himself on tape before a classroom of students. "The weathering, the same kind of discoloration at their bases, the spacing between them, the apparent lack of other construction materials. The engraving aside, there are three possibilities as I see it. One: a hoax or folly erected maybe as far back as Colonial times. Two: aboriginal—American Indian. Three: the work of pre-Columbian Europeans as Hannah claims."

"What's the most likely? Jackie asked.

"From a scientific point of view it's probably a hoax. There's nothing like this in Northeast American Indian archaeology. The Algonquins built stone prayer sites and fish drying stations, but nothing in a circle or on this scale. As for migrating Europeans, that's the most exciting possibility but the least probable."

"What about the Vikings?" Sparky asked. "I thought they came to America way before Columbus."

"That's a disputed claim," Peter explained. "There's a famous Viking settlement in Newfoundland from about the eleventh century, but apparently that's about as far south as they came. The most prudent speculation right now is that the stones are a replica."

"Pretty extreme for a practical joke," Connie said. "Dragging them all the way up here and standing them up." She appeared to be over her resentment about the backhoe. No doubt the excitement of the stones had helped, for they were solid insurance against any reprisal by Flanagan.

"True, but follies and hoaxes of this magnitude have been done before."

Jackie took a swallow of beer. "Either option, what were they for? Stonehenge and the rest? Some kind of temples or observatory, or something?"

"Nobody's really sure," Peter said, still assuming his cool scientist pose. "The Neolithics had no written language. The archae-ology points to several functions—some rather mundane, some clearly spiritual, some astronomical. There's evidence they were used as places of commerce, marketplaces where people traded goods."

"I heard stone circles were also astronomical clocks and calen-dars," Sparky said.

"Yeah," Jackie said. "You're supposed to predict the phases of the moon and where the sun rises and sets."

"There's evidence the stones had some astronomical function for the builders," Peter explained. "In the case of Stonehenge, there are some alignments with the solstitial risings and settings."

"Yeah, but didn't I read some place you could predict the eclipses of the sun down to the second?" Jackie said.

"You probably did, and by the same guy who swore he was kidnapped by Big Foot on a motorbike," Peter said. "To predict an eclipse would presuppose a level of geometry and astronomy far beyond what we know of the people who built the stones. They were very industrious, but quite primitive. Predicting an eclipse would require mathematical ability beyond what the evidence says they had. There's also the problem of how things were aligned. In a circle of stones any two can give you ten alignments—across the tops, right to right, left to left, left to right, right to left, then those same five in the opposite direction. With a circle of ten the num-ber of alignments would be well over a hundred. Almost any event in the sky would have a couple stones lining up."

"So we really don't know," Connie said.

"No."

There's a great power up there. . . . Hannah's words fluttered in the back of Peter's mind.

"Those stones humble me and all my books," Peter said.

"They ever find any human remains in the circles?"

"Some," Peter said. He swallowed more beer. "Apparently the circles served some kind of ritualistic purposes."

"You mean human sacrifices?" asked Sparky.

Peter felt his mind dip. Smoke. An instant later the sensation was gone. He finished the beer. "Something like that. But it's really not my area."

"I think I read how the Celts believed the stones contained the spirit of their ancestors," Connie said. "And sacrifices were made to appease them."

"Whatever," Peter said. "They had an obsession with immortality." He looked at the bed of stones. "Hard to imagine a more impressive monument to permanence than a stone circle."

"Or one more defiant of the impermanence of things," said Connie.

"Too bad we haven't got a phone to call Merritt," Jackie said.

"Merritt?" Peter felt an edge of irritation at the suggestion that nothing had meaning until officially sanctioned by Dan Merritt.

"We're going to tell him, aren't we?"

"We're not going to tell anybody anything," said Peter. "Technically it's still a bunch of boulders."

"But what about the engraving?" Sparky asked.

"The implication lights up my soul," Peter said. "But, why we're here is to authenticate the stones, not the engraving." He had no difficulty imagining a ring of stone pillars standing on that promontory, rising stark and craggy in the gray early morning seamist or luminescent in the warm gold of the setting sun. The images flooded his consciousness. "Unless we find hard evidence to date the site, or no one will take it seriously."

It was nearly six. They had been excavating almost nonstop since seven that morning, and they looked it. They were exhausted and were ready to head back to the cottage.

But not Peter. He had that edgy feeling again and wanted to keep digging. He wanted to get on that backhoe and clear the rest of that overburden if it meant going around the clock. And it wasn't just to clap eyes on the remaining stones. He would bet his life they were there. It was what other stuff lay under the sand that he hankered for: artifactual remains—tools, ornaments, bones—anything that could be carbon dated, authenticated, definitively attributed to the handiwork of migrant Celts just so they couldn't say he had found himself another Mystery Hill. Even once they had cleared the remaining quarter-hump of sand, they still had to excavate the circle floor—where the real archaeology began with picks and brushes and trowels. So much to clear, and so little time. Sixteen centuries they had lain here, and sixteen days to prove it.

He looked at the stones lying helter-skelter in the dirt, and he thought how he would kill to prove it.

It was a fine clear night. All the stars were out, and a tangerine moon began to nose its way out of the sea. Andy was asleep, and Jackie and Sparky were in their room. Peter sat on the porch, drinking a beer, when Connie joined him.

"Peter, about this morning," she said taking a seat, "I never congratulated you on the discovery."

No, you hadn't, he thought. You were too busy resenting my exuberance. "Is that what you're doing?"

"Yes."

"Thank you."

And now, he thought, she'll apologize for having been blind to the urgency of the moment. For having doubted him at the threshold of what might be the greatest archaeological discovery in North American history.

But she didn't apologize. "My real concern is Flanagan."

"What about him?"

"We weren't authorized the use of the backhoe in his absence."

"I'm well aware of that, Connie."

She sensed the reprimand in his voice. "Peter, I'm saying that he might use it as an opportunity to get our excavation permit revoked."

"Am I to take it that you've decided to stay on with the expedition?" For a long moment she estimated him. He tried to keep his expression neutral, but he could feel himself smile with pleasure in spite of himself.

"Yes, I've decided to stay."

"Well, I'm really happy to hear that." The words came out but they lacked the conviction he had expected. As if he didn't give a hot damn if she stayed or left. But inside he knew that didn't make sense. The other night he was half desperate for her not to go. He clearly recalled a warm fondness for her and the sense of renewal they had shared up on the Point that same afternoon. He had even entertained possibilities of seeing her after the expedition was over. Yet, suddenly, she seemed a different person. Or, was it he? It didn't make sense. Something had happened—he had lost his interest in her. He even resented her. Maybe something had taken him over. Maybe . . .

"Be careful, Mister. The dead are always jealous of the living."

A long silence passed as he pondered his change of heart. Sure, she decided to stay on, he told himself. *Now that we've found the Western Hemisphere's equivalent of ancient Troy, she wants to hang around to make sure her name ends up in the credits.*

"But what concerns me," she continued, "is that we still have an expedition left."

"Why wouldn't we?"

"Because I don't think finding the stone will sway Flanagan, not given his hostility. You said it yourself we're messing up his plans."

"You seem to forget that Hatcher's calling all the shots, and I think he'll be very impressed."

"I hope you're right."

I hope you're right. Still doubting me, he thought. But why should Connie Lambert be any different? "It's what I'm banking on."

They were quiet for a moment as Connie settled into his certitude.

The three-quarter moon hung over the outermost island, The Graves, where hundreds of men had lost their lives in ships gone afoul over the centuries. A small warning light pulsed evenly, holding Peter's eye as he sipped his beer.

"I wonder how long it's been since those stones last saw moonlight," Connie said wistfully.

"Or how long 'til they got covered up. We have sixteen days to find out."

"Not much time given what we're trying to authenticate."

What WE'RE trying to authenticate? Already she was making claims on the find. But he let that pass. "We'll do our best."

"In any case, I'm pleased for you."

He looked at her and felt a moment's flush of warmth. "Thank you, Connie," he said. The words were barely out when he felt smoke begin to fill his head. Suddenly a blister of petulance rose up in him. Why suddenly so pleased for him? Just forty-eight hours ago, she was ready to blow her rape whistle on him.

He washed down the irritation with more beer. A minute of silence passed as he watched the moon. He imagined seeing faces in the shaded areas.

"Peter, if you don't mind me asking, are you all right? I mean, is something bothering you?"

He turned his head toward her for an explanation. "Not that I'm aware of."

"I think you know what I mean."

"I'm afraid I don't know, Connie."

"Since the other night, you seem distracted."

"I do?"

"Yes, even the way you're acting now. You seem remote, even annoyed."

He felt himself heat up slightly from the accusation, but he kept it hidden. "Maybe it's because of the pressure I've been under with the dig and Andy. He lost his mother, you know. But if I've been short, I apologize. Let's just say that today has set me back on track with a renewed sense of purpose."

She studied him without comment and nodded.

Another minute of silence passed.

Peter sipped more beer. She was fairly perceptive, he thought. Since the night of Linda's return he had lost all interest in Connie. Furthermore, he had come to nurture a low-grade resentment of her. Like this morning. And that first night in the kitchen, even before Linda had spoken to him. On both occasions Connie had tried to throw up a roadblock to his discovery of the stones. Had he filed a police report on the backhoe as she had insisted, the stones would never have seen the light of day. He took a sip of beer. It was Linda all right. He didn't understand it, but she was seeping into his soul, steeling him against any efforts, action, or inaction designed to keep him from finding that stone circle. About the other night? That was easy, Peter decided. Linda was a jealous woman. Even in death. It was all making perfect sense.

He drank more beer. In the eastern sky he saw a shooting star. And another. And another. Portents, he thought. No. Affirmation.

Connie got up to go. "You know," she said, "Jackie's jumping out of his skin. He's dying to tell the world the Irish discovered America."

Peter smiled. "In due time."

"Good night."

"Good night, Connie." She left, and he sipped his beer, glad for the solitude.

The stars looked so close he swore he could scratch them out of the sky with his fingernails. Just overhead burned the constellation of Sagittarius. He connected the dots to make the hunter's arrow.

When you think about it, it wasn't really a violation the other night. Sure, he had gotten a little carried away, maybe a little rough. But that wasn't your everyday garden-variety kind of sexual intercourse. In fact, she really should be flattered. Not every day a woman is treated to ménage à trois with an angel.

He finished his beer and went up to bed.

He slept like a newborn.

chapter
Twenty-five

At first Peter didn't know what to make of it.

It looked like a small sapling growing out of the center of the arc of boulders. It was barely noticeable, and he wouldn't have spotted it had the sun not made of it a neon V against the brown earth.

He stepped over one of the megaliths and into the circle. A forked branch, its bark stripped clean, the ends dark and shiny from gripping. It had been stuck there upright in the dirt like a directing sign.

Hannah's divining rod.

Her boot prints were all over the place. Sometime in the night she had stolen up here and planted the rod in the dirt a few feet above the sixth stone.

Peter pulled it out. The end was a whittled point. There were no signs of disturbance. Just the divining rod. If she was spying on them now, she was nowhere in sight. No face among the oaks, no blue boat on the horizon. But the message was clear. It was a marker to dig.

Jackie and Sparky went below to get the backhoe keys from Flanagan's trailer. Meanwhile, Peter and Connie removed the plastic covering from the stones. Since last night, he had set his mind into a bland neutrality toward Connie. He could understand in the abstract how she had appealed to him—bright and pretty, pleasant and sensitive, a good sense of humor, et cetera, et cetera. But now that the veil had slipped from his soul, he saw her in a different light. He felt nothing but a chaste indifference toward her. Since she was no longer a danger, the petulance was gone.

Andy, however, was a different story. He had awoke in his I-wanna-go-home mood again and whined through breakfast about not liking the island, about being scared. Peter tried reasoning with him, but it didn't work. Six-year-olds didn't reason. Even Connie and Jackie tried, but he wouldn't bend. He just screwed up his face and folded his arms and scowled at his Cheerios. The more he squawked about wanting to leave, the more Peter heated up. But he did not lose it as he could have—probably because the others were there. When he couldn't stand the whining anymore, Peter sent him to their room until it was time to head to the Point.

Andy sulked all the way to the site, then took to his blanket by the toolbox, where he dug in the sand with his shovel, not talking to anyone. Just as well, Peter decided. Better than moaning about going home. He had enough to worry about with Flanagan. The site was a clutch of foxholes, nothing four adults with shovels could have dug in a month of Sundays. One look and he'd know they'd used the backhoe. Peter was banking on the man's contempt to keep him below; that and the fact the Point had no immediate importance to the rest of the construction, at least not for fifteen days when Flanagan would blow the whistle to raze the hill.

But Flanagan never showed.

"Hey, man, he's taken the day off," Jackie announced when he returned from below. "They said he's meeting with Hatcher in town and won't be back until tomorrow."

Relief washed over Peter. They could roll.

Jackie dangled the keys of the backhoe. "Jimmy P." He grinned. "And from what I can tell, he couldn't give a damn what we do up here as long as we don't drive off a cliff."

Jackie looked at the divining rod in Peter's hand. "What's that?"

Peter stuck the rod back into its hole. "It's where you're going to start digging."

For most of the morning Jackie worked the machine while the others used shovels. In that time he cut a six-foot-long gully about three feet wide and two deep from the outer arc of the stones. The rod sat in place. What he removed made a large bank which passed through the sifting screens in sample buckets. It was not textbook methodology, digging with backhoe and sample buckets, but nothing about the excavation was textbook. The thought that conclusive data lay buried buzzed in Peter's head like a wasp.

Andy moped for an hour near the drop-off. Every time Peter looked at him, the kid flashed his hang-puppy face. But Peter ignored it. He had enough anxiety trying to document in two weeks the greatest archaeological discovery in the twentieth century. He didn't need this. On Connie's suggestion, Peter set him up with his sand molds. He resisted at first, but when they were alone Peter squatted beside the boy, and under his breath he said, "Andy, I'm going to tell you this just once—you're going to sit here nice and quiet and build a sand castle with your tools, and if I hear one peep about going home . . . I'll . . ."

What?

You'll what?

(Cut his throat)

Rumble and smoke.

The spell snapped off.

"Just do it, okay?"

Andy's lips quivered. "Okay, okay."

"Good." And Peter walked away, shaking, his head sour with fumes.

Andy never moved from his spot. He worked on his castle, then napped on his blanket when he got tired. His protest was over.

Peter and the others worked for three hours and turned up nothing but more shells and sand. Not a single artifact of human craft. Peter was beginning to feel frantic. It could take forever, and he didn't have forever. If he didn't come up with something to date the place, it would all be lost. Stonehenge of America—bulldozed off the face of the earth because they couldn't turn up a datable clue.

A little past eleven Jackie hit something hard.

He pulled back the hoe, and Peter leaped in for a better look.

He whisked away the sand with a brush. "Another stone," Sparky said.

With shovels they cleared away the flanks. Although still partly covered, it was narrower than the others—maybe a foot and a half wide and about a foot thick. But what was unusual was its color. The surface was blackened, as if veneered with carbon, but the material beneath surface scratches was pure white.

"Limestone," Peter said in dismay.

"Is that unusual?" Connie asked.

"The nearest limestone quarry is in Vermont."

"You think it could have been carted all this way?" Connie asked.

"Sure," suggested Jackie. "Enough horses and a big enough carriage."

"Except that limestone wasn't quarried in Vermont until the late eighteenth century," Peter said.

"What are you saying then?"

"I'm saying the next closest limestone quarry is southwestern Ireland."

They cleared away more of the debris—over five feet of it with shovels, trowels, and brooms. More lay hidden under the four-foot covering—Hannah's divining rod still in place above where they had begun. The material was soft and brittle and had to be cleared with greater care than the granite. It lay a few feet within the arc of ring stones—a solid pillar of limestone.

A limestone phallus, thought Peter. Fertility stone. My God!

The pillar they had burned Brigid against.

The exposed flank was covered almost uniformly with that black skin. Peter inspected a few chips from where the hoe struck. The discoloration looked like permanent stain leeched into the pores from the soil. Yet the covering material was yellow brown, and the stain was black. Peter didn't need the soil charts to tell him the content was nearly all carbon.

He put a few chips in a sample bag. At least he could date the execution. It was a start.

With a trowel he dug a little below the stone and into the original ground bed. For nearly half an hour he gently worked the trowel and small hand shovel until he exposed a small cross-section of the material the stone rested on—a thin black stratum that made a definite vein through the yellow sand-soil mixture. He took a sample of that for chemical tests.

Then along one flank of the stone he spotted hairline fractures. "Heat cracks," he said.

"Could be where they torched her," Jackie said.

"Yes," Peter said.

"From the looks of those cracks, it was a pretty intense fire."

"It was," Peter whispered, still digging. It was. I was there.

"Think this is what she wanted us to find?"

"Possibly."

"But how could she know there was a limestone column here, or that it meant anything?"

"She had a divining rod," Sparky said. "Maybe she picked up some kind of energy vibrations."

"Too bad stones can't talk," Jackie said, "or you could do a natal chart on it. 'Strong, solid, the real quiet type. Prefers cool, dark places. Going to need a good bath.' "

"And you're going to need a new set of *cojones*," Sparky said to him.

But Peter paid no attention to their banter. He fingered the blackened earth.

"Now we play real archaeology," he said softly. What he needed was just below the surface. He could feel the heat.

"Maybe not just yet," Connie said. She was looking over her shoulder at the water.

The large white prow of the *Kingdom Come* was slicing into the cove.

chapter
Twenty-six

"Shit!" Hatcher was the last person Peter wanted to show up.

On deck with him were Fred Goringer and a man Peter did not recognize. They climbed off the boat and onto the small dock.

"They're coming up," Sparky said looking over the drop-off. "Wait 'til he sees this."

"As far as he's concerned, it's still a bunch of foundation stones."

"We're not going to tell him?"

"No. We don't have hard evidence yet."

"But it might be worth a couple days' extension, man," said Jackie.

"We've already cut into their schedule by three weeks. Any more, and Poro might take legal action against him. We're not speculating yet."

Hatcher, dressed in a wheat suit and open-necked blue shirt, led Goringer and the other man to the top. He said hello to Andy who was sitting on the ground playing with his Power Ranger figures and some small rocks.

"We've got some design details to work out below," Hatcher said. "Thought I'd drop by to see how you were doing." Then he noticed the stones. "What the hell you come up with?"

"We're not all that certain," Peter said. Professional restraint was all. He wished they'd leave.

"Damn, look at those things, they're massive. One, two, three . . . eight, no, nine of them. What the hell are they?"

"We're being open-minded," Peter said. "Maybe the foundation of your ancestral chapel, maybe something else."

The third man, introduced as Tom Rice, an architect, carefully stepped up on one of the stones for an overview. "I could be wrong, but I don't remember any round chapels being built in Colonial times. Or any other time, for that matter."

"No, but there were some polygonal structures—mostly octagons, but a few with ten and twelve sides."

Rice nodded vaguely. He still didn't look convinced. Hatcher looked at Peter. "What about your Indian theory?"

"That's another possibility. We're being flexible."

He turned to Connie. "And what do you think?"

"I'm just along for the dirt and sweat." She wiped her brow on her sleeve.

Hatcher smiled at her like a mongoose regarding a cobra. "You make dirt and sweat look good."

Connie said nothing.

"In any case," said Goringer, "we thought you should know they'll be drilling in the tunnels down below in a few days. So don't be alarmed if you feel vibrations."

"What are they drilling for?" Sparky asked.

"Explosives. The Point's going to be leveled after you leave."

Andy overheard and looked up. "Explosives," he sang.

Hatcher went over to Andy and squatted down beside him. "Yup, and maybe if you and your dad are still around you can watch the men blow it all up. How would you like that?"

His eyes saucered. "Why they going to blow it up?"

"Well, we have to make sure the ground is real solid because we're going to build something pretty neat up here. It's called a 'casino' where people will come to play games and have a lot of fun."

"You mean like the Magic Kingdom?"

Hatcher chuckled. " 'The Magic Kingdom?' Yeah, something like that, but for big people."

Peter froze. Andy placed one figure at the center of a circle of rocks then made an explosion that sent it in the air. "Andy—" he began.

But Hatcher cut in. "You building some kind of castle there?"

"Unh-uh. It's a stone circle, just like the one we found."

"A stone circle?" said Hatcher.

"Sure, 'cept that one got knocked down."

Hatcher looked to Peter for an explanation. "A stone circle?" He stood up and took another look at the boulders behind Peter. "You mean like whatsits in England . . . Stonehenge?" Then he added, "Merritt said you had a taste for the exotic."

"I said it reminded me of the megaliths you see in the British Isles."

"But, Dad, you said the old lady—"

"Andy, why don't you just play with your Rangers," Peter said.

"Old lady?" Hatcher asked, bearing down on him.

"Your past caretaker."

"Caretaker? . . . You mean Hannah Mac Ness?" Hatcher looked to Goringer and began to laugh.

"How the hell she get here?" asked Goringer.

"Apparently by boat," Peter said.

"Jesus H. Christ! What did she tell you, her ancient ancestors built sacred temples out here and their spirits roam the place?"

Peter's face turned hot. He said nothing. Andy pulled his cap down over his eyes.

"Son of a gun," Hatcher said. "Professor, if you take nothing else away from this island let it be this: Hannah Mac Ness hasn't got both oars in the water. She's a nutty old woman who wouldn't give you the right time of day even if she could. So, don't go running to the bank with anything she says because she's loco. You understand?" He tapped the side of his head. "Crazy."

"We're not."

Hatcher glanced at Andy's tiny replica. "Someone is," he said. "I don't know what these stones are, but the only ancient temple you're likely to dig up is a pile of old Guinness bottles. Her grandfather was an immigrant from County Cork. Came over about the turn of the century with the rest of them. My great-grandfather gave him a job at Hatcher-Pearson Press because he was something of an engraver back home. I think her mother was some kind of Indian—Abakenakami, or something. There was a bunch of them living out here, farming, fishing, whatever. When the old man sold the Press, he set them up as tenant farmers and caretakers. Those were her ancestors—fishers and farmers, and they didn't build any stone temples."

Peter's heart dropped into a hole. Suddenly everything was losing definition. The engraving could be a fraud. And the diary. And her sixth-century Celtic claims. Maybe her grandfather was a besotted fruitcake, built the damn site, then forged a seventeenth-century engraving for kicks. He glanced at the limestone column. It was charred and full of heat cracks. Because her grandfather was an engraver didn't render it all a fake. It was real! He knew that. So was Linda. His mind became a fugue again.

But Linda's dead.

No! you heard her, goddamn it. You felt her presence.

Sure, and half the street yellers got Jesus talking to them. What makes my claim any more valid?

But she saved your life and led you here.

That's a conclusion you want so badly to believe you're torturing the evidence to fit. Hannah Mac Ness saved you.

But the place has power. You've been feeling it since you got here. It's gotten into your head, your dreams, your soul.

Then how come I'm the only one?

Hannah felt it.

And she runs around in horns and a divining rod and talks to Druid priestesses. Peter stared at the ground, his thoughts adrift.

"She said her mother was born in the cottage," Connie said. "And her mother before her."

"Maybe," said Hatcher. "But that doesn't make her Pocahontas."

"Peter, she's not even a nice crazy like some of the bag ladies in town," Goringer added. "She's mean crazy. You're lucky she didn't sic on you."

"The way she did Fred here," Hatcher added.

Goringer made a dismissive gesture with his hands. "She kind of took me off guard. Nothing serious."

"That's not what you said when they sewed you up."

He shrugged. "She swiped me with a knife, and that's what I mean. She can't be trusted, she's only half there. Whatever she says, take with a grain of salt."

"What the hell was she doing out here?" Hatcher asked.

"Guess she was curious about the dig." Peter felt faint. What they were saying wasn't true. He had seen things, heard things that pointed to higher truths. That circle was real, authentic, and Linda brought him here. It was his destiny. The fulfillment of his life.

Linda, give me another sign.

"We offered to put her up in a first-rate senior citizens home," Goringer said. "That's when she took a slice out of me. She doesn't like people. Lived out here for seventy-something years, a genuine hermit. The family'd come out here for a picnic, and she'd throw rocks at us. Unbelievable. Woman's a real lulu. She say where she's living?"

"No." Nothing made sense anymore.

"But she claimed you found yourself a stone circle," said Hatcher.

While they talked, Tom Rice had stooped down to inspect the stones. He was rubbing his hands over the surface to clear away the dust. "You find any structural material—mortar, timber, construction stones, nails, stuff like that?" he asked.

"No."

Rice stood up slapping the dust off his hands. "The bottom third of the stone looks discolored," he said to Peter.

"So?" Hatcher said.

"Looks like it might have been underground." Then to Peter, "Do a soil sample?"

"Yeah."

"Match?"

"Yeah."

"What are you saying?" Hatcher asked them.

"Well, I'm no archaeologist, but it looks to me like they were once standing. The top two-thirds are weathered, and the bottom isn't, but it's clearly discolored," Rice said. "Probably was up a long time."

"You too?"

Rice shrugged. "I'm just telling you how I see it, Fane."

"Is that what you think?" Hatcher asked Peter. "That it's a stone circle?"

"It's possible." There was no point in going any farther. When they were certain, then they could sound the carillons. Call in *Na-*

tional Geographic, Time magazine, Rupert Murdoch, Peter Jennings, you name it. Just don't jump the bait, he told himself. "But most likely a folly."

"A folly? What the hell's a folly?" Hatcher asked.

"A hoax."

Hatcher looked around dumbly. "What the hell's he saying?"

"A replica of a Bronze Age stone circle," Peter said. "Built within the last couple centuries."

"Who the hell would do that?" Hatcher asked. "And why?"

"I don't know who," he said. "Replicas like this were not uncommon, particularly in eighteenth- and nineteenth-century England. People would have Gothic ruins built in their backyards to go be melancholy in. Pretty silly, but they did that sort of thing."

"This isn't England."

"No, but it's New England, and there are a few replicas around."

"Why would somebody bother?"

"Nostalgia, a practical joke, who knows? Why did someone bother with the Piltdown Man? Why do people claim they see dinosaurs in Lake Champlain?"

"Maybe one of your ancestors," suggested Connie. She was giving Peter backup. "If somebody bothered to duplicate London Bridge in the middle of Texas, then a stone circle replica here isn't too farfetched."

Hatcher considered Connie's comments. Then he went over to inspect the stones. "If it's a replica, what's it doing flat and buried?"

Peter was humming for them to go. "Maybe somebody didn't like the joke. I don't know. That's history, not archaeology. We've only scratched the surface."

"How about the real thing?" asked Goringer.

"There's no evidence of European migration before Columbus."

"If you were to put money down, what would you say it was?" Hatcher asked Peter.

"A replica until we know better."

Hatcher regarded how much they had cleared in a week.

"Hope you can finish the job by the seventh because the place is going to be blown to kingdom come—pun intended."

Peter felt as if he'd been kneed in the gut. "The seventh? You said we had until the fifteenth."

"There's been a change in schedule. The demolition people can only make it on the seventh. Sorry."

"Sorry? That's one week! How are we going to authenticate it?"

"Guess you'll have to work faster."

"With picks and brushes?"

"If I had my way, I'd give you a month. But I don't call all the shots. On July seventh Bay State Blasting is coming out to do their stuff."

"What happens to the stones?"

"Professor, I respect your professional concern. But I think we can discount an ancestral chapel or any other historical structure. And that was what I was hoping for. If something like that once stood here, it's clear it got blown away in a hurricane. These stones came later, for whatever reason . . . a folly as you said."

The bastard was hanging Peter with his own noose. "But what if it's the real thing—an American Stonehenge?"

" 'An American Stonehenge.' Oh my!" Then he turned to Goringer. "I like the ring of that."

" 'An American Stonehenge.' Yeah," said Goringer, testing the phrase.

Hatcher turned back to Peter. "But you just gave your professional opinion that it's only a replica, no?"

"I said that was my best guess. It's still possible it could be ancient."

"What? On the evidence of crazy Hannah's claims? Come on, man, you're a scientist."

Peter had the urge to smash Hatcher in the face. "We need more time to look for clues to date the site."

"I can't give you more. The schedule is fixed. You've got the backhoe."

"We can't use a backhoe to excavate critical data. That's not how archaeology works."

"Well, that's how I work. If you can't prove your circle in seven days, you've lost." He glanced at his watch. "Dig at night for your data. I'm told you're a dedicated scientist."

You greasy son-of-a-bitch, Peter thought. But he made no response. The man didn't give a goddamn what it was—real or fake, recent or ancient. It wasn't his precious family chapel, so the hell with the stones. Push them over the edge, blow them up. There was no point in resisting him. It was his island, his stones, his time clock. If Peter pressed, Hatcher could ship them out in a moment. And a replacement could be installed to finish the dig—anybody, some grad students from Harvard, or summer help out of Merritt's office, even Mike Flanagan.

As Hatcher led the others away, he tousled Andy's hair. "You're a sharp little guy, you know that? Maybe you'll be a famous archaeologist like your dad someday." Then he headed down the hill with Goringer and Rice.

"There must be something we can do," said Connie. "This could rewrite American history, and they're going to blow it up in a week. Can't we contact somebody—Earthwatch, Merritt, anybody to stop them?"

"Not on a private island," Peter said.

"But those stones belong to history, not to him."

"He's violating everything but the law."

"How are sites declared national monuments?" Sparky asked.

"When they're on government property," he said. "We can't do a thing here. Nothing. They're Fane Hatcher's stones."

"This is criminal," Connie said. "Why doesn't he care?"

"Because he's a businessman."

Seven days. The same number it took to make the world. Then something clicked in Peter's head.

"What do we do now?" asked Jackie. The red glow was gone from his face. He looked disillusioned. As if Hatcher had personally let him down.

Then a soft cool voice whispered something in Peter's head.

He looked back at the circle. It was the rest of his sign. He'd never doubt again.

Three quarters of it was exposed, with the prominent hump waiting to be removed. The white limestone column sat half buried. And the divining rod was still in place.

It had the sublime inevitability of great art.

He nodded at the hump of dirt at the far end of the circle. "We're going to clear away the rest."

"Uh-huh." Jackie was interested.

"Then we're going to raise the stones."

chapter
Twenty-seven

"That means digging out the sockets with the backhoe," Jackie said.

"Correct," Peter said.

"You said yourself that they sometimes buried human remains and artifacts under the stones," Jackie said.

"Peter, that's like fixing teeth with a crowbar," Connie said. "We'll destroy the very data we're trying to salvage."

"Besides, how we going to date them if we raise them?" asked Sparky. "I mean, what's the point?"

They were right, of course. One bite of the hoe, and any vital clues would be crushed, lost. Even from the most liberal scientific perspective, there was no justification for raising the stones. "We'll excavate and reconstruct at the same time," Peter explained calmly.

It was nearly ten o'clock that night. Andy was in bed. The four of them were sitting on the porch, drinking beer and wine. A bowl of fruit sat on the table. Overhead the Big Dipper hung like a connect-the-dot scoop. The bucket of a backhoe, in fact.

Part of Peter's mind was on that mound. The rest was on setting the others at ease. "Seven days is not enough time to find clues, to analyze, and date them. That'll take weeks," Peter explained. "But a standing stone circle might stop them."

"He doesn't give a damn if they're standing or flat. All he wanted was his chapel," Jackie said.

"What's it going to accomplish?" asked Connie. "The man only knows business."

" 'The American Stonehenge,' " said Peter.

"I don't follow," Connie said.

"The way he lit up when I mentioned it. We get them up in seven days, then call the press."

"What's that going to do?"

"He's a businessman in need of good PR. Think of the hay he could make: 'Kingdom Head, site of America's Stonehenge.' Real or fake, he could build his casino around it, ring it with a fancy marble bar. A lot more provocative than an old chapel. Doesn't even have to reconstruct it. We give it to him on a platter. The press will eat it up. And we get an open extension to prove it's the real thing."

"What about artifacts once we tear the place up?" Connie asked.

"Something's bound to sift out."

They talked more. The others protested a little longer, but in the end Peter won them over. What choice did they have? Before they went to bed, Jackie asked, "Just how we going to raise them?"

"With the backhoe and ropes."

"You gotta be kidding. You'd need a crane to get those up." He went inside. Sparky followed him.

Only Connie and Peter remained in the dark of the porch. The small citronella candle burned low. Peter watched as a bug flew too close and sputtered to ash.

A few minutes of dark silence passed between them like a herd of elephants. Then Connie broke the mood. She put her wineglass on the table.

"Peter, what's going on?"

A bowl of peaches sat between them. Peter removed a ripe one.

"What do you mean?"

"I think you're keeping something from us."

He turned his head so that only half his face was in the light. "You do?" Amazing how nearly human the skin of a peach was. He rolled it in his hands.

"Yes," she said. "And why are you talking as if you're some-place else?"

"I guess I'm just distracted with the dig." His knife hung from his belt. He slipped it out of its sheath.

"I understand," she said. "But why do I have the feeling that you're hiding something? that you're on a different expedition from the rest of us?"

"Well, Connie, I really don't know. I think only you can an-swer that." Slowly he began slicing the skin off the flesh.

"Oh, come on, Peter."

"Come on what?" he asked. "What do you think I'm hiding?"

"Let's stop playing games," she said. "Ever since you returned from Hannah's, you've been acting strange. Even Andy's feeling it. Again tonight he asked me to read him a bedtime story because you didn't have time."

"I was making dinner with Sparky." The skin came off in a continuous spiral, like a Dali head.

"I know it's not my business but he's quite upset. He's com-plained about headaches and stomachaches for the last two days. All he wants to do is go home. He's afraid, Peter. He thinks you're mad at him. He thinks that you don't like him."

"Don't like him." The words cut into him, and for a moment he felt his mind wince in pain. But immediately his mind said, Don't let her throw you. Don't let her in. None of them. You know what your priorities are now. He put the knife down. "That's ridic-ulous," he said. "I'm crazy about Andy." Unraveled, the skin made a long curlicue on the table. Carefully he wound it up into a rag-ged empty sphere and stood it on the mouth of his beer bottle.

Hello, Dali, you're looking swell, Dali. It's so nice to have you back where you belong. . . .

The peach was a blank wet face on the plate. "He's just anx-ious to get back to friends his own age, and playgrounds, and TV. That's all."

She nodded.

The blade was sticky with juice.

"Maybe," she said.

He could feel her staring at him. It was clear she had much more on her mind. It was also clear she didn't know how familiar to be with him. Things were a tad tenuous. "It's almost over," he said. He picked up the skinned peach. He cut a precise wedge. The inside was a voluptuous pink.

"Peter, the other night . . ." She hesitated. "The other night on our walk I thought you were a very sweet man. Then something happened I don't understand."

"Well, I appreciate the compliment anyway, Connie," he said.

She looked at him blankly.

Peter slid the blade point into the pink. "Peach?" He grinned, aiming the knife at her.

She stared at it across the dark air. "No."

"Don't let me keep you up."

She rose to leave. "Good night."

"Good night, Connie."

Before she stepped through the door, she looked back. "Peter?"

"Yes?"

"How's it going to end?"

"And they lived happily ever after."

She left, but never asked who *they* were.

He popped the wedge into his mouth.

An hour later Peter was still sitting in the dark. The candle had burned itself out. But he could still see. He drank another beer and wished he had a cigarette. He hadn't had such a craving since he quit seven years ago.

When he was certain Connie and the Kellehers were asleep, he walked down the stairs to the beach. He knew all along he couldn't sleep.

The walk to the Point took only fifteen minutes. The tide was out and the sea was tranquil. As he crunched his way down the sand he felt as if he were reliving the dreams—déjà vu all over again, as Yogi Berra would say. But in slow motion this time.

The night was vibrant, as if statically charged. A smoky tang of expectancy laced the breeze. Overhead the stars burned with outrageous brilliance, and on the eastern horizon a huge blood moon was on the rise. It was the kind of night poets and songwriters celebrated. And as he walked along he amused himself with all the different lyrics he could come up with about the night.

Don't go around tonight.
Well, it's bound to take your life.

In just a couple minutes he thought of a dozen songs alone about the moon—"There's a Moon Out Tonight" to "Moon of Love" to the old standby, "Moon River."

I see the bad moon arising.
I see trouble on the way.

"Blue Moon" by the Marcels, even "Stagger Lee"—all about moons and love. All but that Creedence Clearwater Revival number that kept flooding his head—from Jackie's *Chronicle* CD.

I see earthquakes and lightnin'.
I see bad times today.
Don't go around tonight.
Well it's bound to take your life.

The words blared in his head.

I hear the voice of rage and ruin.

He tried to drown it out with lyrics of other songs, singing one, then another, until he was yelling out loud whatever refrain he could hold.

Hope you got your things together.
Hope you're quite prepared to die . . .

God, why wouldn't it stop? It was like an implant in his brain with the volume turned to max. He started jogging along the water's edge, stumbling through bundles of rotting seaweed. Things squished under his feet.

One eye is taken for an eye.

The words filled his head no matter what he did. By the time he reached the end of the beach, he was wet and gasping for air. And in his head the chorus howled:

THERE'S A BAD MOON ON THE RISE THERE'S A BAD MOON ON THE RISE THERE'S A BAD MOON ON THE RISE THERE'S A BAD MOON ON THE RISE THERE'S A BAD MOON ON THE RISE THERE'S A BAD MOON ON THE RISE . . .

"Jesus Christ!" he screamed.

And it was gone.

Dead-black silence. Nothing moved. He was at the base of Pulpit's Point.

He steadied himself against a large shore rock. His shirt was a cold plaster. He sat there for several minutes until he felt whole again. Another crazy little whirlpool of the mind, he told himself. Another little test of his mettle—kind of like Ulysses against the sirens on his way home to his estranged wife.

But why the trailing sense of guilt? Why the feeling that he'd done something wrong?

It was that Connie and her insinuations that are messing you up, he told himself. You're a good father. You love your son. So what if you've been distant, maybe even a little gruff? There are big things on your mind. Much, much bigger than you'd ever dreamed. Much bigger than your son's sudden attack of homesickness. And maybe, just maybe someplace deep down where the sun don't shine you *do* hold him accountable for Linda's death. Nothing criminal in that. It's only natural. After all, if he hadn't disobeyed, Linda would be alive today.

He headed up the slope of Pulpit's Point. The place was utterly still. No circle of parishioners, no hysterical children, no witch on fire.

Of course not. He was awake this time. *Really awake.* Things were clear. No more CCR mind-jamming. He had his things together, and he was quite prepared to ride.

The moon, up a few degrees, was a gaudy tangerine.

There was no need to ponder. He knew what he would do. He had thought about it all evening. In fact, for most of the last six hours. It was a tad unorthodox, but, what the hell?—nothing about this expedition wasn't unorthodox. Besides, somebody had turned up the rheostat again. The air began to crackle.

Smoke. It cut to his brain. But this time it was sweetly pleasant—none of that acrid sharpness.

Carefully he removed the plastic tarpaulin. The sand was still warm. When the cover was folded and tucked away, he went over to the backhoe. The key sat in the ignition. He climbed in and turned the ignition. The machine roared with life.

He gripped the forelever. It vibrated in his hand. He pulled it back, and the hoe reared its claw like the trunk of a bull elephant.

Automatically his hands flitted across the levers, from one to the next to the next like he'd been doing it all his life. He slipped through the hoisting gates and gear patterns as if the shifts were directing him instead of the other way around. It was amazing. He felt magical.

He switched on the head beams and rolled the machine forward.

Ahead of him lay the first stone they had cleared. It appeared in the light like a fallen idol. With a precise flourish, he worked the levers, and the claw dug into the socket. Yeah, Connie was right: He was probably destroying all sorts of little artifactual nuggets *in situ*. But it was the only way. Besides, stuff was bound to turn up. He'd give the world its evidence soon enough. Then he'd mash Hatcher's nose in it. Merritt's too.

He jumped down to check the hole. The soil was much harder than the sand they'd been digging in. Also, the claw was pulling out lots of small fieldstones. Of course: Footholds for the megaliths.

He measured the base of the stone and got down several times from the machine to carve the hole with a hand shovel. When he had a socket nearly three feet deep, he packed the sides with the original support stones. Part of him wanted to sift through the dirt, but that would have to wait.

By one o'clock he had finished. It had taken him nearly two

hours to get the socket right. He was sweaty and his muscles were sore, yet he did not feel tired. Except for a three-hour dinner break, he had been digging and hauling since seven that morning. He should be exhausted. On the contrary, he felt high and wildly strong. Yes, the place was a damn power plant, all right. He could feel it in his atoms. He felt a crackling alertness, and his body glowed with well-being.

With the hoe extended, he coaxed the stone until it was lined up and overhanging the socket.

He swung the machine around, and with the edge of the bucket he raised the top end a foot. Then he got down and tied the polyvinyl chloride line around it several times. He lowered the stone, swung the machine around, and tied the cord five-times thick to the hoe. When he was in place, he pulled the lift lever all the way back. The stone rose in the air like a rocket.

Suddenly there was a lightning crack.

In the headlights the stone stood high, the yellow lines dangling like snakes. The cord had snapped. Peter jumped off the machine. The stone tilted at a crazy angle, maybe fifteen degrees from perpendicular. Yet the foot had caught the edge of the socket.

For a second he expected it to topple. But the socket gripped it firmly. He grabbed a shovel to fix where one wall had collapsed.

It took him maybe half an hour to get it right.

He walked around the stone, thinking about using the backhoe to finish the job. To get the stone perfectly upright, he'd have to retie it and work it down by gearing back and forth until it nestled in. As he worked out the maneuvers in his head, he half-consciously lay the flat of his hand against the tilted stone.

It was damp and cool from years of stony sleep.

For a long, long time he stood that way, when suddenly a surge of hot lava swelled his veins. It was crazy. He knew it. A twelve-ton monolith of blue granite! Impossible, but he couldn't stop himself. He put his shoulder against the tilting edge, sensing the enormity of its mass—a mass so great that should it give, he'd be pressed to pâté.

He gave a heave.

The stone budged.

Weeeeeoooooo! A thrill shot through him.

He took another deep breath, and concentrating with everything he had, he laid his shoulder and hands against the stone and
pushed again, groaning and straining, his eyes clenched shut, his
lips stretched across his teeth. He felt the muscles of his thighs
swell in his jeans and his neck tendons bulge like anchor ropes. His
whole body shook as he strained and strained against the impossible mass. But once more he felt it give, then he felt it rise with him
under it as he pressed with unrelenting determination, his legs
pushing like great hydraulic lifters.

And the huge stone thudded into place.

The breath exploded out of him. His face was slick and his
shoulder was in agony.

But the stone stood upright—a finger raised to heaven.

He felt no surprise. He knew from the first touch that he
would move it. It was an act of faith, like Samson at the pillars of
the temple, but in reverse.

Peter.

He spun around half expecting to see Connie.

I've been waiting for you.

"Huh?"

There was nobody there. The headlights of the backhoe
sprayed the whole mound. It was empty.

Peter, I'm getting stronger.

"Linda?" He could barely catch his breath. Everything was
racing. "Where are you?" He spun around. Nothing.

I'm near you.

"Where?"

The voice was out there, but didn't have a fixed point.

Here.

He snapped his head the other way and saw the quarter-hump
of sand. The divining rod was a glowing vector.

His first thought was that it was blurry vision, as when you
wake up, or stand up too fast. But his sight was fine. Something
hovered over the divining rod. From what he could tell, it was not
quite a material thing, more like a small pocket of gelatinous air.
As his eyes adjusted, it appeared to be a suspended pinpoint radiat-
ing thick heat waves. An intensely hot singularity, but with no visi-

ble source. Through it the moon rippled—a distorted red jellied thing shimmering against the black like a hot crab.

"Linda?"

Yes, Peter. It's Linda. Your Linda.

It sounded like her, though her voice was void of personality. But, of course. It wasn't the living Linda speaking to him, but her immaterial form, her spirit—the ectoplasm of his Linda. And speaking directly into his head.

Peter, I'm getting stronger.

"Linda . . ." he whispered. He squinted to hold that node of shimmering air. "It was you in the marsh."

Yes.

"You saved my life."

Yes, I saved your life, Peter.

"And you led me here."

To raise the stones . . .

"I'm going to do that, my darling. I promise."

To make me stronger . . .

"Make you stronger?"

To come back to you.

"Come back to me?"

Yes, yes.

"But . . . how, Linda?"

Peter, there's something you must do.

His mind was swirling with dark eddies. He had dropped to his knees from faintness. "Yes, anything."

Somewhere in the black a seagull cried out.

You know, Peter.

"No, I don't know. Tell me."

You do, you've known all along.

"What? Please . . ."

The seagull cried again. Overhead it sliced through the black like a blade and flew out to sea.

Andy.

"What?"

I want him.

"Linda, no. No."

I WANT HIM.

"But he's my son."

In a blink, the air was still again.

She was gone, and in her place a shrunken yellow moon scowled down on him.

"But he's my son."

chapter
Twenty-eight

The sky was white.

He watched the sun come up. It rose out of the water like a bloody wafer. By six, it was hot. A mean white hot. It would be a bad day.

He sat in the porch chair, as he had for the last five hours, watching the moon fade, tasting smoke.

The peach, a single wedge missing, was brown and festering with insects. His knife still lay beside it.

He looked at it, and a small secret voice in his mind said: *Get away from this island. Get away while there's still time. Pack up your son and put as many miles between him and those damn stones as you can. Let them raze the bloody place. Let them blow it all to dust. Just get away. Get away.*

But a hot crackling buzz drove away the voice.

He picked up the knife and went in. Their bedroom was upstairs at the far end. The stairs creaked under his weight. He could hear the others stirring behind their doors. Quietly he slipped into the room and closed the door.

Andy lay in a deep sleep, holding his lamb by the foot. Peter's own cot hadn't been touched. Sometime in the night Andy had removed the night table between them and pushed his cot flush to Peter's. The small pocket clock was buzzing by Andy's head. It was not like him to sleep through the alarm.

Peter turned it off and sat on his cot, watching his son sleep. The knife was sticky in his hand. A shaft of orange sunlight pierced the curtains lighting up the boy's face. How like Linda he looked. He had her thick black hair and feathered eyebrows, her Cupid's bow lips, and long liquid eyes. Peter's reflection was less obvious— a rough of Peter's profile. Peter studied the resemblance for a while. Then his eye caught the configuration of the exposed ear—a tight pink swirl that spiraled down into a tiny black point. Like a miniature whirlwind. It was Peter's ear, too. His eye fell to Andy's cheeks and chin. Amazing how firm and supple children's skin was. No wrinkles or sags, no blemishes or pockmarks. Just tight and creamy with ever-so-fine hairs. Like a peach.

As if it had a mind of its own, Peter's thumb found the blade, tested it. It was a barber's razor.

Twin creases like hairline slits across Andy's neck connected one ear to the other. Peter studied the creases. He could see a fine seam of dirt where the face cloth never seemed to reach. And a thin sheen of perspiration. Even in the dead of winter Andy's pajamas would be damp at the neck—"dream dew," Peter called it, which he'd told Andy came from all his midnight romping with fairies. Peter's eyes fell to the small hollow of Andy's throat. It throbbed to a faint pulse. He imagined a tiny heart just below the surface. He wondered how many times it had beat in Andy's six and a half years. He could probably calculate that easily enough. Then he wondered how many more until there were none.

Do it.

Peter's hand raised the knife. He looked at it half in wonder, as if it were an alien object—his knife, but not his hand.

For a shuddering moment a ray of light shot through the thick smoke. What in God's name am I doing, his mind asked him. What am I doing? Suddenly Peter was watching himself from above, watching as he sat by his sleeping son with a knife poised to kill. It was a monstrous moment without context, one split from the continuum of his life, of the history of his being, of everything he was and believed in. *This is not me doing this.*

He stared in stunned disbelief at the knife.

What is happening to me?

"The dead are jealous of the living."

But Linda wouldn't want this.

His hand dropped to his knee. God in heaven, I'm not doing

this. It's not me. *Not me.* He pressed his thumb into the blade. But it was there. He could actually feel the occupation of his brain, of the smoldering presence spreading like hot pus through the gray matter, filling the lobes and convolutions, searing away the autonomy of his mind.

Linda, his mind whispered.

She's been seeping her way in from the moment you stepped off the boat—twisting you, making you crazy, turning you against people, filling you with resentment and rage and hot unspeakable urges. Like that night on the Point with Connie, like those times with Andy. Like now. Don't let her in, she's poisoning you. But why? It didn't make sense. Linda wouldn't want this. Not her own baby.

She'll get inside your head, make you do things you'll be sorry for.

But not Andy. He looked at his son, his sweet little boy face. And, again, the voice whispered, *Get away before there's nothing left to lose. Take him and go back home.* Andy stirred, and Peter's brain flared.

Do it, she said.

The burning in his head cut his breath.

Now.

Incredibly, his hand jerked up as if remotely powered. He stared at it dumbly.

Now.

A clean quick cut across his throat. It would be so easy.

NOW! she screamed.

Blood throbbed out of the severed veins in Andy's neck.

Andy in a puddle of blood covered with flies.

NOW!

A ring of standing stones. A column of smoke, Linda's arms spread.

GIVE HIM TO ME!

He winced at his hand. He had gripped the horn so hard he felt fused to it.

I'll come to you, Peter. I'll come to you.

His heart ached from the pounding. "Andy." He heard himself whisper the name.

Give him to me.

Why is she doing this? He's her son, too.

NOW!

The blade glinted fire in the sun.

"Nothing crueler in the universe."

The pulse on Andy's neck. *Look at it,* the secret voice said. *Look at your son. Your little boy. You love him. You love him.*

NOW! NOW!

The pulse in the peach.

The pulse.

The pulse you love.

No, Linda. NO. I CANNOT KILL MY OWN SON.

His fingers sprung open as if releasing a demon. The knife clunked on the floor.

"Daddy, what are you doing?" Andy looked around startled.

Peter shook his head. With his foot, he kicked the knife under the cot. "Time to get up."

"Why you looking at me like that?" he asked. "Are you crying?"

Peter shook his head and rubbed his eyes. "Just sleepy." She was gone, but his mind felt blistered from heat. Peter kissed Andy on the soft red of his cheek, his neck. "I love you, little man. I love you."

"Love you, too," he said. "You cut your thumb."

He looked at the small gash in dismay. He'd never even felt the knife. He sucked away the blood. "It's nothing."

"Dad, can we go home today?"

"Just one more week."

"But I want to go today. I hate it here." His face screwed up the way it did when he was about to cry.

Peter held him tightly. "Nothing's going to happen to you. Nothing, I promise."

He pushed Peter away. "You're squeezing me."

"It's almost over."

Andy looked at him oddly. "But, Dad . . ."

"No 'but, Dad.' We have a lot more digging ahead. A lot more." He looked at his watch. "We should be up there right now."

"But Dad."

"Get dressed, Andy."

"Dad, you sure you aren't crying?"

"Sure."

The others met them downstairs. They took a quick breakfast and headed up to the Point.

By the time they got there, Peter's stomach was spasming out of control. Even in life Linda had been keenly perceptive. She had been gifted with a honed sense that would alert her when something wasn't right—when Peter was lying or trying to hide something, whether bad news or a birthday surprise. It was impossible to keep anything from her. She could read it in the micro-expressions of his face, or in some subtle inflection of his voice, or maybe she was cued by a secretion of pheromones. He didn't know how she did it. Linda was like a finely tuned instrument that would allow no secrets. What bothered him was the thought that she'd know what was on his mind as soon as he stepped foot up there. She'd know that he could not let her have Andy. She'd know he could never sacrifice his son, no matter how great the rewards.

But he feared how she'd take his defiance.

"What the hell?" Jackie gaped at the single standing stone.

"I put it up last night."

"How did you do it?"

He told them how he had used the backhoe and cord, how it took him half the night to get used to handling the machine—and not to kill himself. Over and over again he had had to position it just so, dig the socket, recarve it with shovels, hoe up the dirt, repack the footholds when they gave, and on and on. The hardest part he said was getting it to stand upright just so. The damn thing took him to dawn to finish the job.

What surprised Peter was how easy it was to make it all up. He never betrayed himself. And they were amazed.

"It took me two weeks just to get the hoist levers straight," Jackie said.

"Where there's a will there's a way," Peter said.

"You've got one hell of a will."

As the others walked around the single standing stone, Peter looked at the torn-up mound and the exposed stones. No, he had not betrayed himself, but he'd betrayed Linda. And he knew she'd let him know.

But the morning passed without event. Jackie reclaimed the backhoe to clear a second socket, and with a shovel Peter prepared it for the next stone. Like the other, it contained dozens of field-stones for footholds.

Not once did Peter sense the power of the place, nor did the second stone slip home the way the first had hours before. For a second he wondered if that had all been imagined. But he knew better. Under his shirt his right shoulder was capped in a painful purple bruise from the press of the stone. It had happened, all right—a strictly private thing, he told himself. A private thing between a man and his wife. Linda had been here, and though the place had lost its charge, he'd bet his life on her return.

They dug.

The ground beneath the stones was hard, packed dirt, not the lighter beach sand overburden. With Connie and Sparky by his side, it took them hours to excavate another socket. Perhaps it was the grueling labor to clear the holes, but by noon Peter's anxiety had dwindled. If Linda was present, she was not letting him know. It was possible she allowed the magic only at night. Or when no one else was present. But as the morning oozed into the hot afternoon he began to suspect a consequence almost as bad as Linda's wrath—Linda's abandonment. Without her, the fate of the stones was left to chance. To lose her a second time was maddening— almost as maddening as her price.

While they worked, Andy lay on his towel under an umbrella. He napped on and off. Some toys and a pile of books lay untouched beside him. As the hours wore on, his sullenness became more of a distraction to Peter, even a source of irritation. A couple times he walked over to him but returned to the dirt when he realized he was asleep. Peter told himself that he should wake him and make an effort to cheer him up, engage him in activities— maybe a coloring book, or his collection of mazes, or tapes. His phoenix kite lay furled by the towel also. It had not been touched since their day of arrival. But, odd as it was, Peter could not bring

himself to wake the boy. He wondered if on some level his disinter-
est was an unconscious kind of avoidance behavior—that any show
of concern might cue Linda to his betrayal. Or, maybe Linda was
working on him more subtly—seeping back in, numbing his concern.

Whatever, Peter felt the others silently condemn him. He
could see it in their furtive glances at each other. A few times
Sparky went over to chat with Andy. Connie, too. She made him a
late-morning snack, and during lunch she coaxed him into a game
of checkers. Though he played half-heartedly, she got him to finish
the game, letting him win. On the surface all that was nice of her,
Peter told himself. But, frankly, Connie Lambert was becoming just
too goddamn officious. She was playing surrogate mother, and
he'd had had it up to here with her. Linda was Andy's mother,
damn it. Still is.

When Andy wandered off to take a pee, Connie came over to
him. "I know you're under pressure, Peter, but for Christ's sake
acknowledge your son. He feels rejected by you."

Her boldness left him nonplussed. She didn't have a goddamn
clue as to what kind of pressure he was under, he thought. Never
in her wildest dreams. Sure, she realized the import of those stones
to his career, but she could never comprehend his plight. It was
Biblical. He was like Abraham poised between Isaac and God. And
what mere mortal could comprehend that?

Someplace inside, the node sphincter opened again, and
some hot jelly exuded through. "So, what do you recommend,
Connie—just pack up and go home?"

"No, just take the kid for a walk or something."

His impulse was to tell her to mind her own business, that she
wasn't his wife, that he didn't need a goddamn coach to bring up
his kid.

"He thinks you're mad at him." She was hedging.

"What exactly did he tell you, Connie?"

"That you hate him."

"Hate him?"

From across the mound, Sparky and Jackie eyed him. Shit!
They were against him, too. "Connie, you're not a mother, so
maybe it never occurred to you that kids can be very manipula-

tive." Where the hell was he? How much time does he need to take a goddamn leak?

Her cheeks flushed. "I know manipulation," she said in a hard voice. "He's half-traumatized with fright for some reason. He wants to go home badly, and because he can't, all he does is sleep the day away."

His hand rested on the horn of the knife hanging on his belt. "Traumatized from what?"

"I don't know, but look at him. He's withdrawn."

His eyes dropped to the white underside of her throat. He found what he was looking for. Just beneath the thin gold chain—her pulse. He wondered how many beats she had left. Peter grinned. "Well, Connie, he sure doesn't look traumatized to me."

Over the rise Andy returned dragging Jimmy P. by the hand. Connie turned on her heel and walked away.

"Hey!" Jimmy P. came over to them. He had a big grin on his face. "The kid says it's a stone circle. I saw a program on those on Channel Two once." He inspected the erect stone and the second in ropes about to go up. "Jesus, ain't that something. Is it old?"

"What we're hoping."

"Yeah? How old?"

"Don't know," Peter answered. He glanced at Andy on his towel. His head was down and his eyes were closed.

"Well, better you than me, hah?"

"Pardon me?"

"Digging this place," he said. "It gives me the creeps, is all. I told you we had some trouble three, four months ago up here. Yeah, some kids came up one night in their boat. Had their dog with them, hah? Well the thing took off, and they chased it up here. Said the dog just dug itself in a hole, in all this sand you're digging up. And that ain't all of it. The guy—a college kid, Vinnie something-or-other—well, he came around couple weeks later, told us he tried to stop the dog, like it was possessed or something, and gets his hand twisted in the leash, and so help me, God, the dog nearly pulls him in with him. No baloney! He says the force was so strong he thought it was going to suck him under. The dog disappeared. A story like that, you figure the kids're on drugs or something. I wouldn't of believed him myself if he hadn't of showed up. Had a cast on from his wrist to his neck. The force ripped his hand clean off. I ain't kidding. I saw the stump. Hatcher made a settlement with them. It was all hush-hush, they didn't want no publicity is all. But I'm telling you because you're nice people. I'll be glad when they blow it all up. It's crazy, I know, but I got a bad feeling about this place. I think it's evil is all."

Nobody said anything.

The words hummed in Peter's head. Three or four months ago? Was Linda here then, too? Waiting for him?

"Well, I gotta go. If you need some help gettin' 'em up, maybe I can get a few of the boys to give you a hand. The sooner the better, hah?"

Peter thanked him.

Before he went back down, Jimmy asked, "Something the matter with the little slugger today? Looks a little under the weather."

"Just a little homesick," Peter said.

He watched Jimmy walk down the slope.

I think it's evil is all.

Peter picked up his shovel and went back to his hole. "Time to get back," he announced. Nobody said anything. But their eyes scraped him like a rake.

They worked throughout the afternoon, while Andy slept.

By five o'clock, a third socket was nearly dug. And two granite boulders seven feet high stood firmly like an unfinished portal to the sea.

Despite all the digging and sifting, they had found nothing of scientific value. Nothing to take to the labs. Just pebbles and broken shells. Hannah's rod still sat in the middle of the circle on a large hump half burying the limestone pillar. There was so much more work to be done, so much more sand to sift. And so little time.

So little time. How was it going to end?

"Peter! It's Andy."

Connie was at the umbrella. Andy was thrashing around on his towel.

When Peter got there, he could see the boy's eyes were closed. He was still asleep, but muttering and twisting violently like a snake on a hot plate.

Peter took his shoulders. "Andy! Andy!"

Suddenly the thrashing stopped. His eyes snapped open, and he sat upright.

"Daddy."

"I'm right here."

"Daddy." His eyes were huge, his voice very strange—high and tiny, like a baby's.

"What is it?"

"I go see Mommy."

"What's the matter with him?"

"I go see Mommy. I go see Mommy." He said it over and over again.

"He's in some kind of trance," Sparky said. Jackie ran to the cooler for icewater.

Andy's eyes fixed straight on Peter, but they were vacant, unseeing.

"Andy, it's okay. It's okay." Peter poured icewater onto a towel and dabbed Andy's face.

But it did nothing. He just kept staring in that hideous gaze, saying "I go see Mommy."

"Some kind of seizure," Connie said. She felt his head. "He's got a fever."

Peter could feel the heat radiate from Andy's body. "Jesus, he's burning up."

He draped the cold towel on his forehead. Instantly his mind cleared. Andy had gotten temperatures before without warning, but nothing like this. Nothing this fast. Nothing this high. His temperature could be 105 or higher. No wonder he was so lethargic. He could suffer brain damage. Peter grabbed the canteen and dumped the icewater over his hair.

"Andy, Daddy has you," Peter said. He felt frantic. "More water somebody."

Jackie shot to get the cooler.

"It's going to be okay, Pooch. Gonna be okay." Jackie came back with the rest of the canteens, and Peter poured water over Andy's shirt and head.

No reaction. No flicker of his eyes. Just that sightless stare straight up at the underside of the umbrella. And, "I go see Mommy." His mouth worked the syllables over and over again.

"Jesus!" Peter muttered. It crossed his mind to run him down to the water. Total submersion. It was what they did in hospitals to drop high temperatures fast. Before there was brain damage. But this was no ordinary fever. No ordinary seizure. His eyes were fixed, intense, not rolled back; and his mouth was moving, not locked. And, God, why was he saying that?

Linda—she slipped out of you and into Andy.

"No, God, don't do this," Peter cried. "Andy, wake up!" He started to lift the boy to take him below when suddenly he fell silent.

"He's coming to," Connie said.

He blinked the water away from his eyes, then rolled his head toward Peter as if trying to recognize him. His eyes locked on Peter's for a moment, then he pushed himself to his feet. His head snapped toward the stones.

"You okay, Pooch?"

Even before the words were out, Andy dashed for the mound.

"Andy!"

By the time Peter reached him, Andy was on his knees beside the limestone pillar pawing the dirt. "Mommy, Mommy . . ."

The V of Hannah's divining rod blazed above him.

The image so filled Peter with horror that he nearly started screaming. It took three of them to pull Andy out of the dirt, three of them to restrain him from throwing himself back into the small pit he had dug. His fingers were bleeding and strings of drool hung from his mouth.

"Mommy, Mommy . . ." His voice. It was thick, gravelly . . . too big for him.

Peter barely heard Connie's words. "I think we better get him to a doctor."

"I'll get the boat," Jackie said.

"Mommy, Mommy, Mommy . . ." Andy strained against Peter, who did all he could to prevent him from breaking away, his strength like that of a man. "Mommy . . ." A voice too heavy, alien. Full of smoke.

Linda, don't do this! Linda, I beg you.

"Andy, stop!"

"Mommy . . ." His little face was skinned back like a terrified monkey.

Peter swung Andy around, and slapped him hard on the cheek. At the moment of impact, it occurred to Peter in a side thought that this was the first time in his life he had ever struck his son, that his hand had ever made violent contact with the boy's flesh.

For a brief second, the boy stared at his father in total shock. His hand floated up to the fire in his cheek. Then his face screwed up and he began to cry. "Why'd you hit me?"

He hadn't remembered a thing.

"Why did you hit me, Daddy? I didn't do anything," he wailed. "You're mean. I didn't do anything."

They walked him to his towel and coaxed him back. He was mad that his clothes were all wet, and he was outraged that Peter had struck him.

Peter held him while the others sat in a circle, trying to comfort him. They explained in rough what had happened, that he had been dreaming, like sleepwalking, and started digging in the sand as if he had lost something. Peter said that he had had a sudden fever and was delirious and that a slap was the only way to snap him out of it. After a while he accepted that. Nobody mentioned "Mommy." Or his fit. And nobody offered an explanation for how his temperature had dropped as mysteriously as it had shot up. But Peter knew.

"Do you remember what you were dreaming?" Sparky asked.

He shook his head.

The images Linda could have filled his mind with, Peter thought. Maybe she had spared him. Maybe it was all a private thing for him. A warning.

Maybe.

She gets into your head.

Andy drank a carton of orange juice and ate a sandwich. It was the first thing he'd eaten all day.

After several minutes, the others went back to work. But Peter stayed with Andy under the umbrella, rocking him in his arms until he dozed off.

Peter sat holding his son, wanting to sob himself into oblivion with him, and wondering how it was going to end.

chapter
Twenty-nine

The blast of a horn shattered the spell.

Peter lay Andy's head on a folded towel and went to the drop-off. Below, a gray police boat pulled into the cove.

Two officers remained aboard as Dan Merritt got off and climbed up the slope. Hatcher had called him. He slowly took in the two erect stones and a third waiting at a crazy angle in its hole held by cables to the backhoe. He walked the periphery toward Peter.

"Very impressive," Merritt said. "I suppose if you can't find one, you might as well build your own."

"One way of getting attention."

Merritt said nothing. He leaned over to check how the stones had been dressed, how they had been raised. "Somebody worked hard at making it look authentic."

He was baiting him. "Seems so," Peter said. He could feel the tension crackling in the air.

"Hatcher said you mentioned something about European origins."

"I was talking resemblance." Peter glanced over to Andy. He was sound asleep.

"Uh-huh." Merritt looked at him suspiciously. "He seemed to think you harbor possibilities."

"That's not what I claimed."

Suddenly a nasty thought leaped to his mind. Merritt was here to announce that some muckety-muck from Harvard or the Smithsonian was coming to take over the dig because Peter wasn't big enough, because he didn't have the credentials. Because the site was too important for Peter Van Zandt to handle.

Merritt took off his sunglasses and massaged the bridge of his nose. "He did say you mentioned the possibility of a hoax."

Peter made a flat grin. "I was having a fit of reasonableness."

Merritt smiled. "The screens turn up anything yet?"

"No."

"You think it's a replica?"

"Might be."

Merritt nodded. "What period?"

"I'm not yet sure."

Merritt turned something over in his head. Below, the MBTA boat idled. His face darkened. "I'm afraid you're not going to like this. Hatcher's cutting your time again."

"What?"

"He's giving you until the fifth."

"The fifth? That's two days."

"Says he's forced to, another shift in schedules or something."

"That's bullshit."

"Sorry, Peter."

"Bullshit, sorry. Stop him!"

"You know there's nothing I can do."

"You're state archaeologist, goddamn it."

"That means nothing on private land, Peter, and you know it."

Peter closed his eyes. *They're going to cut me down before I get there.*

"Two days ago he said we had over a week. Now it's two days. What the hell is going on? Why's he doing this?"

"I don't know. Something to do with a mix-up in dates."

"That's a fucking lie, Dan. Something else is going on."

Merritt fixed the glasses on his nose again. "What can I say, Peter? I'm just reporting the news, not making it."

"They don't know what they're doing."

"I tried to convince him to hold to the original schedule, but he wouldn't hear of it. His mind is made up."

"That son of a bitch."

Merritt shrugged. "I tried. Even the excavation of a replica is worthy archaeology, I told him."

Jackie tossed his shovel on the dirt. "It's no more a replica than you are."

"Beg your pardon?"

"You heard me. Tell him what the hell we found," Jackie said to Peter.

Merritt sighed. "Oh, for God sakes, Peter," he said as if his heart were going to break. "You're not back there again?"

Peter wished Jackie hadn't said anything, but what the hell difference did it make now? "It's a possibility. We've found things."

"What things?" Merritt's voice took on a serrated edge.

"Things that suggest the circle is authentic. Okay? There, it's out. Not a replica, not a hoax—the real fucking McCoy, Dan. A stone circle. Pre-Colonial," Peter said. "Pre-Christopher-fucking-Columbus, too. And if somebody can get us some fucking time, I might be able to fucking prove it."

"Prove what?" Merritt said incredulously. "You have Bronze Age artifacts? Some Beaker pots? Chemical analyses? Carbon fourteens? You got any of that?"

"I didn't say Bronze Age."

"Well, just what *are* you saying?"

Peter felt a sour leakage in his gut. "I'm saying it's possibly the biggest bonanza in the archaeological world today. Maybe the cradle of the new world."

"Maybe it's just as well you're leaving."

"Dan, you've got to help us." Peter felt desperate. "All I'm asking for is time."

"In two days, you'll have the rest of your life. And frankly, Peter, I'm a little sick of your Edgar Cayce crap about Pre-Columbian migrants. Grow up."

"Tell him, Peter," Connie said. "Hannah."

"An old woman came by the other night," Peter said, restraining himself. "Her name is Hannah Mac Ness. She used to be the caretaker of the island. Eighteen months ago Hatcher evicted her, settled out of court and gave her a pile of money to live else-where."

Merritt checked his watch. "So what?"

Peter told him about the engraving and her story of her ances-tors settling here years before the historical migrations. But his words turned into lead pellets as they hit the air. Merritt didn't buy it. And there was so much more he couldn't tell him.

"And that's your evidence: an undocumented engraving and the claims of a disturbed old woman?"

"Then look at this," said Peter, pulling him to the limestone pillar.

"A replica like the rest."

"But limestone wasn't quarried in the seventeenth century," Jackie said.

"There are far more reasonable explanations than a fertility stone from sixth-century Britain."

"What about the lunula around her neck?" Peter asked. "From what I could tell it was authentic."

"From what you could tell." Merritt shook his head. "Even if it was authentic, a real Celtic lunula, did it ever occur to you that it might have been an heirloom? Or maybe an antique she picked up someplace?"

"That's precisely why I need time."

Merritt shook his head. "It's a good thing she wasn't wearing a gold death mask, or you'd claim you'd found the tomb of Aga-memnon."

Below the police boat gave a couple of blasts from an air horn.

"Dan, what if it's the real thing?"

Merritt stopped and glared at him, and for a moment Peter thought he had gotten through. "You know, Peter," he said, "I really feel sorry for you." Then he walked down to the boat.

"He doesn't want to know," Connie said.

"What the hell we going to do with two days?"

Peter walked to the edge. Acrid wind whipped him in the eyes. He felt crazy.

Below, Merritt climbed into the boat and took off.

Don't let them do this to me, Linda. Please. Then he looked over at the sleeping figure of his son.

chapter
Thirty

The sun was getting hotter.

Peter woke Andy. He did not expect a relapse, but he wanted
him out of the heat, back at the cottage. He directed the others to
continue troweling around the limestone pillar, where Hannah
had planted the divining rod. He also asked Jackie to find Jimmy P.
and arrange for his men to come up with a crane.

As they were starting to leave, Connie came over to Peter.
"Are you going to be all right?" There was something in her face.
He had dealt her harsh words that morning, and she hadn't gotten
over it.

"Sure," Peter said.

Andy pulled at Peter to go back.

"Want me to come?" she asked.

Whatever had hold of him slipped for an instant, and he almost said *Yes, come, with me. I need you. We need you.* But he shook his
head. "Thanks, we'll be fine."

She did not look as if she believed him.

"I'm sorry," he whispered. "For all of it."

She nodded vaguely.

"We're going to lay low." He tousled Andy's hair. It was still
damp. "Think we need a few hours together."

"Sure you don't need company?"

He nodded. "Thanks anyway," he said and thought how she
was worried about his sudden mood swings, his lack of stability. So

was he. "Things will be just fine. I need you more up here." A voice in the back of his head said, *not true.*

"I'll be glad when this is over," she said.

Peter nodded. Andy took his hand as they headed down the slopes.

The walk back felt good—just being off the Point, away from the stones. Part of Peter regretted not letting Connie come along. But, of course, he could not compromise a few private hours with his son. Yes, he told himself, they would be fine. But in a dark back pocket of his mind he wondered what the night would bring.

Andy went right to his cot when he got back. Peter suggested they play cards or checkers or color in his Jack and the Beanstalk book, but he wanted to nap. So, Peter drew the curtains and settled beside him on his cot.

On the night table beside the coloring book lay a shiny brochure Hatcher had left in the cottage: *Kingdom Head—The New England Riviera.* On the cover was a photo of Pulpit's Point from the water with the sun rising unseen behind it and the artist's rendition of the finished resort—a glittering white casino surrounded by a colonial village painted in exaggerated proportion on the photograph. On the inside cover Hatcher beamed at the camera; behind him sparkled the blue water of the Boston Harbor and the city skyline in the distance. There was in bold white letters across the bottom: "Edgar Fane Hatcher: Harbor by Design."

He had won. By design. It would be over in two days.

Peter closed his eyes. The cool darkness of the room was a relief. He let his bones settle and for a long serene moment he blanked his mind. It was the first time in days that he was able to put aside all the emotional stress, the craziness. He had lost, but he felt peaceful—something he had never felt up on that mound. It was like being away from a contaminated area. Like undergoing psychic detoxification.

While his mind was still a tranquil pool, he wondered about all that had happened—the dark stuff, that is. He wondered for a second if maybe he actually had imagined the whole thing with Linda. That ball of hot plasma up there, her voice. Even raising the first stone. How did he know he hadn't had another amnesia attack? That he had raised it with the backhoe? Sure, his shoulder was a painful mess, but maybe it was the result of a fit of desperation as he tried the impossible. Another hallucination. One long psychic fugue like that first day in the kitchen.

He closed his eyes. And one by one he reexamined the events of the last several days, dropping them like pebbles in the dark well of his mind, watching the waves spread in concentric circles from a pinpoint of light. If only he had a sign. Anything for a sign, he thought.

He rolled his head and opened his eyes a crack. Andy had dozed off, Lambkin in his clutch.

Peter wondered why he slept so much. Maybe, in fact, it was trauma. Like that time when he was two, the day they had dropped Linda off at Logan. She was flying to Chicago for a few days to visit a friend. Not two minutes back in his car seat and Andy was out like a light. Her departure was too much for him to handle, so he had escaped. He had slept a lot after Linda died, too. Amazing how the mind refused to accept. Amazing, also, how it struggled to reconstruct the past.

Peter's mind drifted back to the morning. And what was that all about? he thought. Andy had called for Linda, tried to dig her up, in fact. Said she talked to him, wanted him to visit her. Still compensating? Couldn't be, not after all these years. Couldn't be coincidence either, could it—that they were both imagining things, both crazy? Perhaps Andy had tapped into the same dark zone Peter had.

He let his mind experiment in the dark: Just suppose you had the option. That's right: to bring back your wife. What would be her form? Just some hot shimmering ectoplasm? How do you relate to that? Or, perhaps, a full-fledged spirit, a guardian angel, that could be conjured at will.

Or, would she be back in the flesh? As she was?

Peter, make me stronger.

How was that possible?

There's fire in those stones.

How was any of this possible?

This way . . .

Who was to say that place isn't magical, sacred? And what is sacred? Something or someplace apart from the mundane. A place of divine things. Of powers beyond. Of the spirit. Sacred. You just have to believe hard enough. He tested the word. Sacred. Sacrament. Sacrarium. Sacristy. Sacrifice.

I believe, O Lord; help thou mine unbelief.

He'd kill for a sign.

"Peter?"

He woke with a shudder. She was at the door.

"Peter," she whispered, "I think you better come." The light from the hall filled her hair with fire.

This way . . .

"We found something."

Something important.

Connie.

Andy was still asleep beside him. He checked his watch. It was seven-thirty. He'd been asleep for over four hours. He followed her downstairs.

Sparky was sprawled on a chair. She was dirty and exhausted.

"What is it?"

"You better see for yourself," Connie said.

"You go," Sparky said. "I'm going to crash."

They hustled down the beach. As they neared the Point, Peter counted three additional stones standing. Jimmy's men had been up there with the crane.

They ran up the hill. Jackie was alone in a trench they had dug near the flank of the limestone pillar. The divining rod was lying flat. Treads from the crane covered the Point.

"What happened?" Peter asked.

Jackie shook his head. He was covered with black dirt. He looked exhausted. He nodded to where he'd been digging for the last few hours. "Bones."

"What?"

Jackie stood up to let them see. In a small plot of black carboniferous soil sat a humerus and the exposed side of a human skull. A cold wave rippled across Peter's skin.

The sign.

"Maybe it's what Hannah wanted us to find," Connie said.

"I didn't want to touch it until you got here," Jackie said. "But we couldn't pull ourselves away. It doesn't look damaged." Peter knelt beside the remains.

"I just cleared away some of the top stuff. But I was real careful, like you showed us." Lined up along the trench were ice picks, spatulas, trowels of varying sizes, a whisk broom, and a toothbrush.

Peter nodded. Jackie had done it right. He had dug a trench along one flank so that the remains sat on a platform—just as Peter had described in the field notebook. The remains looked undisturbed, *in situ*.

With the point of a small trowel Peter picked fragments of clam and razor shells out of the exposed ground near the skull. The combination of char, anoxic beach sand, and the acid-neutralizing calcium from all the shells had preserved the skeletal material remarkably. There was little decay. He cleared more of the skull, using only the pick and brushes, being careful not to touch it with his hand, as if it were sacred.

"What do you think?" Jackie said.

Peter did not answer. Instead he fully exposed the skull, then ran the pads of his fingers along the parietal slope. His heart was pounding.

It felt warm.

"I've got you," he whispered.

"Got who?" Jackie asked.

Peter looked up at them. He grinned. "Edgar Fane Hatcher."

"Huh?"

He stood up and filled his lungs with air. "Massachusetts General Law Chapter 7, Section 38A: Any human remains found on an archaeological site must be investigated by the state examiner. And all construction stops."

"You've got to be kidding," Jackie said.

"No. These bones just bought us a stay of execution." *Thank you, my love.*

"Holy shit!" said Jackie.

Connie's face lit up. "That's wonderful," she cried. "Maybe she didn't die in vain."

The low-grade tremors in Peter's head flared for an instant. "Who?" he asked, genuinely confused.

"Brigid."

"Yeah," Peter said. "Brigid." And he gave his fingers a secret kiss. How could he have doubted her? His Linda.

"What do we do now?" Jackie asked.

"Expose as much as we can. I'll radio Merritt tomorrow," Peter said.

"But it's a state holiday," Connie said.

He'd forgotten. July Fourth. He would leave a message on his machine. "Did the men see this?"

"No way they could have missed," Jackie said. "Flanagan himself came up."

Peter nodded. "What'd he say?"

"Not much. Connie laid into him about how they were going to destroy the greatest discovery of the New World. He said he didn't care if Jesus Christ himself walked across the Atlantic and raised them."

"We even tried the Irish slant," she said. "But it didn't work. He spit and said '*Erin go Bragh,*' then walked away. He knew as soon as he saw them."

"Yes." Peter checked his watch. "And Hatcher probably knows, too."

"He must be pissing vinegar," Jackie said. "What about the stones?"

"We'll keep excavating. We still need hard data."

"Least we got the time now."

World enough and time, Peter thought.

While they put away the tools, he walked over to the five stones standing like so many doorways. He put his hand to the one he had put up himself last night. He thought of Moonwatcher at the monolith in *2001: A Space Odyssey*—the pre-human creature who in a transcendent vision glimpsed a four-million-year future. This was the opposite kind of thing. Peter touched the stone, and he felt himself slip toward a resplendent past.

chapter
Thirty-one

The sky smoldered, but the storm would not come until tomorrow.

In the dwindling light, they set up a makeshift tent over the skeletal remains. By the time they were through, the rumbling in Peter's head had picked up momentum, and he smelled the fireless smoke. Also, that nasty irritability was back. And he knew he couldn't distance himself from it.

He wanted to remain on the site while Connie and Jackie returned to the cottage, but he decided he should get back to Andy. It wouldn't look good. He hoped Andy hadn't pulled any more zombie impressions because Sparky didn't seem to have what it took to snap his switch.

It was dark by the time they got back. Andy was listening to a tape on his headphones—Jackie's *Best of the Grateful Dead*. Sparky was on the couch with a beer, checking the ephemeris. A natal chart sat beside her. It was full of calculations. On the top she had written: "Andrew Peter Van Zandt, born January 6, 1992, 12:01 P.M."

"How's it look?" Peter asked.

"It's kind of hard to read," she said. "He was born on a cusp."

"A cusp?"

"The point where the moon begins to rise in a new house."

"Is that bad?"

"Not really a matter of good or bad," she said. "His Mars

squares Saturn, but his Venus and Pluto conjunct. I don't know
what to make of it. It can go either way."

"Could be said for all of us."

"Except he was born on Little Christmas," she said. "Astrolog-
ically, that makes him very special."

Special. Oh, yeah.

They told Andy about Jackie's discovery of the remains. He
wanted to know if it was the bones of the Indian Bride Witch. Peter
said it was everybody's guess. Everybody except for him.

Peter brought him upstairs and put him to bed.

"Dad, are we going home tomorrow?"

"Well, hon, there's been a change in plans. Looks like we'll be
staying a little bit longer."

"What?" His face began to crumple. "You promised. How
come?"

"Because of what we found."

"Because it's the witch's bones?"

"That's right. They can't make us go home now."

"But I want to go home."

"We can't until we finish excavating the stones. You know that.
You know how important it is for Daddy."

Andy dropped his head onto the pillow. "I hate those stones.
They're bad."

"How can stones be bad? Only people are bad." He tucked
the blanket around him.

Andy cried softly into the pillow.

"You'll feel better in the morning."

"No, I won't."

Here he goes again, thought Peter. He gave Andy a peck on
the back of his neck, then turned off the light. Just as Peter closed
the door behind him, he heard Andy grumble through his sobs,
"You're mean, Dad. You never want me to go home."

The words stopped Peter cold. For an instant Peter's heart
swelled with a sadness like grief. As if he had lost something. He
felt the pressure behind his eyes and wondered what deep chord
Andy's words had struck.

But the rumbling in his head clicked up a notch, and all at
once he didn't care. The old petulance bit at his temples.

Now, there's a fine howdyado? Bust your balls raising the kid, and he won't give you an inch when you need him the most. Not a fucking inch, and calls you mean to boot. Should bleed his mouth for talk like that, the little motherfucker.

The rumble got louder.

Yeah, the little MOTHERFUCKER.

You did this to her.

He pushed open the door.

The room was ablaze, and in the middle of it was Linda flailing against the flames with blackened stalks, her hair a crackling plume.

A second later the vision was gone.

"I hate you," Andy said.

"What did you say?"

"I hate you, Daddy. I don't like you anymore. You're mean."

Peter felt his body lurch, but the sounds of the others laughing downstairs stopped him. He took a deep breath and let it out slowly. He was trembling. "Someday, little man," he whispered, "I'll show you what mean really is."

Peter slammed the door shut. He waited a couple minutes to bring himself together. He could hear Andy sobbing into his pillow.

To Hell with him! he thought, and went back down.

The others were joking about something. They seemed to be enjoying a sense of renewal. That was okay. Peter smiled his big principal investigator smile.

"How long you think they'll give us?" Sparky asked.

"Could be indefinite," Peter said. And he explained how the state examiner had to come out to study the bones, then a physical anthropologist came to date the site. When, after another couple weeks, the dating labs confirmed it to be historical, the construction would be further postponed until they finished excavating. "Furthermore," Peter said, "once we document Brigid Mocnessa's Indian blood, Pulpit's Point could qualify as an Aboriginal Burial site. And they're sometimes protected forever."

In a side thought, Peter wished he could be there when Merritt told Hatcher that an injunction had been slapped on his Kingdom Royale—just to see those million-dollar sapphires pop.

Such sweet irony: flogging E. Fane Hatcher with Dan Merritt. There might be a God after all, he thought.

"That's fabulous," Connie said. She got up and poured herself another glass of wine. She had changed into snug white shorts. Peter took in the taper of her legs and roundness of her ass—like twin peach halves. "The relief you must feel."

"I do," Peter said. I feel lots of things, he thought. Almost more than I can contain.

"Now we can excavate the place right," Sparky said. "I can't wait to see them. Are we going to remove them?"

"No, just expose them *in situ.*" He looked at Connie and tore off her clothes in his head.

"It'll be nice to have that awful pressure off us," she said.

Peter nodded, and shoved himself into her up to the hilt.

Connie took her wineglass and settled into a chair with a paperback. Jackie and Sparky were back in their books, too.

During the next hour, Peter pretended to be absorbed in some technical journals while they read.

But his mind was a festering hotbed. He didn't completely understand what was going on, but he loved the heat of decay.

Finally, Jackie announced he was tired and was heading up to bed. Sparky and Connie fell in after him, and Peter put the lights out and followed them up, right behind Connie.

Before she slipped into her room, Connie turned to Peter. "Maybe on our break we can go into Boston."

He smiled. "Sure. That would be fun."

And under him her mouth gaped as he rammed himself into her.

"Let's do Boston." He grinned, and shot a stream of lava through her. "Good night, Connie."

She paused. "Good night." A flicker of uncertainty.

But he stepped into the dark before it took hold.

For nearly an hour, he lay on his bed and watched the Connie tape play in his head on a continuous loop. Yes, it would be fun.

He stared at the moonlight filtering through the curtains. Tomorrow it would be in full blaze. So would he.

Andy did not stir when Peter got up.

There was no need for Peter to change. He had never taken off his clothes.

He opened the door. The place was in a deep sleep.

Softly he crept by Connie's door, stopped for a moment, then decided to put that aside for a rainy day. There were more pressing issues.

He padded down the stairs, across the foyer, and out onto the porch.

The sky had cleared, and the moon silhouetted the tops of the oaks, leaving the porch in thick shadow. But the wooden rail of the staircase at the cliff edge was polished with silver in the moonlight.

He sat there for several minutes, drinking a beer and taking in the night. That cigarette craving was back. He could almost taste the smoke. He finished the beer and got up to go.

"Where are you going?"

Adrenaline burst in his chest. Somebody was standing on the far side of the porch, under the tangle of wisteria.

"Who's there?"

A black figure stepped out. "I know what you're up to."

Hannah.

"What the hell you doing here?"

"You're going up there again."

"I don't know what you're talking about."

"You're gonna raise the rest of the stones." She moved closer.

There was just enough light to make out those eyes. Her head was turned almost to the side so that she could regard him with both eyes. It was like addressing a flounder.

"What business is that of yours?"

"Listen to me good, Mister Archaeologist," she said. "Those stones are bringing her back so powerful, she's gonna make you do things you'll regret."

"I don't know what you're talking about." The rumbling in his head threatened to split his brainpan.

"You know what I'm talking about," Hannah said. "That ain't your dead wife up there. That's Brigid Mocnessa. She's taking over your head."

"No one's taking over my head."

"Maybe you don't even know."

"Maybe I do."

"I told you about the stones because I thought you could stop them from killing the island. But I was wrong. I shouldn't have because the power up there is bad. It's tried to get your boy on the machine, you told me yourself. It tried today. I saw what happened. I'm telling you it's Brigid what's doing it. She knew that power, she used it, she died with it, and it brought her back. They called her the handmaiden of Satan. She's the fire up there, she's the voice in your head, and it comes from them stones. They're dangerous, I'm telling you. They're angry."

"I don't know what you're talking about."

"Sure you do," she snapped. "You gotta tear them down."

"Tear them down? Are you out of your mind?"

She stepped so close to him he could smell her. "Listen to me good, Mister. She wants her cup of vengeance. She wants innocent blood. It's your son she's after because they killed her own. Take him home before she gets him."

For a numbed moment Peter just looked at the woman. "I'll think about it."

"You don't have time to think about it."

"We'll leave when we're ready."

"Then you'll never leave," she hissed. "Never." Before she pushed by him, she shoved something into his hands. "You wanted it." Lydia's diary.

She crossed the lawn to the stairs. Peter followed her. He watched her wade out to her boat. In a couple minutes it puttered off, a dim yellow light disappearing in the distance toward the mainland. He looked at the ledger. He vaguely recalled wanting it, but couldn't remember why.

He looked back out across the water. Hatcher was right. The cockeyed old coot couldn't be trusted.

By the time he got back to the house, the rumbling had leveled off to gentle background music. He slipped the diary onto a shelf in the living room. Maybe he'd look at it tomorrow if there was time. Maybe not. Right now he had nightwork.

He went down the stairs to the dock and hopped aboard the boat. He flicked on the radio phone and made a call to the office of the state archaeologist. He left a voice mail message for Dan

Merritt that they had found human remains which should qualify under Chapter 7, Section 38A. Short and sweet. Tomorrow was a holiday, but he'd be out bright and early the next day. A couple days later the state examiner would show to make sure it wasn't a recent homicide. Then the physical anthropologist would come to take back samples for the dating labs. It was all such tedious red tape, just the kind of bullshit Merritt thrived on.

Then he thought of something wonderful and made one other call.

When he was through, he marched down the beach toward the Point, thinking how fed up he was getting with having to answer to everybody else.

You are the damn PI on this dig, no? The Principal-fucking-Investigator? I mean, could you picture Herman Schliemann having to clear things with his assistants or his six-year-old son or the resident crazy? Cut the crap, man: There's only one engineer on this train and he doesn't make conference calls.

It was a little after midnight when he reached the top, and the rumbling in his head had ceased. For several tranquil minutes he walked inside the half-circle of stones. Between them glowed the distant skyscrapers. Two stone worlds across a black expanse. As he took them in, Peter—the old Peter—could sense their ancient magic emerging. Not the magic of witches and oak-leafed gods, but a quiet magic of space and stone, gaps and substance, windows and doors. A magic that teased the imagination—what the bright stone world across the water was missing. A magic asleep in stone.

Suddenly he felt a wincing rumble of that other magic.

Peter, I'm getting stronger.

The words were not real words, just sound shadows in his head. But he could feel her heat. He turned, and a thin warble squeezed out of his throat.

At the center of the arc just above the burial shaft a column of amber light shimmered violently. The heat was so intense that Peter stumbled backward, his eyes watering. At first, the liquid roiling denied definition; but then the core appeared to coalesce into a vaguely human form—naked. Her head was not full with hair, but round, smooth as if pulled back. The shoulders were slender, the arms extended, and the legs long and parted slightly. He tried to find something to distinguish her. The same small frame. He tried to make out the cesarean scar, but that was impossible. The image kept shifting, holding no lines or substance long enough for the eye. It radiated with blue light against an amber aura. She was the hottest part of the flame.

"Linda?"

Yes, Peter.

His eyes strained to compose her face. "Linda, let me see you."

You must raise all the stones to make me stronger.

The same voice—in his head, like the smoke. The same roughness. His body trembled. "Will I see you then?"

I will come back to you.

"Linda, I'm half dead without you."

I shall come back to you, Peter. Forever.

The words, like a benediction, filled his soul.

"I'll raise them for you. I promise. Nobody's going to stop me."

Eight stones lay in the dirt. He couldn't do them alone, he needed the men. Tomorrow. Yes. He'd get them to put them up.

"Tomorrow, Linda," he said. "And you'll come back to me. You promise?"

Yes, yes, I'll come back to you. Tomorrow.

Peter slipped to his knees, his eyes streaming with tears, the flamed figure shifting through impossible shapes and hues. He wiped his eyes to hold her image, but it was impossible. She was in constant shimmer, an apparition of liquid light slipping out of definition a moment before he had it. "Linda," he whispered, "come back to me. Make it all good again."

All good again.

"I hate my life without you. I need you. We need you."

Andy. Bring him to me.

The words jabbed his mind. "No, not that."

I want him. . . .

He winced from the pain. "But he's all I have."

You want your Linda again. . . .

"Don't make me choose."

Bring him to me.

"But, Linda, how . . . how . . . do . . . I . . . know . . . it's . . . you?"

The shaft flared so intensely that the heat waves nearly blinded him.

You know who I am.

The roar made him cry out.

"But . . . but I have to be sure. Andy is all I have left."

Bring him to me.

He felt he would faint if it didn't cease.

"Linda . . . Andy's middle name. Tell me."

ISAAC.

The syllables sizzled in his head like fat.

For a long time he lay on the ground hearing nothing but the grating of his own breath. When he opened his eyes again, there was only black. He was all alone in the dark midst the stones and the gaping holes.

He rolled onto his back, blinking the water out of his eyes. His face felt sunburned. All those stars. As his vision came clear, he half-consciously connected the fire points of Scorpio's tail.

His head ached, but he would survive.

After several more minutes, he pulled himself up. His legs felt wobbly, like a newborn colt's. But he managed to stumble down the slopes to the beach. He was soaked with perspiration and covered with dirt.

He took off his clothes and plunged into the midnight surf. A chill shot through him.

In the eastern sky, a white crystal moon rose up. Tomorrow it would be full round.

Isaac. Such a nice biblical name.

He'd almost forgotten.

chapter
Thirty-two

One day over coffee some years ago, a colleague from the Sam Adams English Department presented one of those foolish conundrums to Peter. They were sitting in the faculty cafeteria, complaining about their salaries, when out of the blue the man asked Peter what he would do if his wife and son were drowning and he were in a lifeboat and could save only one of them. Whom would he save—his wife or his son?

Peter remembered dismissing the question since it had nothing to do with real-world options. And what did it prove? It was also emblematic of the dumb academic propensity for transforming horrendous circumstances to facile abstractions. So he balked at the problem, saying he refused to commit himself. His colleague kept pressing him for a choice, insisting that it was the kind of decision everyone should be prepared to make. Peter responded that such a decision was impossible to make beforehand, and he would not dignify the question with an answer. All he conceded was that he would try to save both, and probably die in the process. Unsatisfied, the English professor insisted that the conditions of the dilemma precluded saving both. Only one could be saved, and he had to choose. Peter gave him a flat *no*. The guy finally gave up. But before he left, he said that nearly every man he'd polled chose his wife, while the women chose their child.

"Now there's a useful statistic," Peter said as he left. And he thought that either the respondents were as stupid as the guy who conducts such polls, or they answered just to shut him up.

Peter crunched his way along the beach toward the cottage thinking about that conundrum. Thinking about how he was now in that lifeboat. Your wife and your child are sinking fast, and you got one shot to save one. Who you gonna love?

The chill was gone by the time he reached the beach stairs. He climbed to the top, thinking about all those other men who had made the same choice.

Yes, he'd vote the party line.

The cottage was an amber glow from the small light in the living room. It should have been black. When he'd left, all the lights were out. He didn't like that. He liked the dark.

He went inside. Nobody was waiting for him. The place was as he had left it, except for the small light. On the table by the window sat his Randall knife in its leather sheath. He slipped it on his belt and pulled it out of the case. The blade lit up like a tongue of flame. Polished molybdenum steel. "Keen and esoteric, like you, Big Daddy."

He handled it as if for the first time. He felt the heft of the handle, the ridges of the staghorn. Etched on the small gold escutcheon were PVZ. For an instant he was not sure what those letters stood for. He turned off the light.

The stairs creaked as he climbed them.

He felt his way down the hall past where the Kellehers slept (Jackie snoring like a bear), past Connie's room ("That would be fun.") to his door. The sweat slicked the handle of his knife. He took a deep breath and slowly he turned the handle. A slender metal squeal cut the air. He froze, waiting to hear if anyone stirred. Nothing. No movement, no turning over, no nervous voices. Just sweet dead silence. He eased open the door. The moon, now high, cast a pale light through the front window. He closed the door gently behind him. The latch clicked into place. With his back pressed against the door, he waited for the room to settle with his presence. His breathing was hard, and his heart filled his throat. He counted a full hundred beats. Then he stepped toward the dark shape along the inner wall—the two cots pressed side by side, his nice and flat, the other humped with the form of his sleeping son. He took three steps when a shuddering realization stopped him dead. Andy was not in the room. Neither was his cot.

He flicked on the lamp. His own cot sat alone against the wall. And on his pillow was a handwritten note.

Peter—
Andy was having nightmares, so I let him sleep with me. Hope you don't mind. We'll see you in the morning. Sleep well.

Connie

Son of a bitch! That bloody woman. Why doesn't she get her fucking nose out of my affairs?

Peter took a vicious swipe with the knife across the air. *You bitch.* Then he stabbed again and again. Against the wall of her room he saw the shadow of the blade cut down on his outline.

That woman, he thought, was destroying everything he'd worked for. Everything he'd ever dreamed of. And she'd been doing it all along, standing in the way—file a report! Don't use the back-hoe! You can't raise the stones! Now she's working on my son, taking him over, trying to turn him against me like she did Jackie and Sparky. Like she'd been turning Linda against him. I won't have it.

He could see them behind the wall, so snug and cozy side-by-side, Madonna and child. He pressed his eyes shut and hissed at the ceiling. With every atom of his being he fought the urge to kick open her door right now and pull him from her. He'd have to kill them all, including Jackie. And Connie still slept with an axe under her cot.

He stabbed the knife into his pillow. Tomorrow, he told himself. Just a few hours.

He slipped the knife into the case and flicked off the light.

He would need his sleep. Much business tomorrow. July Fourth business. Fireworks.

Peter slept a deep dreamless sleep until seven when Connie's knocking woke him. He changed into a black pullover and jeans and went through the motions of pleasantry.

Andy, in his red shorts and green Celtics shirt, sat next to Connie at breakfast like old buddies. She had him smiling. She had even gotten him to accept the fact that they would be staying a few more days on the island. Maybe her little midnight rescue would pay off after all—especially if it put a cap on his whining.

Sparky and Jackie got up to make the lunches and Peter seized the moment for his announcement. "No need for that," he said, "I'm giving you the day off."

"You are?" Jackie said.

"Hell's bells, you've been killing yourselves for ten days without a break." His voice was easy and natural. "Every Earthwatch expedition is supposed to give its people two days off, and you're long overdue. Besides, folks, it's the Fourth of July."

"Are the men working?"

"Yes, holiday wages. So we won't be lonely." He sipped his coffee. "And look at that sky. It'll be a mess up there." He took a bite of toast. "Besides, we're no longer playing Beat-the-Clock."

"Sounds good to me," Jackie said. He looked to Sparky.

"Me, too," she said. "I brought a stack of paperbacks I haven't even touched yet."

"And I've got comps in six months and haven't cracked a book."

Connie didn't say anything. She just watched Peter and drank her coffee.

"Well," began Peter, "what I had in mind was more of a getaway, kind of an R-and-R. Take the boat to Boston, kick around town, see the sights, whoop it up. And sleep in a real bed. I made reservations for the three of you at the Marriott on the waterfront—and harborside rooms so you can watch the fireworks from your balcony. How's that?" He pulled out the keys to his car and slid them toward Jackie. "And it's on me."

"Hey, man, you're all right," Jackie said.

Sparky said she'd stock up on groceries while in town.

"Consider it a wedding gift," Peter said. And to Connie, "One you can share."

"But what about you guys?" Connie asked.

"Well, Andy and I are going to catch up on just being father and son." He winked at Andy.

The boy looked at him without expression.

"I radioed Merritt about the bones. He can't do anything to-day, he's got it off. He should be out tomorrow or the next day, though. It'll take another day or two for the forensic people to come. So we can't do anything anyway. And who wants to dig in the rain?"

"I'm game," Jackie said.

"And we've never seen Boston," Sparky said.

"Have a ball," Peter said. He poured some coffee and took a sip. "In the summer, Boston's at her best."

Connie studied him.

"Can I go, too," Andy asked.

"Not this time, hon," Peter said. "We're going to lay low to-day. But we'll have a good time, too. Okay, Pooch?"

"But, Dad—"

"No 'But, Dad,' Andy," Peter said. He gave the boy a firm stare. "Why don't you do some coloring?"

Andy's shoulders slumped. He got up from the table. Peter watched as he took the chair by the window where his markers and "Jack and the Beanstalk" coloring book sat.

Peter turned to Connie. "I know how you wanted to see the town." He smiled warmly. "The North End's always fun. You can drop in at Old North Church, and Quincy Market is just across the expressway. You can spend the whole day there; and if the rain holds off, there's the parade around the Common."

She nodded, but she did not look enthusiastic. While Sparky and Jackie went upstairs to pack, she sat in silence, slowly sipping her coffee and looking at Peter across the table. On the far side of the room, Andy was lost in his coloring. After several minutes Con-nie said, "Peter, why do I have the feeling you're trying to get rid of us?"

He shrugged. "You tell me." Then he said, "I think we all need a break from the dirt, from the routine—"

"From us," she said.

Peter took a deep breath. "Connie, we've been locked up with each other for ten days. Ten trying days. We all need some breath-ing room to refresh."

"Uh-huh." She didn't seem convinced. But she got up and

headed for the stairs. She glanced at Andy. His eyes wide, he sat scribbling away with his markers. "You'll be all right while we're gone?"

Peter turned on a sweet smile. "We'll be just fine."

She nodded.

"It'll be good for all of us. And the pressure will be off when you come back."

And what, he asked himself, do you tell them when they return and find Andy missing? He got homesick and swam back to Carleton? Amos and Boris took him for a ride to the Ivory Coast? He went to see his mom? No, while they were gone, you got Jimmy P. to let you use their radio, arranged for a neighbor to pick up Andy from the water-taxi stop. He's gone to stay with his aunt in New York until you're through out here. That'll do it.

He watched Connie go upstairs.

Peter finished his coffee and got up. He took a wide stretch and walked over to Andy.

"And how you doing, little man?"

Andy didn't answer.

Peter noticed the coloring book. It was one of the back pages, the one showing Jack racing to get back home with the giant pounding after him.

"Nice job," Peter said.

But he failed to register how the giant was colored in black and blue, and Jack in red and green. Like Peter and Andy.

Thirty-three

"Shouldn't take you more than half an hour in this water," Peter said. "Just aim for Winthrop. My car's at the marina."

The sky was a heavy underbelly of dark clouds, and the sea a sheet of iron.

"I don't think you'll see rain for a while."

Jackie pulled the boat away from the dock. "See you tomorrow. Probably around noon. Gonna sleep late for once."

"You do that."

Jackie maneuvered the boat around. Peter made a happy face. "Have a nice day!" Then he looked up to the top of the stairs. "Hey, Andy," he shouted. "Say good-bye."

The boy looked down at the boat pulling into the harbor. He made a weak wave and turned back to the cottage.

Peter shrugged. "Needs a good night sleep."

They waved. Jackie was at the wheel, Sparky beside him and Connie, stiff in her yellow slicker, sat at the stern looking back. She nodded, but didn't wave.

For a few minutes Peter watched the boat pull into the dark water, all the while singing quietly to himself, " 'Saturday in the park, you'd think it was the Fourth of July. . . . And I've been waiting such a long time for today. . . .' "

"The others were a piece of cake going in," Jimmy P. said. "Practically stood up by themselves, hah?"

"Amazing." Peter grinned. "Then you'll have no trouble putting up the other seven."

"No sweat," Jimmy said. "We'll get 'em up before the rain comes."

"Good."

"We're gonna need you to show us how you want them."

"We'll be here all day."

"The others gone home?"

"Just taking the day off."

"Uh-huh. I see you found a body up there."

"Just some bones."

"Some kind of cemetery, or something?"

"Possibly." Peter checked his watch. If the crane could get up there by ten, and a man on the backhoe, the stones could be up by mid-afternoon. Just as long as the rain held off. The sky looked bad. How was that when everything was going so well?

"Probably why the place gives me the creeps."

Peter nodded. Jimmy was beginning to get on Peter's nerves with all the creepy-peepy crap. He didn't have a clue to what was up here.

"If those bones are old, lotta people gonna hit the ceiling."

"Well, they're probably recent."

"Looked old to me."

Jimmy looked over at Andy staring off over the water. "How's the slugger today?"

"He's just fine, thank you. Don't let me keep you, Jimmy."

Jimmy nodded and left.

A little after ten, three of his men showed up with a high crane.

Andy, in a folding chair, colored in his book, while Peter directed the workers. The backhoe claw dug out the remaining seven sockets, leaving small piles of dirt and foothold rocks. When the sockets were all dug, they removed the hoe claw and attached an assembly with a two-foot-long steel spike: a hoe-ram, used for smashing concrete. This the men used to shape and pack the walls of the sockets with the field stones. Only in a fleeting thought did it occur to Peter how much data was being lost to the machines. But he didn't need data anymore. The project was beyond data. Beyond archaeology.

They worked through the afternoon and the stones went up one by one. And while the place shook under the growls of the backhoe and crane, Andy sat sullenly in his folding chair, working on his coloring book; and when that was done, he went down to the beach to fly his kite. Then a short while later he came back up to his chair, where he just watched the men raise the stones and his father clear the rest of the skeletal remains with a brush and his knife.

When the men and machines were gone, thirteen granite megaliths stood in an even circle like a crown rising out of the crest of Pulpit's Point.

Peter walked around and around the circle. Thirteen stones and gaps. An endless circle of open doors to draw you in. It was small and crude by comparison to other monuments, but it had the topography of myth. He thought how this was the first time in three centuries the megaliths had pierced the sky. He wondered how many more they had stood since that weary clan of voyagers first raised them against forces they could neither understand nor control.

He crossed to the center to the limestone pillar which rose out of the dirt like a bone. He recalled the rust-red engraving of the Druid priestess and the sacrificial child. Through one portal he spied Andy gazing at him like a ram in the thicket.

Boston sat in the distance under a sky the same color as the granites. The rain had not come. Yet, distant thunder rumbled. The nightwork would be in rain. Keep things clean.

They waved at Jimmy and his men as the utility boat left for Boston. Then Peter took Andy by the hand back to the cottage. He prepared a supper for the both of them. Andy's favorites: spaghetti and lamb chops, with the last of the bread from the freezer. Peter set the table with candles. He had a glass of wine with his meal. He let Andy take a sip. He said it tasted bitter. But that was okay.

They ate quietly. Andy wasn't hungry. He barely touched his food, just a little crust. That was okay, too.

After dinner, Andy wandered upstairs, and Peter washed the

dishes, humming the Chicago song to himself and thinking about what lay ahead. Things were good.

But sometime around eight-thirty, he heard the sound of an engine. At first, he thought it was coming from inside his head. There was a lot of that of late.

But this was different.

He ran outside. A light rain fell. He went to the cliff, his heart pounding against the awful expectation of a boat pulling up. But no boat.

Yet he could still hear the muffled sound through the rain. But where?

The sound was familiar, but not like one of the construction machines.

He shot back into the house and up the stairs. Andy was in deep sleep on his cot. The coloring book was opened on the floor. The last page—a sketch of Jack and his mother hand in hand heading for their cottage. Not a spot of color on it. He'd left it blank.

Peter closed the door quietly.

His knife on his hip, he ran down the stairs to the beach.

The rolling roar in his head was indistinguishable from the thunder. He raced down the sand, the rain lashing his eyes.

With each step, the rumbling seemed to click up a decibel. But the sound of that engine was gone.

He was soaked to the skin by the time he reached the end of the beach. He cut up over the dunes to the flats where backhoes and trucks sat like supplicants at the base of Pulpit's Point.

It was there he saw the small black helicopter.

He tore up the slope. Why hadn't he thought of it? Where in hell was his mind? Of course!

When he got to the top he let out a shout that whipped around the stones like a whirlwind.

They were in the middle of the circle. Three of them.

Hatcher stood on the limestone pillar under an umbrella, watching Goringer hold open a large garbage bag while Flanagan shoveled in the exposed charred bones.

"That's my wife!" screamed Peter. "What are you doing?"

"Party's over, asshole, and you're out." It was Flanagan.

"You can't do this."

"Tell it to the angels," Hatcher said.

Peter heard a sharp click. "But you don't know what you're doing," he said. "You don't understand."

"No, *you* don't," Hatcher said. "Your fucking bones could have cost us everything. Sorry, Professor."

But Peter's mind was too full of smoke to understand what he meant. "But that's my wife." He pulled his knife.

"The crazy fuck's gotta knife."

"Then we don't have to sweat our cover," Hatcher said. "Shoot the bastard."

Goringer raised the gun as Peter charged. A loud crack filled the bowl of stones, and Peter felt a punch to his left arm. Before the pain registered, he made a flying leap behind the nearest boulder. He splashed onto the mud, then rolled several times, the piles of dirt shielding him.

In the dim light he could not tell blood from the driving rain, but he knew the flesh under his shoulder was torn.

"Where the fuck he go?" Flanagan came around the first stone with the shovel raised to hack him.

Goringer shouted, "Go back. I'll take him."

Peter saw Hatcher take off down the slope. Out of sight below the chopper revved up. They'd left the pilot inside.

Peter slithered through the mud toward a far stone, a feral excitement quickening his moves. He raised his knife and waited. Against the leaden sky he saw Goringer come round the stone just five feet in front of him. His gun arm poked the air first, then his huge belly. But just as Goringer swung the gun toward him, Peter sprang up from the mud like a jack-in-the-box. Before Goringer could shoot, Peter brought the knife down full force with both hands nailing Goringer to the ground through his shoe.

His shrieks shattered the air, and his arms flailed wildly, the gun flying far out over the water. He plopped down in place, screaming and trying not to twist his foot against the blade. Wildly he groped to pull it out. But it was in up to the hilt.

Peter got up. Flanagan was already halfway down the hill behind Hatcher. He looked at Goringer. The man was yowling, his hands flapping at his foot like birds with broken wings. His foot spiked in place through the arch. He wasn't going anywhere.

The helicopter was at maximum rev. Through the sheets of rain, Peter could see the craft lights. They'd be off as soon as Flanagan got aboard, leaving Goringer here to finish the job, then pick him up later.

Peter raced across the circle to the backhoe. He turned the key, and the machine growled to life. With a push of the forward lever, he raised the bucket behind him. Then he swiveled his seat 180 degrees. The hoe arm was up already. He turned the machine around and raced down the slope.

While the machine rolled, Peter raised the hoe-ram spike straight out, the full twenty feet, like the horn of some great cryptozoic rhino.

Flanagan was just getting into the copter, when Hatcher leaned through the open door and shot at Peter.

The bullets ricocheted off the spike.

Peter flicked on the headlights and trounced on the accelerator.

Hatcher pulled Flanagan into the craft and then fired off three more shots. Peter was no more than thirty feet from them when the copter lifted off the ground.

For a brief moment the chopper freed itself of gravity. But Peter raised the spike and snagged the landing structure. In the lights the copter made a crazy curtsy in the air, screaming protest, but it was not enough for the backhoe. Peter yanked the hoist lever, and the chopper slammed down in place.

But he wasn't through. Before the pilot could lift the vehicle again, Peter backed up, pulled the spike free, then swung it into the whining blur of blades.

The impact created a burst of sparks and a brilliant staccato ringing that sent shrapnel in all directions. The copter flopped on its side with a thud, twisted stumps making a pathetic pinwheel in the air.

Before they could get out, Peter backed up, then drove the spike through the plastic windshield clear through the cockpit. Peter pulled back on the lever and, full throttle, he lifted the chopper off the ground.

Flanagan's body fell out the door. His head was gone.

Peter roared on up the slope with the copter raised in the air like a bug. Halfway up, he turned the wheel hard to the right—toward the drop-off. He could see Hatcher fighting to climb over the pilot to the door. There was a flurry of movement under the backhoe arm, when suddenly Hatcher leaped to the ground to the right. The pilot rolled out the other side. But Peter continued with the machine, racing toward the drop-off. It crossed his mind to go over with it, but at the last moment he jumped; and the backhoe with the skewered chopper stumbled over the edge to the rocks below.

In the crash, Peter could not hear the shots from Hatcher's gun. Nor would they have stopped him. He was running on pure adrenaline. Down the slopes he chased after Hatcher and across the dark flats toward the Poro trailer.

At about a hundred feet, Hatcher came to a sudden stop. He dropped to one knee, slipped a new clip into the gun, took position, and opened fire at Peter. But it was dark and the rain lashed so hard against him that he could not get Peter on target. And Peter was wild with fearlessness. He charged the man, leaping and turning impossible zigzags. He was burning with more power than he'd ever known.

No more than sixty feet from Hatcher, Peter let loose a hideous animal cry. Terrified, Hatcher stood up with the gun held in two hands. He shot wildly into the dark at the oncoming yowls. Bullets burst in flame from the barrel. But Peter flew through them untouched.

Hatcher slipped in a new clip and raised him in sight when Peter tackled him across the waist. They splashed down hard in the mud. In a lightning stroke, Peter chopped the pistol out of Hatcher's hand, then smashed him in the face with his elbow. Hatcher rolled to get up when Peter hit him on the right temple with both hands clenched. It was over in seconds. The impact knocked Hatcher out instantly. Or maybe it killed him. Peter didn't care which.

He had to get back up there. To his Linda. They had violated her.

He tore back across the mudflats to the base of the slope. Up he ran nearly stumbling over the headless corpse of Flanagan. The pilot had run off into the woods. Several times Peter fell in water cascading down the incline. But he leaped back up, thick with mud. He rounded the top. Goringer was still on the ground.

When he saw Peter blackened with mud he held up his hands. "Noooo. I beg you."

Peter felt like an animal.

"Where's Linda?"

"Who?" whimpered Goringer. "Nobody else up here. Please . . . I'm bleeding to death." His foot hadn't moved.

Peter looked around wildly. Suddenly he dropped to his knees and yanked out the knife.

Goringer let out a keening screech. Peter raised the knife to the bulb of flesh under Goringer's chin. "What they do with Linda?"

"N-n-n-no!" screamed the man.

"Tell me."

"I don't know any Linda."

Peter lay the blade against his throat. "You were digging up her grave."

"Oh . . . over there. He dropped the bag over there." A limp hand flopped toward the circle. "Don't kill me. please."

Peter slipped the knife into the sheath and ran to the center of the circle. The black bag was on the ground, its contents spilled in the puddles.

Peter dropped to his hands and knees. He felt in the mud for the scraps of bones. "What did they do?" He ran his fingers through the puddles, the mud, feeling for the fragile pieces of bone. They were all over the place, mixed with shells and rocks.

He gathered what he could find and made a small pile by the burial shaft, too consumed in his efforts to notice Goringer hobble away. In fact, he noticed little else in the world. For maybe an hour he clawed through the mud—fingering pieces of bone, gently removing them, washing them in the puddle, and placing them like gems in the pile. Even if it took all night, he would find the rest of her. Then she would come back, from the tibias and femurs and charred, shattered ribs. She would come back, just as she'd promised. All the while he dug and gathered her pieces, a thin animal warble squeezed out of his throat. But he never heard himself, or the whipping rain nor the wind howling across the stones like a lunatic calliope. All he was aware of was Linda naked beside him in the dark, promising impossible, wonderful things. That and the bass note rumbling in his head.

His fingers worked the mud like tiny animals.

The cruelest thing in the universe is the death of a young mother.

His fingers shredded themselves against rocks and the shells.

If there's a way back, I promise I'll find it. I could never leave you.

And the smoky rumbling grew deeper.

Never leave you.

Suddenly his fingers felt it. The smooth unmistakable contours: Linda's forehead. He felt the soft hair, still wet from the shower. She always showered before they made love. His fingers worked furiously to clear the back of her head. It was still so warm. He could feel her temples and cheek bone and chin. Eagerly he cupped her face, his tears mixing with the rain. Then ever so gently he lifted her head from the pillow.

"My Linda," he said. And he kissed her face again and again and again. "You've come back."

"Peter."

"It's okay. I've got you now."

He lifted his head. The bright figure emerged from a stone.

The figure slowly approached him. "Peter, what are you doing?"

It was Connie.

chapter
Thirty-four

Peter clutched the skull to his chest. "Connie, I found Linda."

Connie froze.

"Nothing to be afraid of."

"Peter, I think we better go back."

"Back where?"

"To the cottage." She stepped closer and held out her hand. "Peter, please."

"No." He pressed the skull to his chest. "They tried to take her."

"Peter, Linda is dead."

She doesn't understand the power of great love, Peter.

"Not anymore," he said. "There's a great power in these stones, Connie, and she brought me to them so I could raise them and bring her back."

"Peter, that's not Linda. That's Brigid Mocnessa."

"No, Connie, it's not. I was confused, but I know better now."

"Okay, but please come and we'll talk about it back at the cottage."

"But she wants to see Andy, or she won't come."

"He's at the cottage, and Dan Merritt's with us."

"Dan Merritt?"

"Yes, we called him at home and told him about the bones. He came out because he wants to help. If they're authentic, Hatcher might try to remove them to prevent a work stoppage."

"He won't be removing anything," he said. "Or Flanagan. They're dead."

Connie recoiled. Peter raised his face to her, the skull in his hands like a black egg. "I have to get Andy," he whispered, "or she'll be mad."

Connie started moving away.

"We'll walk back together." He started to get up, but Connie backed out of the circle. "Where you going?"

Suddenly she turned and ran for the slope.

"Connie?"

But she had disappeared into the black.

"What are you doing?" he shouted. "Don't take him." He stumbled out of the circle after her. "CONNIE . . . STOP! SHE'S HIS MOTHER!"

He stumbled down the slope and across the dunes. He could see the yellow slicker in the lightning flares. She was down the beach, racing toward the cottage.

Several times he tripped over seaweed, nearly dropping the skull. But he got up again and pounded down the beach, the skull tucked in the crook of his arm.

Over Boston the sky had cleared and the full face of the moon burned through the storm clouds.

As he reached the cove, he saw their boat bobbing at the dock. And it suddenly hit him. They had come back. And like Hatcher they were going to try to stop him. But they didn't know what they were dealing with. This was holy war.

He ran onto the dock. With a swipe of the knife blade, he severed the fuel line. Gasoline emptied all over the boat. In the small compartment on the dash, he found a butane lighter. He slashed the boat free of the ropes, then set it ablaze, pushing it out into the water to burn. Halfway into the cove, the fuel tank exploded.

Up the steps he bounded, the skull in his left hand, the knife in his right. Across the lawn and up the three steps in one leap. He kicked down the door. The living room was empty. He bolted to the kitchen, and in a subliminal flash, he saw Andy standing in the middle of the floor, smiling at him, a clean bloodless slash across his throat. "I go see Mommy, Daddy."

In a blink it was gone. On the counter he noticed Lambkin, its seams like swollen sutures. He vaguely remembered it.

Peter shot upstairs. The place was empty. The bastards. Even Andy's backpack was gone. But they could not get far unless they planned to swim.

He leaped down the stairs and onto the porch. Where'd they go? They could hide anywhere. The woods behind the house were shallow, and on the other side were truck trails and flats that stretched almost to the other coast. Too much exposure. Too much construction stuff and blind pits in the interior. The other way were the woods and the swamps. They were too smart to risk those places with a kid.

Then something clicked in his head. Like a sign from heaven. They could run, but they couldn't hide.

He ran into the house to get something. Then he was back down on the beach, racing at full speed. The moon white-washed the sand. With huge gazelle leaps he cleared the bundles of sea-rot. He had never felt so powerful, not even in dreams—as if any second he might leap into a shallow orbit.

He came to the end of the beach. He was slicked with sweat, but not the least winded.

Up to the right the stones hunched against the stars. The hard-faced moon floated above them. Silver-laced clouds rolled back over the sea like a canopy retracting. Stars, so many stars, he thought. A dreamy stillness had settled on the place. But he had no time for that now. The nightwork had just begun.

Instead of cutting back up the dunes, he headed for the shore rocks at the base of the Point. It would not be easy going with the slimed rocks and tidal pools. Could slip, crack an ankle, or break a leg. He would have to take it slowly.

But for some reason, the footing was easy. He didn't even have to look; his feet seemed to find the right holds. Like his hands on those levers. He was running on autopilot again. From one rock to the next he flitted like a ballet star, the skull in one hand, the knife counterbalanced in the other.

Around the base he came, up to the high rocks and onto the small landing.

Then he stopped, crouching in the dark for cover.

There they were, just as he'd guessed. Jackie and Sparky ducked in first, then Merritt. Then Connie pushed Andy ahead of her. They were going to hole up in the tunnels until morning when the workers returned.

They're bad people, a smoky voice whispered. *They're trying to turn you against me, Peter. Trying to break the family circle.*

Peter wiped the blade on his pants. Well, they weren't going to get away with it.

Up to the rise he climbed, to the access road and into the mouth of the tunnel. Instantly the temperature dropped. But Peter barely noticed. He slipped the knife in its case and pulled Andy's Laz-R-Lite from his rear pocket. The batteries were low, but it threw a dim light. He had told Andy not to waste them, not to leave it on all the time. He never, never listened! But it didn't matter. A road map of the place lit up in dull green in his head. Like seeing in the dark.

He padded his way down the main tunnel toward the muffled voices. He could hear Andy's high little pitch. He was probably asking them what Peter was up to, if he had to work late tonight. Daddy's little boy.

He scraped along the walls. They were slick with a mucinous slime. It was like slithering through the innards of a huge animal. A monstrous birth canal.

He came to a turn in the walls. He flicked on the flash. High on the walls just below the ceiling vault he spotted deeply drilled recesses. For a moment he didn't know what to make of them. They had been evenly spaced every several feet. Dozens of them, as far as he could see into the black. Then it dawned on him. It was where the charges had been set for leveling Pulpit's Point. It was all ready to be blown tomorrow.

The thought produced a ripple of urgency in him. He had to reach them.

In the dim light he passed side chambers containing many barrels of fuel. The odor of gasoline was nauseating. They were to be removed in the morning, stored elsewhere so the place could be razed. But Linda had changed all that.

He reached the junction where the tunnel forked. He could hear voices, but they were too faint to get a bead on. And the rumbling in his head disoriented him. He began to shake with frustration. He had reached a cusp—*could go either way,* he had heard Sparky say. Christ! which way? He had to get to them. He had to get Andy up on Pulpit's Point before she got angry and did something. He was about to turn right on sheer intuition, when he heard it.

This way.

He let out a whine of joy. "Yes," he said giving the skull a hug and shot down the left-hand tube.

He trailed after the voices he now heard, moving smoothly through the passages, making quick turns around corners with radar keenness. The voices grew louder. The tunnel suddenly narrowed so that the ceiling was just a couple inches above his head. He passed a row of small prisoner cells, remembering how, the first time, they had horrified him. He turned off the light, and ran on his own.

Garbled voices ahead, then, suddenly there was a loud crash of metal on metal. He felt a shock of adrenaline. "Stop!" he screamed.

"It's my Dad."

"Andy, don't let them take you. Andy." His voice rumbled down the tunnels. "Come to me now!"

A door slammed shut.

"Andy!"

Then he heard something else.

Above him. All around his head. The air was alive with movement. And a kind of high-speed ticking sound, almost electronic. Then something like muffled fluttering.

Bats.

He was in a swarm of hundreds of them startled into a frenzy by the sound of his voice. He growled with rage and flicked on the light. A cloud of flapping black bodies swirled around him like leaves in a wind tunnel. Peter pulled his shirt up over his head and held his light on the ground.

The creatures had impeccable sonar, but their sheer number were forcing them into him. He slid along the walls, keeping his head low. He tried to hold the flash up, hoping the light would act as a deflector. But they fluttered into it like moths. He thought about making a run for it. The others were minutes ahead of him; they could be out of the tunnels by now. But the air was a thick frenzy of bats.

Suddenly one flapped through the torn neck of his shirt. It slipped inside, fluttering against his stomach. He let out a yell. Sharp claws and wings flittered across his skin. It spilled down his side and crawled around his back. He could see his shirt flapping. He wanted to smash it through the shirt or press it against the wall—anything before it took a rabid bite out of him. But the thought of mashing it against his flesh was revolting. He tore his shirt out of his pants. The thing was caught by its wing hooks. He couldn't reach it, but he felt it crawling against his spinal column. In a violent flash, he pulled off his shirt and squashed the creature under his foot.

Half-naked he felt phantom wings flitting across his skin. He crouched to the floor with the skull and torch. Like stroboscopic visions from Hell, tiny rat faces with jabbering pink mouths flicked in his face. He was caught in a rapid of them. He dropped flat to the ground, pressed into a pool of evil-smelling water, his face half-dipped into the stuff. An acrid stench stung his nostrils. A soup of bat guano. His stomach began to spasm and he felt his supper rise. He fought to keep it down, but it was impossible. In a gagging fit, he raised his head and vomited.

And the bats kept coming.

For what seemed an hour, he lay there pressed into his own vomit. When the air cleared, he got up and shuffled to the end of the tunnel. He was at the same far chamber where Hannah had disappeared days ago. Gently he laid down the skull, pulled out the knife, and opened the door.

He jammed the flash inside. Empty. Four blank stone walls. The light was a dim orange, but he painted every inch of the place. Solid walls of heavy stones. Concrete ceiling. Concrete floor. Everything covered with that fungoid muck. How could they just disappear? He was ready to scream. The rumbling in his head would split open his skull any second. Linda was coming alive just fifty feet above him. And she demanded Andy. He growled at the walls.

Then he spotted their secret.

It was just to his left, on the floor at the rear of the cell. One of the large rectangular wall stones. It looked like all the rest, except that it was not flush with the others. It was depressed, by just an inch. And the black muck of its face was smeared.

Peter dropped to his knees and held the light to it. Footprints. The treads from Jackie's work boots. And the mud on the floor in front of it was fresh.

Peter rolled onto his back in the mud, put his feet against the stone, then pushed.

He felt a slight give. That was it! He hummed with joy. Then he took another breath and pushed again. The block might have weighed three hundred pounds, but it sat on mud and slid all the way as if greased.

He rolled onto his belly and slithered halfway through the opening, flashlight first.

His light stunned them: five faces in an alabaster frieze.

"Knock, knock: You're dead!"

chapter
Thirty-five

"Oh, my God!" cried Connie.

Peter crawled through and stood in a crouch. He was half naked and covered with blood and vomit and foul mud. His face was a black mask, his hair matted spikes on his brow, his arm gashed and streaming blood. His eyes darted at them like an animal's. And in the crook of his arm, a charred skull and a red plastic light; in the other, a long flickering blade. He grinned at them. "Cozy."

Sparky was pressed against Jackie, Merritt behind her. In the rear with her face full of horror, Connie was pulling Andy into the shadows.

"Daddy."

Peter didn't say anything. He just grinned while assessing them. They had no weapons, nothing to attack with. Just two flashlights.

"Come on, put the knife down, man," Jackie said. "Everything's cool."

He held his hands out to show they were empty except for the flashlight. His arms were big. But the knife was a razor.

Sparky's eyes were wide. Her nostril stud blinked foolishly. "Peter, there's nothing to be afraid of," she said.

He said nothing. Connie was fading into the black with Andy.

Stop her!

But the others were blocking him. He aimed the torch down

the tunnel. Someplace far in the thick black he could see another figure with a lantern. Hannah.

"Peter, we have a lot to tell you," Jackie said.

"That's right," Merritt said. "Everything you said about the stones was true. Look over here."

Don't let them fool you, Peter.

It was only then that he became aware of his surroundings. They were in a low cylindrical tunnel, maybe six feet in diameter, lined with brick, slimed black and dripping. A shallow trough of stagnant water ran down the length as far as his light would reach. The place smelled of decayed marine matter, and the air seemed void of oxygen. It was like breathing sewage.

"Andy, come to Daddy," he said.

"But, Daddy . . ."

"No 'but, Daddy.' Now! They want to hurt you."

"Peter, wait," Merritt said. "I'm sorry I questioned your judgment. I didn't know. It just sounded impossible, but you were absolutely right. It's the real thing: a Celtic stone circle."

Merritt put his hand out, but Peter hissed and slashed the air with the knife.

"Let us show you," Sparky pleaded. "Please, Peter. Please."

"Yeah, man," Jackie said. "It's unbelievable. Over here." Slowly he and Sparky backed up with Merritt while Peter fanned the air with the blade, waiting for the first false move. They backed past a passage, a large square opening to a side chamber, making enough room for Peter to inspect it. Jackie held his flashlight on the inside.

Peter waited, studying them. Their faces were fixed. Then he took a step. Nobody moved. The opening was between him and them. It was a trick. They were going to make a charge for him as soon as he got closer. He held the knife at arm's length, then crouched lower to spring full force. If they tried to run he'd be on them. He'd get Jackie first, then Merritt. A piece of cake.

He reached the opening, another gaping mouth. Quickly he swabbed it with light. No trap floor, no secret iron door to pull down on him, no cops with guns. He turned the light back on them, when suddenly the interior of that chamber took form in his brain.

Skulls.

He swung the torch inside again. *A trick,* the voice said.

The chamber, maybe thirty feet long and six wide was filled with human remains—skulls and bones all filed neatly in individual cubbies from floor to ceiling. Peter swept the light in disbelief. In some were only skulls or partial skulls—mostly adult, but some smaller ones, children, even infants—gaping down on him. Hundreds of them. Peter's mind was flickering in and out of consciousness, trying to make sense of what the light was taking in. A few were still white, with full sets of teeth. But most were darkened with age and fungal murk, gap-toothed, with lower jaws missing. They were ancient with discoloration. The odd thing was that they were all arranged very neatly, all facing the same direction.

"Hannah," Jackie said. "They're her ancestors. She dug them up from the west end of the island so they wouldn't be destroyed."

Peter felt crazy. He looked at the skull in his hand.

They're trying to confuse you, Peter.

But they looked nothing like Linda. He would know those large black eyes anywhere.

"She arranged them so they looked toward the north," Sparky said. "That's the way they buried them in the cairns. Toward the north. It's the only dead part of the sky. The sun and moon never enter it."

By reflex, he glanced north.

Merritt inched his way behind them. He picked up one of the skulls very gently, holding it like a dinosaur egg. In the light he tapped the occipital lobe. It collapsed to dust. "They're ancient," he said. "Hundreds of years old."

Peter clutched his skull closely to him. The sight of Merritt flicking his fingers clean of dust sickened him.

"That's not all, man," Jackie said.

Peter gaped at him. Jackie's light dropped to a trunk sitting on a stack of cinder blocks. An old standard shipper. Peter backed up suspiciously. Here it comes. One of Merritt's cops was going to jump out at him. Peter got ready with the knife. He'd chop him down before he knew it.

Slowly Jackie pulled back the top. He dropped the light. And it blazed back at him.

Inside, neatly arranged, were stacks of insert trays full of artifacts, some in shell and stone, some in bronze and gold. There were daggers with mother-of-pearl handles, pins, lapis amulets, gold torques, and more lunulae. Jackie picked up a small chalice and held it in his light for Peter to see. It was fashioned in tight geometric patterns of angles and spirals, and the untarnished metal glowed like a piece of the sun.

"They were buried with the bones," he said.

"They're the real thing, Peter," Merritt said. "I have no doubt. You've got two thousand years of ancient craft here. More Celtic archaeology than the Museum of Fine Arts. It's unbelievable, a real bonanza. Congratulations!"

The circuitry of Peter's mind was crackling. "It's a trick." He slashed Merritt across the gut with the knife. Merritt let out a yell and folded in the middle. Jackie caught him with one arm.

There was a flurry of movement, lights swinging, voices shouting, and Peter felt a blow to the back of his neck. He fell and dropped the knife. Jackie. The bastard had betrayed him. He was on Merritt's side. Peter dove at Jackie's legs, but stumbled against the far wall and slid to the ground. He rolled and found the knife. Another chop to Peter's shoulder loosened his grip. Somewhere he heard Andy cry out not to hurt his daddy. Peter got to his feet. Jackie was up in front of him with his hands raised.

"I don't want to fight you, Peter." He was panting.

Behind him Merritt leaned against Connie and Sparky. His shirt was a spreading red blotch. But he was still on his feet.

"Let's cool down, man, please." His arms were like hams.

Peter sprang for him, but Jackie deflected him. Peter went back, spun in a circle, then slammed his fist into Jackie's midsection. Peter heard a deep-throated grunt and Sparky crying out. Jackie folded slightly in the middle, and in that moment Peter turned to find his knife. As he was about to leap for it, Jackie pounded him with both hands on the back of his shoulders.

Peter went flying facefirst onto the floor. He landed painfully, and for a moment lay breathless in the muck. His flashlight was some feet away, and in the light his hand scuttled like a crab for the knife. He could see Jackie pull away. In a moment they were all running.

But he'd catch them, the traitors.

He sprang to his feet, but his shoulders came up hard against the underside of the shelves. The wooden plank gave way, and the whole rack of skulls crashed down on him. He let out a howl. His head was cut and he sank to the floor. His knife was still clutched in his hand, but he had dropped Linda.

Blind confusion. Someplace in the distance, like a voice in a fog, he heard Andy cry out that his daddy was hurt. But the words shot through his mind. He was a membrane away from panic. All he knew was that he had lost Linda. He pushed away the timbers.

From under the pile he saw his flashlight glow. He reached for it, feeling old skulls pop to dust under his weight. He was covered with them, hundreds of black powdery crania and bones. And somewhere under them was Linda.

He let out a cry of anguish. He couldn't lose her again.

Frantically he dug through them, feeling them mush in his hands, tasting the sour dust. He could barely see. They all looked alike, all black. Where were those large bright eyes?

The voices outside were fading.

His light was almost gone. He stood. He was covered with black dust and bone fragments that stuck to his body like leeches. He could never find her and still stop them.

The light was a dull orange ember. Maybe a minute of illumination left. He shook his feet free, and left, the crunch of a hard bone lingering ghostlike in his feet as he ran.

Linda.

He turned left and splashed down the tunnel. His blood pumped so hard his eyeballs hurt. A dull glow of light in the distance. He turned off his light. Someplace in his mind under all the black clouds it occurred to him what this place was—an escape passage built by Union soldiers in the event the harbor was overrun. It cut clear across the mudflats, maybe two hundred yards, to somewhere under the oak woods.

The light at the end grew brighter. He could see the others' vague shadows.

The first figure he made out was Merritt. He was walking in a crouch from the gash, hanging on Jackie and Sparky.

Peter raced toward them. He'd take them all on if he had to.

The tunnel stopped at a wall.

"Noooo!" Connie cried. He had caught them. Stunned faces. Merritt's shirt was a red slash—a flesh wound.

Above them was another brick cylinder leading straight up. He had caught Connie lifting Andy up to iron cleats embedded in the bricks. Someplace above them was another light. Peter looked up. There was a lantern and the face of Hannah. Behind her, stars gleamed.

"Climb!" Connie whispered.

"NO!" roared Peter.

"No more hurting, Peter," Jackie said. He held up Merritt. The man glared at him. His eyes were wide. So much blood, Peter thought. Much blood. Blood. What have I done? he asked himself.

Peter, don't let them stop you.

"Andy?" Peter held out the elbow of his knife hand. "Come to me."

"No, Andy," said Connie. Her eyes were wide with terror. She held him to her.

"Daddy, I'm scared."

"Nothing to be scared of. I'm here now. They won't hurt you."

Jackie and Sparky pleaded with him. Merritt groaned in pain. He flashed the knife toward them. But his eyes were on Connie. She stood between him and Andy.

She's trying to turn your own son against you the cagey bitch. Don't you see? Trying to poison the well. But this *well runs deep, and it's thicker than water.*

"Don't cry, Andy. It's all right. Nobody's gonna hurt you."

"But, Daddy . . ."

"No 'But, Daddys!' "

"But, Daddy, you're scaring me."

He snapped the flashlight on him. It was nearly dead. But in the light he saw his son's face—his eyes puddled with tears, his little mouth quivering. Peter felt his heart lurch.

Then his light died, and Andy's face was hidden in shadow.

"You can't have him," Connie said.

Peter's mind filled with magma. "Give him to me!" he bellowed.

Peter lurched at her.

"Daddy, no!"

Something scraped behind him. He flicked the blade toward Jackie. He was just about to jump him.

"Try it and you're dead and her, too."

Sparky screamed. "No. Don't hurt him, please. Peter, don't."

He slapped the flashlight out of her hand. "Get back," he said. "Back! Back! Back!" He slashed the air in front of her with the blade.

Sparky pulled Jackie and Merritt back down the tunnel. Jackie still had his light. He held it on Peter.

Peter looked up, Hannah was gone. Just stars.

"I know what you want to do," Connie said. She pressed Andy to her side.

"You know nothing. We're going home."

She was crying. "Peter, you're not in your right mind." Andy whimpered beside her.

"Andy, come to me." He crooked his elbow at him again.

"No!" Connie said.

Peter hissed at her through his teeth. "Now, Andy! I have a big surprise for you."

Before Connie could say anything, he aimed the knife at her face.

"Make up your mind, Andy."

"Peter, I beg you not to hurt him."

"Hurt him? He's my son. I'll take care of him. It's you who wants to hurt him. All of you. You're bad. Andy, are you going to come to Daddy, or am I going to have to make you?"

"Daddy, you're bleeding."

Peter felt his heart flood.

Peter! the voice insisted. *Don't weaken.*

He closed his eyes a moment until it passed. "It's nothing, just a little scrape."

"Andy, your daddy isn't well—"Connie began.

"Get out of my face!" Peter roared.

"He's sick," she continued. "He doesn't know what he's do-ing. I think he wants to—"

"Shut up! Your daddy loves you."

". . . hurt you."

A fucking face-off! Peter raised the knife to swipe her across the eyes.

"Daddy, no!" Andy shouted, and he pushed his way to him.

Peter took his hand. "That's Daddy's good boy," he said. Then he lifted him up to the cleats. "Climb up. I'm right behind you, Andy." He held Sparky's light up, and slowly Andy made his way up, looking back down at them. "Don't stop. All the way up to the stars. That-a-boy."

Peter flashed the light at Connie. Something in those green eyes touched him for a moment. Something he dimly recalled, as if from a distant time, from a different realm. But for the life of him he couldn't remember what.

It made no difference now. Linda was waiting.

He turned and scrambled up the insides of the wall, taking care not to slip on the cleats. They were slimed. His mind raced as he made his way up. Scraps of thoughts pulsed through with flash images and sounds. Screaming and rumbling. He heard fire roaring, a sick sizzling sound, things exploding. He heard a woman crying. He heard his son call him.

He climbed. Maybe ten feet from the top, a cleat came off in his hand. He gasped, nearly tumbling back down. He steadied himself against the one below it. He caught his breath. He slipped his knife back in the case. The cleats were loosening under his weight. They had been in the walls since 1860, a hundred and forty seasons of rain and freezes.

The light of the moon spilled through the opening when suddenly it occurred to him that maybe he wouldn't reach it. Above was the silhouette of his son against the white light. Peter's temples stung.

The next rung under his foot held. He took a breath and pulled himself up to the next cleat. He felt it slightly give in his hand. Christ! And Andy was just feet above him, and Linda waiting on the hill. They were moments away from being whole again.

Then something occurred to him. The silo was little over a meter in diameter. He pressed his back against the one side and his feet against the other. The bricks were slick with rot, but he could do it if he pressed hard enough. It worked. The next minute he shimmied his way toward the top, yanking out the wall cleats one after the other. He let them clang on the concrete below. By the time he reached the top, he had stripped a gap of maybe eight feet. They'd never climb out. Jackie might do it the same way, but not the others, especially Merritt with his belly split. He had them.

Peter pulled himself up and over, not the least bit distracted by the shredded mass of flesh the bricks had made of his back. He was feeling no pain.

Air. The sweet scent of the sea night. He took a deep breath to flush his lungs of the rot and gasoline.

The night sky glittered with stars through the oaks. The tunnel had led from Pulpit's Point clear under the other hill and up into a small clearing in the woods.

Andy was standing alone in the shadows. On the ground Peter found the huge iron manhole lid. He raised it and clunked in on the opening. Even if the others got back out the other way, it would be too late.

"Andy?" He held out his hand toward the dark.

Andy came and took it. His hand felt small.

Peter looked across at Pulpit's Point. The circle of stones made a white cage under the moon. He smelled smoke. Sweet woodsy smoke.

"It's time to go see Mommy."

chapter
Thirty-six

They walked hand in hand, father and son, out from the moon shadow of the high trees, down the sandy slopes, onto the mud-flats, and toward the incline of Pulpit's Point.

"But, Daddy, Mommy's dead."

"No she isn't, silly goose." Peter's voice had the immemorial patience of a father confronted with his young son's stubbornness. "Not anymore. She's coming back to us," he explained. "She's waiting for us up there."

"She's really up there?"

"Of course. That's what I've been trying to tell you. Daddy doesn't lie," he said. "If you look real hard you might even be able to see her."

A firey spider lit up the sky. Then another and another, followed by huge crashes of thunder.

Peter felt a shudder. "There!"

"But, Dad, those are fireworks."

Somewhere offshore in the Inner Harbor sat a barge where rockets were ignited. Flakes of orange fire traced high into the black, and the sky lit up like an aurora gone wild. An invisible crowd roared approval.

"Well, she's up there," he said, feeling the tooth of doubt take a nip.

Silently he moved on toward the base of the slope. He held his son's hand. His other rested on the horn of the knife.

While they walked along, Peter watched the heavens light up.

Great percussions boomed after each flare. Andy was right this time. They were fireworks. He remembered as a kid waiting for the big sonic flash-booms. That was the best part. His dad would take him just like this to the Esplanade every Fourth of July. This year, the fireworks were held at the waterfront and the concert in Christopher Columbus Park.

Plumes of colored fire lit up the harbor sky, and thundering booms rocked across the great bowl. The grand finale. The best part, what everybody waited for.

In the glare of liberty's celebration, Peter led his son toward the stones. They passed the corpse of Flanagan, but Peter distracted Andy's attention to the fiery flags floating on barges near the waterfront. There were two of them: one in red, white, and blue; the other in red, white, and green.

Smoke cut to Peter's brain as they climbed to the top. It was stronger than ever. Acidic. Hard to breathe. Filling, numbing his head. He held Andy's hand but could barely feel it. By the time they reached the top, Peter's body was shuddering uncontrollably. He felt dizzy with nausea. No more little nips of doubt. Something was wrong. Dreadfully wrong, out of place. He felt fright. He shouldn't. It was his Linda. They were a family again. In the protective circle of stones. Just the three of them. Nothing to fear. She was here to watch over them, to take Andy. And he wanted to go to her. A boy needs his mom. She was a great mother, a better parent than he. Besides, Andy barely had any time with her; he was only three when she left. Only three. And now, he's only six.

Only six.

He felt fear. He felt something was wrong. He felt the heat in the middle of the circle by the standing pillar of limestone.

Great heat.

"You can't be scared, Andy," he whispered. "Mommy's made of magic tonight. She'll be here, and she'll take care of you."

"I don't see her."

"You will. I promise."

Before he got the words out he saw light. Not fireworks. Linda's light.

It started as a dull red, then rapidly flared orange. By the pillar, a separate column of glowing air rose out of the ground. It took form and substance. A flash of fire and arms separated from the glowing mass, then legs and a head, like a being forming out of a geyser of lava. Overhead the sky was exploding in the fireworks finale.

Andy pressed himself to Peter. He was shaking.

"It's okay. It's Mommy."

The figure in the circle held out her arms toward Andy.

Peter dropped to his knees and pulled Andy to his chest, facing Linda.

He held one arm tightly around his son's waist. With his free hand he fumbled for the knife.

The light was nearly blinding.

The air was flashing and pounding from the volley of rockets. Andy was trembling. He brought one hand to his face, peeking up through his fingers.

In his head Peter rehearsed how he would do it. He had to get it right so it happened fast. And he couldn't give it thought. No thought. Just let his hand follow the directive. His duty was beyond worldly morality, beyond judgment.

His hand felt wet. But it wasn't perspiration. His wound had opened up in the climb out, and blood was streaming down his arm. His hand was slick on the handle.

The circle was a blaze of orange.

Send him to me, Peter.

He hesitated.

Now.

"I see you." He squinted and raised the knife up behind Andy's neck.

Give him to me.

His body was quaking out of control. Something was not right. Something was holding him back.

Now!

He felt his hand jerk. The blade nearly trembled out of his grip. Tears ran down his face. He could taste the salt.

The blade just grazed Andy's neck. He could hear him breathing excitedly as he watched and waited for his mother to come out of the magic fire. Peter wondered how much he remembered of her. In the intense light Peter studied the soft baby white of Andy's neck. And the little pulse beating rapidly at his throat. For his mom.

Through the bubble of tears Peter whispered, "I love you, Andy."

Now and forever.

Yes, now.

"But, Daddy," Andy screamed, "that's not Mom!"

Peter squinted against the light.

"It's somebody else."

At the core of Peter's being the realization blossomed.

The rumbling in his head snapped off.

It was not Linda.

Not Linda.

Not Linda.

And it never had been Linda.

Peter made an agonized cry. He pulled Andy back from the phantasm.

Another woman, whose face filled his eyes, twisted and sputtered with rage, her body splitting from the fire, black flaps of skin fluttering, sizzling in the flames, her head a charred skull: Brigid Mocnessa, roaring in fury.

Andy turned to see his father raise the knife high above them.

"Andy, your daddy's been bad, but he loves you more than you know. He really does."

The circle flared up.

I curse you to hell.

Peter's hand plunged the knife to his heart.

chapter
Thirty-seven

"NO!" Andy threw his arm up, deflecting Peter's, and the blade slashed into Peter's side.

All the pain so long numbed suddenly raged through his body. He nearly fainted. But Andy tugged him to his feet, pulled him away from the hot light and out of the circle of stones.

Behind them the roaring flame flailed its arms.

At the edge of the circle, Peter fell. His side was in agony. The ground seemed like shifting plates, impossible to stand on. He was going to black out, his mind flickering on and off.

Voices. He heard voices, sensed others coming. Then he felt his arms pulled up. The pain in his side screamed. It split open and the night air smacked the nerve endings.

He was being dragged. Connie and Andy. In the pulsing bursts of light filling the sky, they appeared as figures in a triptych.

"Jesus Christ, what's that I smell?" Jackie said.

"It's all the fireworks," Sparky said. Connie shook her head. "Let's get him out of here."

Sparky grabbed Peter's legs.

Peter felt delirious. He could hear them shouting. He could feel them carrying him. The sweet smell of gasoline cut through the smoke. Huge tongues of flame filled his eyes, mad shadows capered across the stones. He tried to talk, to tell them it was Brigid. He tried to say he had been dreadfully wrong. To say he was sorry, but nothing was working right. The pain had bled away his strength. His mind flitted in and out of consciousness.

Down the slopes they ran with him.

He noticed the stars above. The white crystal moon.

He closed his eyes. When he opened them he was somewhere on the flats, Pulpit's Point rising on the left and the twin hill of oaks on the right.

"She's up there," somebody shouted.

Peter jolted. He looked across the flats to the stone circle. For a moment he thought he saw Linda raise her arms above her head. He'd left her up there. God, no!

"What's she doing?"

"Hannah!"

She was standing in at the center of the arc of stones. A column of angry red light lit up the pillar of limestone before her. Over her head she raised her oil lantern.

She shouted something Peter could not make out. Then she flung the lantern at the pillar.

It smashed against it, and liquid fire exploded over it.

At that moment rockets made red, white, and blue blossoms in the sky.

Then the snake grew.

From the base of the column, a thin line of fire ran around the ring of stones down the side of the cliff. A giant wick of gasoline-soaked rope led from the sacrificial pillar and into the tunnels below.

"Why doesn't she get out of there?" Connie cried.

Peter reached up to take Andy's hand. The boy's gaze was frozen on the stones. Beside him, Peter saw Connie. He remembered how he had liked her, that she had wonderful green eyes.

Then it happened.

In a sonorous concussion that made the stones dance in place, the whole eastern cap of Kingdom Head erupted.

From the woods there was a huge blast from the escape tube that in an instant was a roaring silo of flame amid the oaks. At the same time from the tunnel entrance on the far side of the Point, a brilliant yellow mushroom exploded out over the sea filling the harbor with a false sunrise. Here and there on the slopes where the bedrock was thin and the machines had cored it, fiery blow holes opened up, spewing out roaring geysers of liquid fire. The heat was so intense that the mild sea breeze was instantly a hot whirlwind that rapidly constricted into a vortex of smoke and debris and snaked up the slopes and into the ring of stones. There, locking into the contours, it doubled in size—a roaring demon tornado of flame and smoke that towered into the sky.

At the top of Pulpit's Point Hannah stood in the circle of stones, thick black smoke whirling around her, and fiery sprays making of it a lunatic auroral storm. Before she fell, Peter could see her head rolling against the flames, her arms held up in a supplicating V. There was a second internal explosion and the whole cap of Pulpit's Point rose upward from the pressure, the stone circle neatly in place appearing to rise out of the inferno and into the heavens on its own power. Still intact, the circle climbed its own height almost to the point of separation, the thrust of the roaring exhaust appeared to propel the thirteen stones free of the tyranny of the earth. Yet, the fire was not great enough, and the next moment the circle settled for a split instant where it had stood for centuries, then collapsed with thunder into a huge maw of bellowing flames, pulling Hannah with it.

And from someplace over the black water half a million people said, *"Waaaaaaaaaaaaaaw."*

Epilogue

The moon was a frozen ghost over the harbor.

On the other side of the sky, the late morning sun, already arcing above its winter orbits, climbed the blue and warmed the shore.

It was Easter Sunday.

Peter and Connie and Andy walked from the Aquarium, where an attendant had let Andy throw a fish to the seals. They flowed with a gathering crowd along Atlantic Avenue, past street musicians and photographers with big bunnies and caricaturists with charcoal and easels. They stopped at an outdoor cafe for lunch, then poked through some stores and antique shops.

It had been nine months since they had last walked these steps. And there had been much healing. Peter's shoulder ached on occasion, but his soul had been purged. Since leaving the island Peter had felt like his old self—no more smoky fugues nor spells of dislocation nor paranoid rage. And no more sensations of supernatural intercourse. What had taken hold of him out there defied rational explanation; and he accepted that and put it away for good.

The island had cooled, and life had returned.

By fall, Poro Construction had removed all of its equipment and construction material, down to the last scaffolding pipe and brick. What had already been constructed—the few poured foundations and open frames, sewer lines, and pilings—would eventually be removed by the state.

Throughout the winter, a team of lawyers and scholars presented documents to the Suffolk County Court demonstrating evidence of Hannah Mac Ness's blood lineage from Brigid Mocnessa and her husband, Josiah Indian. The island, once rightfully theirs, had been unlawfully taken from them by Reverend Jeremiah Oates following her execution in the summer of 1692. Yet, in 1709, the year of the death of Margaret Oates, wife of the then long-deceased minister, the land had been willed back to the offspring of Lydia Mocnessa, who had since moved to the mainland. Though she had no knowledge of the bequest, the island was legally Mocnessa property by replevin. It was clear to Peter now, why Hatcher had tried to kill him that night. Hatcher couldn't let Brigid's bones be uncovered.

The court accepted the evidence and since there were no known next of kin, the state assumed receivership of the island which was, like the other thirty, now a national park. The name would remain Kingdom Head.

Hannah would have been pleased, Peter thought. The diary of Lydia Mocnessa, as it turned out, was a compilation of several journal entries of Lydia and three generations of descendants. Original deeds and accompanying documents ultimately proved critical to establishing Hannah's lineage and rightful ownership. The courts also convicted Edgar Fane Hatcher to seven years of prison on various counts, including fraud and conspiracy and attempted murder. In a plea bargain, Fred Goringer had admitted their attempt on Peter's life. The helicopter pilot substantiated the confession. Flanagan's death was ruled self-defense.

They walked to Waterfront Park and stopped at the statue of Christopher Columbus. Something had always bothered Peter about it, and now it came to him: The artist had sculpted the head too small for the body. He lacked presence.

They passed on to a playground area with a large wooden climbing structure fashioned after the bridge and masts of an old sailing vessel. Andy slid down the mast and cavorted with other kids.

For two months after leaving the island, he had slept with Peter until the night terrors had passed. On that Fourth of July he had seen his father turn monstrous and he watched an old woman go down in flames. He was also led to believe that he was going to see his mother again.

It sickened Peter that at six years of age his son had experienced such horrors. But those wounds, too, had partly healed over the seasons. And Connie was part of that process, closing the circle left gaping since the death of a mother Andy could hardly recall. In those nine months, the three of them were together most weekends and holidays. Connie was also talking about moving to Boston someday. Although, for good reason, she had been wary of a relapse, she had come to accept Peter's mental collapse as the consequence of the extraordinary confluence of natural forces—a singular phenonemon that could not repeat itself. Under the strain of trying to save the stones, he had somehow convinced himself that at stake was also the reclamation of his dead wife—and he had simply snapped. He agreed to her suggestion of psychiatric care, making weekly visits which helped his repair. He had revealed to the doctor his visions as well as Hannah's claims of the malevolent presence of Brigid. But as they were both men of science they shared the conclusion that Peter had undergone a psychotic dysfunction brought on by the combination of stress, grief, and abiding guilt over Linda's death—a kind of ambulatory nervous breakdown—and *not* a supernatural experience. Ghosts and demons were simply products of the human mind. That Peter had remained stable since leaving the island—in fact, that he rallied in light of his remarkable discovery—convinced Connie to put their troubled beginning behind them. Peter was a new man with her. Of course, she did not know the whole story; but it made no difference now. The circle was closing.

They walked along the water to the waiting MBTA boat. Dan Merritt greeted them and they rode out into the harbor toward Kingdom Head.

It was the first time Peter had returned since that night.

Through Dan Merritt's binoculars, Peter saw two milky humps floating in the blue. On the left, Shepherd's Island—and were the magnification great enough, he might have caught the face of E.

Fane Hatcher watching the regreening of Kingdom Island through prison bars. On the right, Kingdom Head. Despite the black crater and scalped hills and slabs of concrete, life was reclaiming the island. The pylons and support beams and half-walls, like gawky land reefs, were becoming overrun with vines and scrub where birds and small animals had returned to nest.

Dan Merritt had suggested that in light of the discoveries, Peter might want to put together another excavation team and tackle what was left of Pulpit's Point. The island was now under state proprietorship, and Peter could take all the time he wanted to unearth from the rubble what he could. The stones were still under there. So was the extraordinary treasure-trove. Merritt would also be able to get him substantial funding.

But Peter said he was not interested. He had agreed to today's small press conference as a way of forever putting matters to rest.

"Hard to believe anything would be left," Connie said.

Peter put his arm around her and watched the island grow on the horizon.

"In their last letter, Jackie and Sparky said they'd sign up if you changed your mind."

Peter nodded. Then he leaned over and gave her a kiss.

"I stopped looking."

"We all did," she whispered.

"Why are you whispering?"

"Because we're getting hokey again." She squeezed his hand. "You know what I want to do when we get back?"

"Anything."

"I want to stroll through the Common and the Public Garden and catch the Easter promenade down Commonwealth Ave. Then I want to stop at that ice cream place in Harvard Square and have a hot fudge Porky Special."

"You have no shame."

"Would I be holding you if I did?"

He smiled, "And then what?"

"Then back home to cook the paschal lasagna."

"Then?"

"Then light a fire and snuggle up with *James and the Giant*

Peach." They had read the first chapters of the book to Andy last night.

"You would like that?" he asked.

"I would love that." She looked at him and his heart flooded.

"Have I told you in the last seven seconds that I love you?"

"No."

"I love you."

She lay her head against his shoulder. "That sounds so good."

"You know what we could do after James?"

"What?"

"Put a few more logs on the fire when Andy's down, and spend the rest of the night jumping on each other's bones."

"Peter, you weave such a romantic turn of phrase."

"Your sweet *derriere!*"

A short time later the boat pulled up to the dock below Pulpit's Point. It looked like a miniature Vesuvius. Peter felt a sudden chill.

They got off the boat and slowly climbed the slopes. A skin of blackened ash covered everything. Part of the slope was collapsed from the internal eruptions. Peter had later learned that some ten thousand gallons of gasoline and diesel fuel had blown that night. Peter could almost smell the fire. He wondered what remained under there.

He wondered.

A small clutch of photographers and reporters stood patiently at the top. There were three cameras from local television stations. A woman named Ginny MacDowell from PBS was shooting a documentary. Earthwatch PR people grinned proudly and shook his hand.

For nearly an hour Peter answered questions about the expedition. He enumerated the evidence they had found, concluding that enough existed to convince him that Europeans had migrated from the Celtic British Isles—probably Ireland—during the fifth or sixth century. They had retrieved none of the artifacts or human remains, but Dan Merritt confirmed their existence.

Peter felt a little self-conscious about his brief celebrity. His story had been run on CNN and the other network news shows, and been featured on all the local TV magazines. There was also a long cover piece on "America's Stonehenge" in *People* magazine. He had even received an offer from a Hollywood producer to do a movie about their discovery. For fifteen Warhol minutes he was famous. Of course, nobody knew the whole story.

Peter moved to the far edge of the pit's rim to pose, the mouth yawning before him, with Boston in the distance.

Some things don't burn. Stone for instance.

From the opposite side, Andy waved while Connie snapped some shots through her telephoto.

And great love.

While the cameras clicked, Peter's mind was aflash with images. The ring of thirteen megaliths brooding against the sky; Brigid and her baby; Andy digging; Connie under him; a blood fire moon; and Linda rising in flames.

Linda rising. What only Peter saw. What only he knew. A special communion.

He glanced at Connie and wondered if Linda approved.

"Hey, Dad!" Andy squealed from across the pit. "Smile."

Connie poked her camera at him. Her last shot. "Smile," she mouthed.

Peter watched her fuss with the setting, and the moment flared.

Officious, he thought.

She took aim, and his lips skinned back over his teeth. She shot and waved him over. She tapped her watch. Time to go.

Officious. Always trying to control. To pull me away.

Instead, he dropped his gaze to the pit. He knew exactly where to look.

Someplace in the dirt a black mouth sphinctered open, and a smoky voice whispered,

Peter, I've been waiting.